Praise for *Night Fires*

"Ms. Harbaugh brings a remarkable originality to a genre steeped in tradition, and the result is a sheer reading delight." —*Romantic Times*

"I was totally blown away with it. I was expecting great things, but [*Night Fires*] exceeded even my expectations. *Night Fires* is an extraordinary book, full of sensuality, surprise and dark danger. One of the most original books in recent years, it delivers on everything it promises. Karen Harbaugh writes with delicacy and power, and her characters sing. Quite possibly the best book of the year. God, it was fabulous! Utterly and completely divine." —Anne Stuart

"*Night Fires* is riveting—The best historical romance I've read in a long, long time. Karen Harbaugh breaks new ground with this enthralling tale of two haunted people—Simone, the Frenchwoman pledged to preserving life, and Corday, the Englishman dedicated to taking it. Joined on a dangerous mission, both may rediscover their lost souls—if they can survive long enough for love." —Mary Jo Putney

"*Night Fires* is the splendidly different romance that readers have been seeking. Don't miss it." —Jo Beverley

Dark Enchantment

Karen Harbaugh

A Dell Book

DARK ENCHANTMENT
A Dell Book / January 2004

Published by Bantam Dell
A Division of Random House, Inc.
New York, New York

ISBN 0-553-58421-9

Manufactured in the United States of America
Published simultaneously in Canada

OPM 10 9 8 7 6 5 4 3 2 1

I'd like to dedicate the de la Fer series—
Dark Enchantment and *Night Fires* (so far)—
to Deb Stover and Barbara Samuel,
whose timely kicks in the pants made me realize
that I needed to publish these books.

Dark Enchantment

Chapter 1

SHE WAS A CREATURE OF MUD AND DIRT, and though from time to time light glinted in her corner of the alley, she did not see it directly. Sometimes the light would catch the edge of her blade and it would startle her, stirring a faint memory. It would stir something around her heart. But it hurt, this remembering, and she would push it away into a dark part of her mind.

Instead, she scrabbled for what food she could take from the rats when she could not find a dropped coin, and tried to avoid notice. Occasionally, she received kicks from passersby if she strayed too far from her corner, but the pain from this was only slight, nothing compared to the pain she felt when she saw pain in others. So she closed her eyes and tried to sleep when she was not searching for food.

She did not know what day it was, only that light and darkness passed one after another, and that it was very cold. When it became too cold, she was forced from her corner in the alley to the church, where she could sit in a far corner of the sanctuary and look at the light of the candles when she was sure no one was looking. This was more comfortable than the alley, to be sure, and sometimes she would find a piece of bread that someone must have dropped on their way to confession. And . . . it eased the pain in her heart to be there, and she did not bleed from her hands, and her back did not ache when she slept underneath one of the pews. But a church was not for one such as herself.

It was on one such cold morning that she awoke to the sound of the priest yawning and opening the sanctuary. She stayed still underneath the pew until she was sure the priest had passed by, and she crept—she thought—noiselessly out the door.

"You, boy, stop!"

She looked wildly about her and stared for a moment at the plump, black-frocked priest who had called to her. He looked surprised, then shook his head.

"Are you the one who has been sleeping here at night?"

Fear clutched her heart, stopping her voice, but she nodded slightly. "I am sorry, *ma Père*," she managed to whisper after a while. "I will not do so again." She looked away, fear overcoming her once more, but this time the fear gave her legs motion and she ran.

"Wait!"

She would not wait. She knew what waiting would do. Waiting led to a place where she had no way to escape except through more pain. She ran to the alley that was her home, her sheathed blade tapping against her hip, hoping that no one had claimed her corner.

But just as the street she followed turned into the alley, she stopped abruptly. Tears began to build beneath her eyelids and she drew in a deep, harsh breath as she looked at the scene before her: a young girl sobbed while a man hit her across her face and another man shoved her against the wall and pushed up her skirts.

Pain sliced across her back, making her gasp, and her hands prickled with the first flow of blood from them. She pulled out two strips of cloth from her pockets and tied them around her shaking hands. She slowly, carefully pulled out her sword while rage built underneath her ribs, rapidly pulling the air into her lungs.

It was the only way. The only way to stop the blood, the pain, and the rage.

She ran to the girl and to the men, snarling in her anger and at the almost blinding pain that surged across her back. It was the sound of fury, the sound of a cornered animal. The men turned, and she lashed at them with her sword.

"Get away from her." Her voice was a growl. "Get away, or I will kill you." She could feel the cloth at the palms of her hands dampen with blood, and pain grew there, as well.

"Stupid boy. Go away—unless you want some, too." One man—short and dark—sneered and the other, taller, man turned back to the girl, leaned down, and thrust his hand underneath her skirt. The girl screamed.

The scream lashed at her, and she jerked as if whipped. She gripped her sword tighter, then her hand lifted and the blade's tip scored the back of the dark-haired man's neck. *His* scream lessened the pain in her hands and he released the girl, putting his hand to his neck and then looking with disbelief at the blood on his fingers. The man's scream made his friend loosen his hold on the girl; she fell to her hands and knees, than scrambled out from between the men's legs. She ran, screaming and weeping, as the taller man tried to hold her by her apron skirts, but her apron came off in his hand. His sneer grew into a frown, then he rushed with a knife at the intruder who had spoiled his sport.

Her blade sliced at his hand and knocked the knife from it. He cried out, and the pain on her back began to fade. She almost let down her guard in relief, but the other man came for her, as well, more cautiously. He, too, had a knife. *"Jesu, Marie,"* she whispered. She had not ever taken on two men before. She had the advantage of a rapier that was longer than their crude knives, but her pain slowed her, and she knew if she were not swift enough, the strength of these large men would overcome her. She hoped her skill would be enough, as little as it was.

The second man circled her, and she could see he was trying to maneuver her so that her back was to his friend. If she could keep both of them in sight—

She turned the other way, but it did no good; both men had their knives in their hands now, and she was not sure she could deal with both of them. At least her back was to the street, not the alley. It would be possible to run if she needed to, cowardly though it was.

The thought of the two men raping another girl made her stomach turn, and the pain across her back increased. No. No, she could not let these men go free.

The men lunged as one at her, and she had no choice. She ducked under the arm of one and thrust her rapier, clumsily, at the other. A roar from the man on whom she'd used her sword told her that she had cut him. She glanced quickly at him and saw that he was clutching his stomach, his clothes showing a spreading blotch of blood. Good.

She turned to the other. This man still had his dagger, and now had a large stick in his other hand. She bit back a groan—the rapier felt heavier to her now, and she had not the rage-induced strength she had long ago before she—before she … She shook her head, trying to dispel the mist over her memory … in the beginning of this fight.

She raised her rapier again, flexing her knees as she should, put her other hand behind her back to reduce fatigue, and wished she had learned to fight with a dagger, two-handed. But she had not learned, and her dagger was still strapped to her leg.

"Come, *cochon,* you pig," she called out. "You can fight me now or later, but either way you will die. Make it quick, so you will not bleed slowly to death like your friend." She jerked her chin toward the other man, who groaned and vomited blood on the cobblestones.

The ruffian looked uncertain, but only for a moment before he rushed at her. She was not so quick this time, and his dagger sliced her arm before she had a chance to move to defend herself. Fatigue washed over her, and she was glad her hands had stopped their bleeding and that the pain in her back had faded with the dispatching of the first man. This remaining man was wily and stronger than the other … and what was worse, looked more well fed than she. Hunger gripped her stomach at the thought, and her knees trembled.

Relief showed in the man's eyes—he had seen her trembling. He struck.

Again she put up her rapier in defense, and she whipped her blade at him—too slowly, for she barely escaped another cut of his knife. Blood dripped from her arm and sweat stung her eyes. At least it was not her hands that bled, or her back that stung now.

Her arms and legs ached, and the breath wheezed from her lungs. She could not stand much longer, she must fight with all the strength she had left. She swallowed down a sob, and made a desperate lunge.

She missed and fell to her knees, her sword rattling on the street from her fatigue-numbed hands.

She would die now. It would be a blessed relief. She closed her eyes and waited.

And waited.

The killing thrust did not come, only the *thud* of a body hitting the ground. She opened her eyes to see a different man, cleaner, better dressed than the two she had fought, and frighteningly handsome. She looked blearily around her—the man she had fought was on the ground, a knife sticking out of his throat.

"Damned shoddy fighting," he said. "Bravely done of you, boy, but shoddy." He spoke French well, but she could hear an accent—English, she thought. "Not that my method was particularly elegant—a thrown dagger, you see." He grinned suddenly. "Fine aim, though, if I do say so myself."

He peered at her, then offered his hand. She could not seem to stand—her legs would not move. But she would not touch him. She sat, then willed herself to push up to her feet and take a step away from him.

The Englishman's eyebrows rose, but he gave an

elegant bow. "Sir John Marstone at your service." He smiled at her, and his eyes were kind.

She closed her own eyes briefly. It was a long time since she had seen kindness. She remembered her mother had been so before that good lady had died, and had been gentle in her words and her touch. Remembering the kindness made her remember something else, as well.

"I ... *merci*, monsieur," she said, and sank into as much of a precise curtsy as she could, though she knew it would never do for a formal curtsy at the king's court. But this was not the court, or even her ... home. The Englishman's brows rose higher. "My name ... my name—" A sob escaped her. "My name is Catherine de la Fer." Pain, old shame, fatigue, and hunger sliced through her, and her sight grew black. *"Dieu me sauve,* my name is Catherine de la Fer," she whispered, and fell into darkness.

Jack Marstone gazed at the still form before him and frowned. Damme, but this was inconvenient. It'd be best if he left this alley; he'd hardly want to be caught with two dead bodies should anyone in authority decide to come down this alley. However, if he left the girl here, and said authority found her alive with the two ruffians—with a bloodied sword, no less—then she'd be as good as sentenced and dead. It'd be a waste of his efforts, and he disliked wasted effort.

Then, too, she was a mystery; he was curious about her, and he rarely resisted his curiosity.

He nudged the girl with his boot. "Up, girl, 'tis morning and no time to sleep. Indeed, we need to be awake on the moment if we're to get away with our skins."

The girl did not move, and Jack grunted in annoyance. God's blood, it looked like he'd have to carry the child.... The girl looked not much more than a child, with her thin, delicate face. He bent over the still form and felt sticky wetness when he touched her arm. Blood. Worse, the girl was wounded.

Jack sat back on his haunches and shook his head. Good intentions were a damned nuisance. Well, there was nothing for it but that he'd have to take the girl to his lodgings. He'd patch her up, get some food into her, and send the girl on her way to her mother, with a warning against playing with knives.

It was easy to pick her up and carry her over his shoulder—the child was as light as a feather, her bones easily felt through her clothes. He wrinkled his nose. She also stank. She'd be better for a washing. If he brought her back to her family in this state, they might just think he was less than a good Samaritan...and he intended to be a well-paid Samaritan.

Unless she was an actress and trollop and stole the clothes from some patron, she could very possibly have come from a good family. There was nothing coarse about her voice, her refined curtsy, or her manner, and that she displayed them even in the midst of extreme circumstances showed that she must be from a noble family. If so, then there had to be money in her return, and he was never behindhand in acquiring funds where he could.

The thought of money cheered him, and he whistled a tune between his teeth as he made his way through the narrow alleys to his lodgings. He garnered a few startled looks from passersby, but his rueful grin and response of "He's as drunk as a louse in a whore's bed" gave him a few chuckles, as well.

His landlady only rolled her eyes at him when he entered the hotel, and he winked at her. "Yes, yes, Madame Felice, yet another one of my charity cases, but this one will bring me into funds, you'll see." He jerked his chin toward his room upstairs. "I'll need some water for a bath—this one's filthy and possibly full of vermin."

"And you say this boy will bring you into funds, monsieur?" The plump landlady wrinkled her nose. "No doubt he will bring fleas into my house, and I will not stand for that!"

Jack grinned. "Aye, the faster the bathwater's brought up, the better. And it's a girl, not a boy, possibly run away from her family."

Mme Felice frowned and put her hands on her hips. "*En vrai*, she will bring you trouble, not money. Her family will not want her if she looks like this."

"True." Jack hefted the girl more comfortably on his shoulder. "Therefore, I must have the bath." Mme Felice shook her head and threw her hands up in exasperation, then bustled off as he went up the stairs to his room.

Once there, he lay the girl on the floor—Felice was right, there was no need to risk a good night's sleep to fleas—and removed the belt that held the girl's scabbard, sword and dagger. He examined the sheath and the sword—both old and of excellent make. She could not have come from anything but a well-to-do family. Surely they would pay a goodly sum for her return. The thought occurred that she might have been cast off from her family—but no. She must have run away, for a family would hardly have given her men's clothes or a sword.

Hope rose. He'd ask for a hundred livres, maybe more. It'd be enough to buy his way back to England—Cromwell and King Charles be damned. That much added to his savings would be enough to offer pay to enough of an army to take his lands back from the Roundheads, with promise of more once he controlled his estate again.

Or so he wished. His future lay with his king's fortunes. Jack closed his eyes wearily. Sometimes he wished he did not have the obligation to regain his estate or support his king, but he was a Marstone—"seize and hold" was his family's motto, and he had failed to do just that, and worse.

He opened his eyes, gazing down at the girl at his feet. No time to think of the past—it'd not gain him the funds he needed, and this girl would. Carefully he peeled her jacket from her unresisting body and threw it in the fire. It was beyond repair and beyond cleaning, as were the rest of her clothes. He frowned at her lack of movement and took her frail wrist in his hand, then breathed a sigh of relief. She was still alive. Good. It'd be too bad if he lost this chance to reclaim his inheritance.

A knock at the door sounded. "Come!" he called out, and the landlady peered around the door, her expression suspicious. "I'll need some help getting the rest of her clothes off, Madame Felice, if you'll be so kind. She's been hurt."

Concern and pity replaced the suspicion, and the woman bustled in, two footmen and chambermaid following with a small tin bath and hot water. Once the water was poured, Mme Felice shooed the maid and footmen out with an order to bring back ointments and bandages, then turned to Jack.

"She is not a woman of the streets, eh?" she said suspiciously.

He put on a pained expression. "My dear landlady. You know me better than that. The ladies I bring to my room are far better dressed and better smelling than this poor rat."

Mme Felice frowned, then suddenly chuckled, slapping his arm. "You are a bad man, monsieur. I have indeed seen you with your ladies, and this *pauvre petite* cannot compare. Ah—!" She gave a little cry as they peeled off the girl's shirt from her back, and crossed herself. "The poor little one! She has been badly treated."

A crisscross of healing weals covered the girl's back. Jack's lips twisted. *There* was the reason she had run away . . . if indeed she received this from her family. Perhaps she was married—no, there was no ring on her finger, although she could have taken off the ring and sold it.

He shrugged. No matter. A woman belonged to her husband, and either way, he'd be paid for returning her.

He caught Mme Felice's worried look as they turned over the girl's body. He shook his head. "You need not worry that I have any lustful thoughts about this chit—I prefer plump beauties, as you know." He gave her a wink, and Mme Felice slapped his arm again and blushed.

"Eh, you think to charm me with your manner, but you know I am as one with my dear Robert, silly man."

He grinned and returned to the girl, gazing at her thin form. It was true; he could not be attracted to such a skeletal thing—her ribs were prominent above and below her thin breasts, and the bones at her shoulders and hips stuck out like the bones on a newly hatched baby bird, featherless and vulnerable. He shook his head. How she even managed to lift her rapier and kill a man, he did not know; it seemed a miracle she was alive at all.

Mme Felice sighed and clucked her tongue as she removed the simple cross the girl wore around her neck, and then gestured to Jack to lift the girl into the warm bath. "Ah, the poor one! She has a sweet face; whoever beat her so must have been *le Diable* himself—who but a monster would have beaten such a child?"

A soft pity moved in him . . . well, who would not feel such a thing? But it was a useless emotion. There were larger things at stake in his life than the fate of a gutter-found girl. He needed to remember that. He settled the girl in the bath, slowly, half afraid she would break.

He moved away to bring over the sponge that Mme Felice had put on the bed, but a sharp gasp brought his attention to the girl again. She had awakened, and her hands gripped the side of the tub with whitened fingers. She looked frantically about, then caught sight of him.

He could not help staring at her. Firelight flickered in her eyes, dark-fringed and green as grass. He had never seen the like—irises so green that they had no other color in them to mar their purity. The girl gazed at him, and her hands loosened from the sides of the tub, chastely covering her breasts, then slowly, finally, she looked away.

Jack closed his eyes and turned from her, fumbling with the towels, then remembered that he was going to give Mme Felice the sponge. He did so, averting his gaze from the girl.

"Shhh, shhh, mademoiselle." Mme Felice's voice was soft and soothing. "You need not be afraid. M. Sir Jack, he is an honorable man and will not harm you, nor will I." The girl said nothing, but he felt as if she were looking at him again, her eyes boring into his back.

I hope she is not married, and it was not her husband who beat her, he thought suddenly. He sat stiffly on a nearby chair, not quite looking at her except from the corners of his eyes. Yes, she had been staring at him, as if he were a wild animal sure to attack. Attack? he thought, disgruntled. Why, had he not saved her from certain death? He would hardly attack her, especially since she was the means to bring him funds for the reclamation of his estates.

A thread of guilt wove its way through his thoughts, but he thrust it away. He was getting soft, and he could not afford that. There was no room for softness in the life of a mercenary. He turned and coolly gazed at her, as if her eyes had not affected him at all, and examined what the tin tub did not cover.

She met his eyes and her gaze did not waver, but he forced his mind into an analytical vein and stared back. She was indeed too thin, as he had noted before, but she had a wide, intelligent brow, a stubborn chin, and a sensitive mouth. His gaze lingered at her lips, and he briefly wondered what it would be like to kiss them, for they were plump lips, unlike the rest of her. She gasped again as Mme Felice brushed the sponge against her back, but she bit her lip and closed her eyes as if exerting discipline over herself. It worked; she had no emotion on her face when she opened her eyes again and looked at him, and he felt at once sorry and admiring of her fortitude. Surely she must have come from a noble family; few else were trained to such discipline except those groomed for King Louis's court.

"Ah! I am sorry, mademoiselle," Mme Felice apologized. "I will be more gentle with your hurts."

Jack thought he saw a flicker of shame before the girl's face became smooth again. "It is nothing," she said, and he noted her voice was low and husky, smooth and sweet as sherry. "I thank you, madame, for your care of me."

Mme Felice chuckled and shook her head. "Ah, it is not I you should thank. It is M. Sir Jack who brought you here and commanded that I bathe you."

"Why?"

Mme Felice raised her brows at the stark question and looked at Jack, clearly expecting that he answer. He stared at the girl coolly. "Because if I had not, you would have been killed, or at the very least taken to the authorities and accused of murder." The landlady gasped and crossed herself, but the girl merely looked at him.

"Ah," she said. "I thank you."

He turned to Mme Felice, grinning. "Do not worry, madame. She is not a desperate criminal, but fought in self-defense."

A concerned look came into the girl's eyes, and she gazed earnestly at him. "Did you see a young girl—she was in the alley, and dressed like a chambermaid? I hope she was able to get away—"

"She ran from the alley as if a devil were after her, mademoiselle, if she was the one who left her apron behind."

The girl relaxed and closed her eyes. "Yes, that was the girl. I am glad she escaped." She was silent and did not open her eyes. Jack was glad—her gaze disturbed him, making him feel as if he were not in control of himself, almost as if he were drowning, for his breath grew short looking at her. He had thought her hair a dull muddy brown, but Mme Felice had washed her hair and rinsed it, and now it was a deep red in the light of the sun that streamed through the windows.

She is too thin, a scarecrow of a girl, and just a girl at that, he thought. Girl... he could not think of her as "the girl" forever. She had a name... ah, yes.

"What brings you to Paris, Mlle de la Fer?" Catherine de la Fer, he remembered.

The girl's eyes opened, and a flicker of fear appeared in them, quickly suppressed. "It feels like a long time since I have been called that," she said softly. Mme Felice cast an encouraging look at him over Catherine's head, obviously curious about the girl's background. He hid his smile at the landlady's curiosity and waited patiently for the girl to speak.

There was a long silence as the girl looked absently into the fire. "I had forgotten I had come to Paris." She looked at him briefly, then into the fire again. "I came to... look for work."

Jack looked at her skeptically. When he had felt her wrist for her pulse, he had noted that though her hands were wounded and chapped from the cold, they were hardly those of a young woman used to working. What roughness she had was on her right hand, the kind a swordsman—swordswoman—would have.

"You did not find work," he stated.

She glanced at him again. "No, I did not, not honest work, and I would not stoop to any other kind."

Mme Felice looked approvingly at the girl. "Of course, honest work is difficult to find... without a reference. Sometimes one's former employers are bad-natured, and will not give any such."

"I had no...no, they were not good-natured," the girl said.

Jack hid his smile. His landlady was clever. It was clear now that the chit was not a runaway servant, but one who came from a family of privilege. Mme Felice grinned triumphantly over Catherine's head and raised her voice. "Now you must turn your back, M. Sir Jack, for I must dry off mademoiselle and cover her."

His lips twisted. "I *have* seen her unclothed before, madame," he protested, but turned his back—not before he caught the girl's blush, however.

"You may turn around," Mme Felice said at last.

He turned to see the girl sitting next to the fire with a large cloth wrapped around her. She did not look at him, but continued looking at the fire. Irritation pricked at him. At the very least she could acknowledge his presence—he was not an insignificant piece of furniture, after all. He watched as Mme Felice combed the shoulder-length hair, becoming absorbed in the repetitive motion through the slowly drying, curling hair, until a knock at the door startled him.

"*Entré!*" Mme Felice cried, and the chambermaid came in with a set of clothes. "*Et voilà!* The clothes. If you will stand, I will dress you." Catherine stood, unresisting except for a slight trembling, and Jack grinned. Yes, she was obviously of aristocratic stock—she took Mme Felice's offer of dressing her as if she were used to being served.

The girl looked at Mme Felice. "Thank you," she said softly. But well behaved, he thought. Then, too, her experiences must have humbled her if she had not had a gracious manner from the beginning. Mme Felice gave him a stern look, and with a grin he turned his back.

And turned again when the girl's voice rose frantically, saying, "These are not my clothes! I must have my clothes back!"

She clutched the cloth to her tightly, shaking her head, and looked anxiously around the room.

"My dear mademoiselle," he said. "Your clothes were filthy, torn, no doubt vermin-filled, and not worth saving. I burned them."

Fury burned in her eyes as she looked at him. "They were *mine*. *My* clothes! And my sword and dagger! What did you do with them?"

He eyed her coolly. "You will wear the clothes you are given. As for your weapons, they are here. I cleaned your sword."

"Give me my sword," she demanded.

"I will not," he said.

"Give it to me now."

He looked her up and down. "What, do you think you will use it on me? In the state you're in? Put on the dress, and I will think about it."

She stared at him, grinding her teeth, and one hand opened and closed as if she wished to feel the haft of the sword in it.

"Hush, mademoiselle!" Mme Felice said soothingly. "You must put on these clothes for now—if you wish to wear boy's clothes, you may, but later, *hein*? Put these on, and eat what Marie will bring us for our breakfast, and then we may talk of finding other clothes for you."

The mention of food closed the girl's mouth, and her eyes shut briefly as she visibly trembled. "Very well," she said.

Jack turned his back once again, until Mme Felice's satisfied, "There!" gave him leave to turn. The clothes were too big on the girl and hung on her as if she were a child trying on her mother's dress. But they were clean, warm, and covered her well.

She looked at him, her expression grave, and held out her hand. "I would like my sword, please," she said.

He hesitated, wondering if he should give in, for it was clear she still needed food and rest. But though her face was still and composed, there was a pleading in her eyes, and it occurred to him that her sword was one of her very few possessions. He lifted it, and held it out to her.

She came forward and took it, and for one moment held it up as if poised for battle. But her arm trembled, then shook, and the sword's point fell to the floor.

She stared at him. "I am weak," she said, and her voice was bitter. "An idiot, and nothing but a weak woman."

He wanted at first to agree with her; she'd been foolhardy for taking on two strong men when she was indeed exhausted from lack of food. But he looked into her eyes again, and thought instead of her courage.

"You did well, considering your state," he said. He grinned. "Clumsy, but I'm sure with time and practice, you'll improve."

She looked sharply at him, and then her lips opened as she took in a deep breath. "Do you think I can?" she asked.

Hope made her eyes widen, making her look almost pretty, and Jack suddenly felt a sinking feeling in the pit of his stomach.

"Of course," he said. Mme Felice looked at him in dismay, but he avoided her eyes.

"Can you teach me? Teach me to be the best with the sword?" the girl asked, her voice eager.

"Of course," he said, ignoring both Felice's whispered mutter and crossing of herself . . . as well as the creeping feeling that he was putting himself to more trouble than the girl was worth.

Her face brightened, and she smiled at last, hesitantly at first, then widely.

She was lovely when she smiled. Jack suppressed a groan. Women were trouble, and pretty ones the very devil.

But he had always taken on the devil and came away richer for it. He forced a smile on his face. "I promise it, mademoiselle," he said.

Chapter 2

CATHERINE WATCHED SIR JACK FROM the corner of her eyes as she wolfed down the food Mme Felice had brought her. She paused only briefly in her survey of him to close her eyes and savor the food—*tiens*, it was heaven, this delicately herbed and spiced chicken, and the bread was rich and thick with butter—better than she had tasted even at . . .

Her mind sheered away from the remembrance and she gazed at Sir Jack again, then looked away. He was alarmingly handsome, and she did not trust him. His looks guaranteed that he would get his way—were not people fooled by a man's or woman's good looks? And she knew that no one gave aid to anyone without some advantage to themselves.

Therefore, Sir Jack wanted something from her, and no doubt he expected to get it easily. Well, she was somewhat grateful for the clothes, and very grateful for the food, but she would not make it easy for him to get what he wanted from her. She had learned better than that.

Memory pricked at her, but she focused on the food again and her assessment of Sir Jack. He was tall, and clearly strong, and stubborn, Catherine thought, and when he closed his well-sculpted mouth it was with firmness, which gave his words a finality that brooked no disobedience. She wondered if he had been a soldier at some time—a scar marred his smooth left cheek. It did not really detract from his looks, but gave him a rakish air ... which was another thing she did not trust.

And yet, he had looked at her with his very blue eyes, and the expression in them was kind. She found herself staring at him again, and he was looking at her, his gaze assessing. No, no, surely she had been mistaken thinking she had seen kindness. He wanted something from her, she was sure, and no doubt it was not going to be to her advantage.

However, he had offered to teach her how to fight, and she would hold him to it. A slight niggling thought told her that she should return something for the lessons he promised, but she gave a mental shrug. If he came through with his promise, then she would think of something.

Her stomach began feeling full, but Catherine still ate. She could not know when she would eat next, after all.

"Eat too much, too fast, and you will make yourself ill, *mon enfant*."

She looked at Sir Jack sharply, but there was nothing but that kindness again. She wondered if the kindness was an attitude he assumed to disarm her. Her stomach did feel tight, however, and perhaps it would be best if she stopped. She took a piece of bread from her plate and put it in her pocket for a future meal, then set down her fork. She eyed the knife next to the plate—it was well honed and had a sharp point. It would work well as a weapon should he try anything she did not like; she was alone with him, for Mme Felice had left, even though she had protested.

She could see he watched her carefully; she thought she saw pity on his face when she put the bread in her pocket. Anger made her hands turn to fists. She needed no pity. Quickly, she thrust her hand in her pocket again and returned the bread to the plate.

"It is always wise to keep provisions for another day," he said gently.

She gazed at him steadily—why had he said that? To warn her that she may not have more food? To let her know she would shortly be let out into the streets? It could not be because he wished to preserve her sense of pride.... She took the bread again and put it in her pocket, watching his expression.

He frowned. "I will not bite, child," he said.

"I am not a child," she said.

"You cannot be more than fifteen."

"I am twenty, monsieur."

His brows rose and he rocked back in his chair. "You are trying to seem older than you are, I believe."

Irritation rose, and she stood from her chair. "Not at all. I am quite grown, and as you see, taller than most women."

He stood then, and she forced herself not to flinch as he rose above her. "You are a mite, a flea, a little thing, easily picked up in one hand." He reached out for her, but she stepped back and seized the knife on the table.

He held up his hands and laughed. "Little fire-eater. No, I will not pick you up and spoil your dignity." He sat again, and crossed his leg over a knee, then waved his hand at her. "Sit. I believe you, and yes, you are taller than most women. You are very thin, however, and your form suggested a young girl rather than a fully-formed woman." His voice was bland, apparently uninterested.

Catherine looked away, feeling a blush creep over her face, and then confusion. She felt embarrassed, but glad he did not find her attractive, yet indignant that he did not. She glanced at him—his gaze still measured her. In truth, she should be glad he did not find her to his liking. It was safer that way.

She sat then, and stared at the leftover food on the plates before her. It was clear he could afford good food, enough to feed his tall body as well as a hungry stranger, with no concern that there was food leftover. Was he a procurer of women, and Mme Felice his accomplice? She cast back into her memory . . . no, he had called Mme Felice his landlady, and they had not the sly, furtive demeanor that often lurked beneath the whoremasters' and mistresses' so-called charity she had hidden from since she . . . since she had gone through all her money.

She probed her memory a little more and shivered. She had thought she could find a paying occupation, but she had no skills other than reading and writing, and there were clerics enough to do that for the unlettered. For anything else, she needed either to have apprentice papers or references from former employers, and she had neither. She was not even able to find a job mucking out stables, for she was also expected to handle horses, and she had never saddled one in her life, for all that she thought she had ridden many.

"Mademoiselle."

The sound of Sir Jack's voice jerked her out of her recent memories and she looked up at him.

"Mademoiselle, tell me of yourself, of your family."

"Why?"

He smiled slightly. "It is clear to me you are not commonborn, but of a good family, perhaps even a noble one. I do not know why you came to the state in which I found you, but it seems reasonable that your family would want to know where you are, and if you are safe."

Fear lanced through her, and she stood, stumbling, overturning her chair on its back. "No," she said, and her voice shook. "No. I—" She forced control over herself, clasping her hands together so that they would not shake. She made herself gaze steadily at him. "I do not remember my family, or where they are." She tested her words in her mind... they were true, more or less. If she allowed herself to push back the veil that seemed to shroud her memory, she could possibly remember, as she had remembered her name. But madness lay beyond that veil, and she did not want to disturb it.

He gave her a skeptical look. "You know your name—Catherine de la Fer—and I am sure it is your true one, for you gave it in extremity. It is not a name for a commoner."

"How do you know?"

His smile was ironic. " 'De la Fer'—'of the blade.' It is a name for a knight, a *chevalier,* not a peasant."

She nodded, accepting his statement. It made sense. If she had been a peasant, or any kind of commoner, she would have had some kind of practical skill she could have used... unless she had forgotten. She tested the veil over her memory... no. She had no skills other than reading or writing, and what little sword-skill she had.

"So, who are you, and where do you come from?"

She shook her head. "Monsieur, I assure you, I do not remember. You must be right about my name, and I think I might have said that I was from Normandy. But beyond that, I do not remember and . . ." She took in a deep breath and gazed at him steadily. "The pain of remembering is so great that I fear it will take time."

He nodded. "Yes. The wounds on your back—they are severe. I am not surprised you would not want to remember it, but surely you remember something of the whipping?"

Fear pierced her, not as strongly this time, and she shook her head. "No. I remember only fear, monsieur."

"Are you a Huguenot, then, trying to escape punishment?"

Catherine smiled. This, she remembered. "No, I am Catholic, and—" Panic seized her, and she looked about the room, searching frantically. "My cross, my rosary—where is it?"

"Peace, mademoiselle." Sir Jack put his hand in a pocket of his coat. "Here it is." He dangled the cross and rosary in front of her, but jerked it away when she tried to grab it.

Anger flared. "Give it to me," she demanded. "It is mine."

"So you remember that, at least."

"Yes. Give it to me."

"No. Not unless you tell me more about yourself." His jaw had tightened, his eyes had grown cool, and there was no kindness in his face now. "I will have the truth, or I will most certainly return you to the alley where I found you. Where did you come from, and why did you run away? That is the only reason I can see for a gentleborn lady to be starving and dressed as a boy in the alleys of Paris."

She kept her eyes on the rosary that swung in front of her. "By the cross, M. Sir Jack, I do not know. Perhaps I ran to escape another beating." Yes, that felt right. She nodded. "Yes, I believe that is true."

"Did you try to escape your husband?"

Fear arose in her with that question, and yet...it did not seem correct. She frowned. "No...I do not think I have been married. Perhaps I was going to be married." Nausea twisted her stomach, making her clench her teeth. She looked up at him. "Yes. I think I was going to be married, and I did not want to be." She took in a deep breath and let it out again, dispelling the sick feeling in her belly. "Trying to remember it makes me feel ill in my stomach."

Sir Jack's lips turned up for a moment, and then he chuckled. "I do not blame you for feeling so. I have avoided marriage these five years since my majority for that very reason."

Catherine allowed herself a smile, then held out her hand. "May I have my cross and rosary now?" she asked.

He gazed at her for a moment, and the measuring expression she had seen before crossed his face.

He held out his hand and dropped the cross into hers. Profound relief made her sigh and press the cross to her lips before she tied the rosary to her waist and tucked the cross on the necklace under her bodice. Strength bloomed under her breastbone, dispelling fatigue, and this time her smile when she looked at him was not forced.

"*Merci*, M. Sir Jack," she said.

"You are welcome."

There was silence for a while, with only the soft crackling of the fire making comment, and it felt oddly companionable to her. And yet, Catherine was sure that Sir Jack wanted something of her. She waited.

He stirred from his contemplation of the fire and looked at her. "Do you want to find your family?"

Emotions flooded into her—fear again, panic, revulsion. But there was also yearning, and a concern for . . . someone. She did not know who it might be, but she was sure it was someone younger. There was no urgency, however, except perhaps beneath the fear that she not return. She looked at him. "I do not know," she said honestly. "I think it is best that I do not return home at this time. There is . . . danger."

"Ahhh. Danger." A flicker of light gleamed in Sir Jack's eyes, and he grinned. "I would think you'd be the sort to take on danger, M. Fire-Eater."

His words made her smile; it warmed her that he thought her fierce and brave. But she shook her head. "No. I am not that much of an idiot, M. Sir Jack. I do not seek danger, but *Dieu me sauve*, it seems to seek me out."

"It amounts to the same thing," he said, shrugging.

She grinned. "And I think you are the sort to seek it out?"

He laughed. "Aye, devil take it. It's the reason why I'm best suited to the life of a soldier than a gentleman farmer." His expression darkened for a moment, showing a weariness beneath it.

"Ah," she said. It was as she thought—he was a soldier.

He laughed. "You think you discern much about me, do you, *mon enfant*?"

She grinned, feeling relief that they had come away from discussing her background. "Yes."

"How so?"

Catherine gazed at him, up and down, giving him as thorough an assessment as he had given her. "You are well formed for such an occupation, and the scar on your cheek—clearly recent—tells me that you had suffered it either in a duel or in war. Your hands are soft except for the calluses I would expect from a man of war, but well muscled. You were quick to come to my side when I—" She took in a quick breath at the memory of her recent fight, and let it out slowly. "When I was fighting in the alley, and you were quick with you knife. You must be reasonably well-to-do if you do not stint on feeding a complete stranger such as myself. You also have an English accent. Therefore, you are not just a common soldier. You must have come to France in King Charles's court, biding your time until the Lord Protector—" Sir Jack made a small growl and looked as if he were about to spit, and she paused, waiting for him to do so. She had never seen a gentleman spit, and she was curious to see if the barbarian Englishman would do it. But he did not, and she continued. "Until Cromwell leaves or dies." She sighed and looked at him. "*Tiens*, that is a difficult name to say—'Cromwell.' "

His face looked grim. "I'd be pleased if you did not say his name in my presence, mademoiselle."

She nodded. No doubt he had suffered in the war against the usurper and did not want to speak of it. She shook her head, however. "We might need to speak of him at some time. What am I to call him if we must?"

"You can call him a bloody damned—" Sir Jack finished his sentence in a string of incomprehensible words.

Catherine bit back a laugh, as she was sure he had said some very bad words, but she looked at him innocently. "I do not think I can pronounce those words, M. Sir Jack. They are very English."

He stared at her for a moment, then burst out laughing. "Aye, so they are, and not a thing for a lady to say in good company, *mon enfant.*"

"Are you, then, not good company?" she asked, putting on an innocent look.

He grinned. "You will find that I am very bad company. You need only ask Mme Felice or her husband, Fichet." His grin faded, and he looked into the fire. "Beware, *mon enfant*, for I am a bad man, indeed."

Catherine looked at him, at the scar that formed a sure line down his cheek and the grim look that had settled over his mouth. She was certain he could be very deadly; had she not seen how he had so swiftly killed that man in the alley?

Yet for all her wariness of him, she felt, deep down, that she did not mind. She did not understand it, for she also felt she could never trust anyone, especially a man.

She looked at him. "Do you mean, M. Sir Jack, that you might betray me at some time?"

He returned her gaze, and his eyes were cool. "Most certainly, *mon enfant*, I will betray you. Beware."

She nodded, and wondered at herself, for she did not really mind. Perhaps it was because he told her so instead of hiding it. She could prepare for such a thing if she was told about it first, and she appreciated him telling her outright.

"Very well," she said. "I will beware."

He chuckled. "That's all? I would think a little thing like you would run as soon as I looked at you."

She considered him, dispassionately this time, and shook her head. "No. Because you told me, I shall be prepared."

He looked at her curiously. "'Prepared'? And what will you do if I were to betray you?"

She looked at him calmly, deadening the feeling she had allowed to grow in her heart. "I shall kill you," she said simply.

A slow smile formed on his lips. "Will you, *mon enfant?*"

"Yes. If you betray me, that is."

"Should I teach you the art of the sword, then, if it will only end in my death?"

She gazed at him and nodded slowly. "Yes, of course."

"Why?"

"You promised to do so, and you are not the sort to take back promises."

He sat back in his chair, away from the fire, and the dimness of the room obscured his expression. "Perhaps I might, if I would also be the sort to betray you."

She gazed at him, glad she had stilled her feelings. It made her feel in control of herself and this conversation, and she would never let another have control over her again. She gazed at him, still coolly. "You will, however, because it will be profitable for you."

He moved forward again, and she could see that

his smile had grown, and now he seemed amused. "How so?"

She paused, for she was not sure at first, but she gazed at her sword set aside next to the fireplace. The firelight glinted off the metal of the haft, the color of silver and gold coin, and it set off a spark in her mind.

She turned to him, smiling slightly. "I will duel for money."

His expression turned skeptical. "You will lose, and be killed. How profitable is that?"

"You will train me—you said so yourself." She put a challenge in her voice.

He did not bridle or take up the challenge as she had hoped, but pursed his lips, his look still skeptical. "And what man will want to fight you?"

She leaned forward. "No one, unless you fight me yourself. Teach me, and we will put on a demonstration—it will be a novelty, and Parisians love a novelty, and gambling most of all."

He was silent for a while, assessing her again with his eyes, and then he grinned, then chuckled.

"Ah, *mon enfant*, you get ahead of yourself. You haven't even received your first lesson."

"Teach me," she said, her voice low and as fierce as she could make it. "Teach me, and you shall see."

He gazed at her up and down, and it seemed he truly looked at her for the first time. "I think . . . I think perhaps I shall," he said slowly, his smile fading though his eyes still twinkled. "I think I shall."

An old rebellion flowered in Catherine's heart, and she held out her hand, steeling herself against flinching when he took it in his. She squeezed it hard and shook it firmly.

"Then it is a bargain, M. Sir Jack."

He brought up her hand to his lips, kissing it gently, and she pulled away from him, thrusting her hand behind her back.

He grinned. "A bargain, Mlle de la Fer. And do call me Jack."

Catherine looked away from him, rubbing on her skirts the hand that he'd kissed. She might call him Jack in time, but she would not allow him to kiss her. No, she would never allow that.

She gazed at him again, and tried to soothe the unsettled flutters that suddenly twisted her stomach. He still stared at her, and his expression had changed to amused kindness again...and something else that caused his jaw to set stubbornly again.

The thought occurred to her that it did not matter what she wanted. Sir Jack would get his way, one way or another.

She pressed her lips together firmly. Not if she could help it, she thought. Sweet heaven, not if she could help it.

Chapter 3

IF JACK THOUGHT THAT HE MIGHT change the girl's mind, he was wrong. He watched as he set Catherine—Mlle de la Fer—through her paces. She was a gentlewoman indeed; everything spoke of it. Every movement of her body was well considered and deliberate, as befitting someone groomed for the court of King Louis. Even the lifting of her hand to pour tea was done in the prescribed manner, but done as if it were second nature to her.

She was practicing the lunge now, again and again, sweat pouring from her brow despite the frost limning the edges of the inn's stable yard. Her breath came from her in a fog, so heavy that it formed brief clouds in the air before they dissipated in front of her, sliced through by her sword and the fierce movements of her body.

"Now your defense," he called out, and she moved her arm up, over and over again, as if to deflect a phantom opponent's lunge. He could see her tiring; she began gasping for breath, and her arm became slower and trembled as she moved it up and down, up and down. Still, she did not stop. A reluctant admiration flowered in him. If she had been a man, he would have hired her gladly as a fighting companion, someone to help him regain his estates in England.

But she was not. Her legs now hesitated as she moved through the different fencing positions; it was not through lack of knowledge, for she was a quick student and memorized each step and movement as if it were a catechism. But it had only been a few weeks since she had begun practice, and she had been a skeletal thing when he had first found her.

In truth, she was surprisingly stronger than he had thought she would be, and her strength grew daily. But he sometimes cursed his idiocy in promising that he would train her to be a sword-fighter. Still, a promise was a promise, and a Marstone never went back on a promise . . . or almost never.

He moved away from the grim mood that would attend him if he went to those kinds of thoughts, and watched Catherine again. It would be cruel to work the girl further, and she would practice until she dropped, he was sure.

"Stop!" he called out. Catherine continued to practice—she clearly had not heard him, such was her concentration. He shook his head. If he did not stop her she would work until she literally dropped from fatigue—he knew, because he had let her alone once during her practice only to find her on her knees, near fainting from overworking herself. He shook his head and walked up behind her.

"Catherine," he said, and touched her shoulder.

She whirled, stepped back, and he found the tip of the blunted sword at his throat. "Don't touch me." Her voice came out harsh and low, hissing between her teeth.

He put his hands in the air and raised his eyebrows. She had fast reactions even when she was fatigued; a good attribute for a sword-fighter. "My dear mademoiselle, you ask the impossible. When I called to you to stop, you would not. I then had two choices: either I wait until you dropped from exhaustion, or I tap your shoulder to get your attention." He looked her up and down, and a sense of mischief made him linger over her thin body. "In either case, I would have to touch you, and I expect I will continue to do so if you are so inattentive." She blushed, looking away, and he was suddenly certain her thoughts were not innocent, for there was fearful understanding in her eyes. Had she, then, known a man? His curiosity rose. If so, it must not have been pleasant for her.

He caught sight of Robert Fichet, Mme Felice's husband, however, from the corner of his eye, and knew he'd have to wait another day to satisfy his curiosity, for Fichet was clearly as full of portent as the small man could be. Jack nodded to Catherine and gestured toward the inn. "Go wash, and have your luncheon, then rest." She opened her mouth to protest, but he cut her off impatiently. "Don't argue. If you truly wish me not to touch you, then you will obey me." A rebellious light came into her eyes, even as she stalked off into the inn. He was glad, for certainly rebellion was better than the fear she tried to control.

He waited until Catherine disappeared into the inn, then strode over to Fichet, grinning. The man shifted from foot to foot, looking as pleased as a terrier that had caught a very large rat.

"It is as you thought, M. Sir Jack," he said, whispering quickly. "Come, we shall talk inside, for *la dulce* Felice wishes to hear, as well."

Jack's grin grew wider—Fichet's thin mustache fair twitched with impatience, and his chest puffed out just a little with pride. The man must have found something valuable indeed about Mlle de la Fer.

Fichet took Jack to a far corner of the common room, ignoring the cries for service from his customers who sat at other tables, or giving them a stern look if they were too insistant.

"You will lose your customers if you do not attend them," Jack said, grinning.

Fichet waved an imperious hand. "They will wait. If I do not attend them, then one of our maids will, and if that does not satisfy them, then they may leave."

"It is a wonder that you have any customers at all."

Fichet gave Jack a haughty look. "They will return because there is no inn better than that of Robert Fichet. I have said it; it is so."

Jack's grin grew wider. "I think I have heard your own King Louis speak in such a way. It makes me wonder if there is not some blood connection between you two."

Fichet appeared to be much struck by this notion, for he paused before he sat at the table and his mustache twitched again, this time into a contemplative frown.

"I cannot say," he said after what seemed like a slight struggle. "On one hand, there is a nobility of character in the Fichets that speaks of more than common blood. On the other, my family is a virtuous one, and would not stoop to illicit affairs." He gave Jack a stern look when a laugh escaped him. "It is a serious matter, monsieur, and a puzzle I must re-solve in time." He looked up, and his expression cleared. "Ah, it is Felice!" He rose again, and took his wife's hand in his. "*Ma doucement, ma chère* Felice." He sighed as if he were a youth with his first love, which brought a blush into Mme Felice's cheeks. She clicked her tongue in a dismissive manner when her husband kissed her hand, but love was clear in her eyes. She sat down, and patted the chair beside her.

"Come, *mon cher*, sit, and tell us what you know of mademoiselle, for if you do not, you would burst with it, I know."

Fichet sat, and seemed suddenly seized with in-decision. He frowned, then handed Jack a folded pa-per, with a very recognizable seal on it. It was from King Charles. Jack's heartbeat quickened. Was it good news? Perhaps Cromwell's rule was over? He hastily broke the seal and read the missive... and nearly crushed the paper in his hand.

The king had written nothing of returning to England, but had merely summoned him to Breda, in Holland, where he held court. Hope rose... he spoke of funds, however. Of course, the king could not speak of any return to his homeland; there were too many of Cromwell's spies about, and it was too easy for them to intercept a letter. Jack grimaced. The spies would not make anything of a request for funds; that Charles asked for money to support his poverty-stricken court was nothing new and all too frequent.

"Well?" Fichet demanded.

Jack looked up from the letter and shrugged. "I am summoned to my king, in Holland."

"And what of mademoiselle?"

Jack raised an eyebrow. "What of her? I assume you have news of her family?" He grew conscious of a tension in his shoulders—he had felt sure she was who she claimed, but not entirely.

Fichet leaned forward eagerly. "It is as she said, M. Sir Jack. She is Catherine de la Fer, of Normandy, an old family, the daughter of the Comte de la Fer. They live not far from Rouen. She is thin now, instead of plump, but it is clearly the same lady, for her height and features are the same, and she has been gone for a good seven months. The mother is long dead, the brother and heir is away at school, and it is said that the father has been very ill."

Jack sat back, the tension gone. So, she was not a fraud, but the lady he perceived her to be; Fichet had more sources of information than King Louis's own spy-ridden court, and it was rare the innkeeper mistook his facts. "Would they welcome her back, do you think?" he asked, almost reluctantly. He would not like to see Catherine leave, he realized. He found he enjoyed teaching her how to fence, and her company was intriguing at best, bracing at worst, and even then her acerbic words amused him.

Fichet paused for a moment before speaking, giving Jack a measured look. "The father had been saying that after a brief engagement to the Marquis de Bauvin, she has gone back to the convent at which she was schooled. But the good convent sisters denied that she had returned, and so now the story is that she has run away. It is clear the engagement has gone awry."

Jack remembered the weals on Catherine's back. "Quite clear." He sighed, but it sounded even to himself that it was a sigh of relief. Nonsense, of course—

he was more exasperated than relieved. "They will not want her back, then."

Fichet's frown grew puzzled. "I would not say that. There is a younger sister, thirteen years old, but she will be fourteen in two months. It is said that the marquis is content to wed her upon her birthday. Nevertheless, the family has offered a reward for Mlle de la Fer's return . . . and de Bauvin is behind the funding of the reward."

"He is a rich man, then?"

"Very rich, M. Sir Jack."

Jack tapped his fingers on the table for a few moments, contemplating the possibilities. A rich nobleman could have some influence at King Louis's court. On the other hand, Louis trusted very few of the aristocracy and kept most of them at arm's length. Either way, Jack could use the situation to his—and King Charles's—advantage. If de Bauvin was a trusted courtier, then returning Catherine would not only garner him funds but perhaps the ear of King Louis, and help turn the king from his apparent appeasement of Cromwell's government. If de Bauvin was not a favorite at court, then perhaps he himself could be persuaded to contribute directly to King Charles's cause. Jack had heard that Cromwell's son would be a weak and reluctant ruler. If Charles's forces could not defeat Cromwell, they could surely defeat his son's, and Charles would return in due course. There was always wisdom in supporting a triumphant king.

Even if the marquis was not interested in any king's favors, there might still be some financial advantage to returning Catherine to him, for it was well known that young girls did not bear children well, and perhaps the marquis would prefer someone of more mature childbearing age.

"How old is this marquis?" he asked. Fichet still gazed at him intently, and Jack was sure that the innkeeper wished to impress something upon him, but did not want to reveal it outright... before Fichet had married Felice, he and Jack had been comrades on many military campaigns; there was little he did not know about the innkeeper.

"He is thirty-five, more than twenty years her elder."

"He likes them young, I suppose?" Jack dismissed his disgust at the thought of the marquis's cradle-robbing. Girls of the nobility made marriages as their parents thought fit, and clearly the de la Fers believed this was the best alliance for their daughter. Few would refuse a high title for their daughters, after all.

Fichet's brows knitted together in a frown. "He has not seemed particular in the past, M. Sir Jack. And it is not as if the de la Fers had any great wealth. They are ... how do you say it? In the basket."

Jack grinned. "That's the phrase. Down on their funds, then?" His grin turned into a frown. "Then there's something else the marquis wants, and it's not young girls, for he was content with Mlle Catherine when she was offered."

Fichet nodded. "*Oui.* There is something else."

Jack waited as the innkeeper paused, for there was a hesitancy in the man's manner, and Fichet was rarely hesitant when relaying information.

"It is rumored—rumored, monsieur—that there is some power contained in, or possessed by, the de la Fer family. And it is *rumored* that the marquis desires this power, for he has an ... interest in sorcery."

Mme Felice gasped and crossed herself. "I have heard of such regarding the court; indeed, did not a lady at Versailles try to gain the king's favor with black magic? But I had thought it was idle gossip—"

Fichet smiled warmly at Mme Felice. "Such is the goodness of my wife that she dismisses what could be base slander—" He kissed her hand again. "But though it is indeed rumor, the de la Fer family is an old one, and has been well-to-do and unusually lucky until this generation."

Jack lifted an eyebrow. He did not believe in luck other than what advantage a man might make for himself. It did not matter, however; if a man believed a thing, it was as good as true if he acted on that belief, and perhaps the marquis believed he would acquire some sorcerous power if he allied himself with the de la Fers.

That, however, was none of his, Jack's, concern. If de Bauvin coveted some power or secret that was somehow connected to Catherine or her sister, then it was all the more reason for him—or the de la Fers—to wish to have Catherine back.

An image of her thin, beaten back came to him, and he gritted his teeth. It was a family concern and none of his; a young woman belonged to her family and then to her husband once she was wed. It was the right thing to do.

The thought that money made the right thing to do more attractive niggled at him, but he thrust it to the back of his mind. Regaining his estate and supporting his king against the Roundhead usurper was more important than one mere girl. There was the missive from King Charles himself that Fichet had given him, requesting his presence two weeks hence at Breda in Holland.

Jack looked up and caught Fichet's look again, and decided not to ignore it. "Very well, what is it?"

Fichet cast a glance at his wife, and she spoke up. "You did promise to teach her to fight with a sword, M. Sir Jack." Fichet smiled and nodded approvingly at Mme Felice.

Jack let out an irritated breath. "And so I have. I never said for how long."

He looked from her to Fichet and met only disapproving gazes. He cut the air with an impatient hand. "She is a runaway girl who belongs to her family. I am only doing the right thing, and if I gain a reward for her return, you know it will go to aid the cause of my king."

Their disapproving expressions did not change, although Fichet's softened with understanding. "Ah," the innkeeper said. "So loyalty to your king is worth the sacrifice of a young woman—*une belle jeune fille, non?*—to a family who beats her?"

Jack felt a definite prick of guilt this time, acknowledged it, and gazed at Fichet and his wife with exasperation. "Very well. You have succeeded. I feel ill at ease about sending the girl back to what may be unpleasantness. But that is not my concern, as I have said. Her fate is her family's business, not mine."

Fichet nodded. "So said the good Samaritan when he found the wounded man in the ditch." His gaze was blandly innocent, but his voice, ironic.

Guilt-fed anger forced Jack to his feet, tumbling his chair backward to the floor. "God's blood, Fichet, I am no saint and you know it, so don't expect me to act like one. I'm bound to my king, not some gutter-found wench, and a promise to my king is a far sight more important than what might happen to her."

Fichet raised a calm hand. "Peace, M. Sir Jack. I

only wished to see how far she has come into your affections."

Jack sat down again, shaking his head. "Fichet, my friend, you pry too much."

Fichet raised his brows haughtily. " 'Pry'? No, M. Sir Jack, it is more a concern about mademoiselle's virtue. Did I not say we Fichets are of a remarkable virtue? *Bien!* It is natural, therefore, that I should act as a father to her, and my dear Felice as a mother."

Mme Felice nodded vigorously. "*Oui*, it is true. *Pauvre petite!* Who is to take care of her, when she has not her family?"

"I remind you that I intend to return her to her family."

"But she has not a mother," Mme Felice said triumphantly. "Surely she needs that. Also, what kind of family allows one to be beaten so? She is not a bad girl, I am sure."

"You know nothing of the sort, madame," Jack said impatiently.

Mme Felice frowned, and Fichet gave him a look of offended fire. "If you were not my friend, M. Marstone, I would call you out for that. My dear Felice is a wise woman, and I defy anyone to say differently."

Mme Felice smiled and patted the innkeeper's hand. "Peace, husband. Not all men are as perceptive as you, *mon chou*. Eh, he does not even know he has fallen in love with the girl."

Jack groaned and clutched his hair. "God's blood, have you no ears? Have I not said she is not to my taste in women?"

Felice smiled complacently. "Perhaps. But we have eyes, M. Sir Jack. We have seen how you look at her. You have not looked at any woman in such a way."

"So I have looked at her. Anyone must look at her to speak to her."

The landlord and his wife exchanged a smug look. "What is it that your Shakespeare has said? You do 'protest too much.'"

Jack clamped his mouth shut over more protesting words, then waved his hand in dismissive defeat. "Very well, you may think what fantasies you like. Mlle de la Fer's fate must rest in your hands for the while, however, for my king has called me to Holland—I hope, to say we may go home to England."

Fichet's brows rose. "You will not be taking mademoiselle with you? You will be passing through Normandy, after all."

Jack looked down at his fingers drumming on the table again before he answered. He would be rid of the girl sooner and gain his funds faster if he gave her back to her family on the way to see King Charles.

"She is not yet well," he said shortly instead. "I would have her in full health before I return her to her family. She will fetch a better price well than ill." He said it brusquely, so they would put off their teasing. It worked—almost—for though Fichet frowned and pressed his lips together, Mme Felice did not look away quickly enough to hide a wide smile. Jack decided to ignore it.

Mme Felice nodded. "You are right, of course, M. Sir Jack. *La pauvre petite* is still weak and thin, perhaps too much so to travel. We will take care of her until you return."

He did not quite trust Mme Felice's innocent gaze, for she was as canny as her husband claimed.

But he let it rest; there was nothing she could do if he left on the morrow and without letting either her or Fichet know when he would depart.

He nodded. "It is settled, then. I shall leave in the next few days or so, and send word of when I shall return. Feed her well, madame—and Fichet, be sure to tutor her further in the art of the duel." Fichet was as good a fencer as he was, and expert in both the French and Italian ways of dueling.

Mme Felice smiled. "But of course. I promise you we shall take care of her as long as you are away from her."

Fichet only shrugged his shoulders. "Eh, if you are not here to protect her, we shall do so."

Jack looked at him suspiciously, for they had given in too easily, but the man's expression was bland. He rose. "I suppose I will have to tell the girl that you will be teaching her how to use the sword while I am gone." The inn-wife only continued to smile at him, and Fichet's brows raised as he bowed slightly in acknowledgment. "That's all I am going to do, damn it."

Fichet bowed again, and with a growl, Jack turned and went up the stairs.

Catherine often felt she was still the creature of the alley; she was painfully attuned to sound, taste, touch, sight, and any other sense that allowed her to survive. And food...dear heaven, food. She would have killed to have such food as she had now. She extended her hand from her bath and took a handful of raisins from the bowl on the table beside the tub, and pushed the fruit into her mouth. She closed her eyes at the sweet stickiness that flowed over her tongue, and groaned. Food. So much food. She still had trouble keeping herself from gorging on what Mme Felice provided her every day, but remembered that eating too much gave her the stomachache, and interfered with her training.

She sank down into the bath, newly drawn for her by the chambermaid, letting the hot water cover her like a blanket. Warmth, dear heaven, warmth. She had felt cold forever, it seemed, and now she could bathe and be clean and warm as she pleased. The heat soothed her muscles, sore from her fighting practice. She let the sounds of the hotel below flow over her: muffled voices of guests, shouts of the ostlers outside, the hesitant knocking and *thump* of closed doors out in the hall as chambermaids and bootblacks performed their duties. She had come to understand over the weeks that they were friendly sounds, made by people who wished her no harm, at least not at present. She had become good at ignoring them; she would ignore them now and let her creature-in-the-alley senses be flooded by the bounty she had before her. She never knew when it would be taken from her, after all.

She took a small slice of cheese and let it lie on her tongue and melt for a while, savoring the saltiness before swallowing it. She moaned again—the taste was exquisite. There was more food, a little farther away—little biscuits and slices of dried winter apple. She frowned. She would have to come out of the water if she wanted some of it, but she would be back in the warmth quickly enough. She rose and leaned over the edge of tub, ignoring the drips of water that fell to the floor.

A harsh sigh sounded a little behind her, and she

turned lazily. Perhaps it was Mme Felice, come with her new clothes—

It was Sir Jack.

For one moment, she stared at him, at his eyes that were so very blue, and the silence stretched out long between them. The snap of firewood seemed to startle him, making him blink, and his eyes drifted lower. He let out another harsh breath.

Her gaze went to the food she had been eating. Perhaps he was here to take it away; she was still hungry, and she never knew when there would be food next. She looked at the knife she had been using to cut the cheese.... Quickly she slipped the knife into her hand and sank into the water. Food was important, more than anything else.

However, Sir Jack was not looking at the food but at her, as if she were something to be eaten, rather than the cheese and the fruit. She was not used to a man looking at her; her face flushed hotter than warranted by the heat of the bath. A flurry of words too numerous and confused to speak, stopped her tongue, and she sank farther into the water, up to her neck. She bit her lower lip, vexed. The silence aggravated her—what did he want of her? She should have heard him enter, but had ignored the sounds of the inn, to gorge herself on food.

"I—that is, I thought you were—" The words came out as scrambled as they had been in her mind.

"I-I did not know—" Sir Jack said at the same time. His voice sounded strained. Was he angry with her? She shrank farther into the water, up to her chin, and clutched the small knife with which she had cut the cheese, but she was not sure how much damage she would cause if she used it. If he were angry, and decided to hurt her...But he made no sound, and she dared to turn slightly to look at him.

He was gazing at the ceiling, breathing in deep breaths. He had not come any closer to her, however, so perhaps she would not need the knife for now. She glanced at him again. He was still breathing deeply.

"Are you well, M. Sir Jack?"

He gave a sidewise look, then nodded curtly. "I am well, thank you." His voice sounded stiff, formal. "And you?"

"I am well, monsieur," she replied, equally formal. He nodded again, and another silence stretched thin between them. Impatience niggled at her. The bath was still warm, but she was still hungry, and did not want to expose herself further while getting the apples. She eyed Sir Jack speculatively. He had not hurt her since he had come to her aid in the alley, and had not spoken to her in anything but a moderate tone of voice unless it was to shout an instruction to her in dueling above the clash of swords. He had not touched her since she had requested that he refrain— again, it was during the course of her instruction— but all the times he had, it was with gentleness. Perhaps he could be trusted...at least to bring her food. It would be a test. If he took it away instead of giving it to her, she could cut him and get it back.

"I am still hungry, M. Sir Jack. Will you bring me the plate of apples?"

"Of course." He seemed relieved to have something to do; he walked to the table beside her, picked up the plate, and held it out to her.

She moved up a little to take the food, watching him closely. He watched her, as well, following the movement of her hand to the apple slices, to her lips, but did not move to take any of it away from her.

His gaze lingered on her mouth, and she looked back at him, feeling at once uneasy and...she did not know. She felt at this moment that he was not a threat to her, and that he probably would not be in the future. But she was not entirely sure if she wanted him to look at her. She thought of what she must have looked like when she had been half out of the water—well, she had overheard him say once when he thought she was not near that he preferred plump women. So she was safe from his advances, she was sure. But she remembered someone had said she was unattractive. Her gut twisted; it had not prevented her from being hurt somehow. She felt sure of that, but was not sure what exactly it meant. Not knowing made her feel unsettled...or perhaps it was the way Sir Jack was looking at her. She could not stand it any longer.

"Is there something you want?" she asked abruptly. She gestured meaningfully at her bath. "It is not a convenient time, as I am sure you can see."

He blinked, and seemed to shake himself. "Ah, yes. My apologies. In truth, I should have left as soon as I saw—" He stopped abruptly.

Catherine wondered if she should ask why he had not, but she was still too unsure of him—of anyone, for that matter—to question. She crouched back into the bath and the knife in her hand gave her comfort.

He averted his eyes, gazing at the fireplace instead. "That is, I came to let you know that I will be leaving soon."

She stared at him, a sinking feeling entering her heart. She did not want him to leave. "But you promised that you would give me lessons in fencing."

"Fichet will do it instead; he is as good at it as I am."

His reply should have satisfied her, for it kept the spirit of his agreement with her. But the sinking feeling grew, and she realized she wished to be taught by *him,* not anyone else.

"But you said that Fichet did not know some sword tricks you do, and you promised to teach me those tricks." She frowned. It was not precisely what she felt, but it would work. She wanted...she was not sure what she wanted, but Sir Jack had brought her to this warm place that had food; perhaps if he left she would have to return to the alley.

She thought she saw guilt on his face before he said gruffly, "Fichet has other tricks with the sword; he can teach you those until I return."

"Where will you go?" she asked, feeling desperate.

"Breda, in Holland. My king calls for my service, and I must go."

Catherine nodded slowly. She remembered duty, suddenly, and understood it in her bones, though anxiety gripped her at the thought of his leaving. She had become...used to him. He was easy to look upon, and she admitted she liked to look at him, even wanted to see if she could bring the light of kindness and humor into his eyes that she had seen before. She had seen Fichet and Mme Felice bring laughter to him—they were his friends, he had said. Perhaps he could be her friend as well some day.

She drew in a long, slow breath at the thought. She had no reason to trust anyone, let alone men. It frightened her a little to think of it, but she had seen the affection and friendship between the innkeeper and his wife; perhaps it might not be an impossible thing for her to have a friend and that friend be Sir Jack.

"I don't know how long I will be gone, Catherine."

The sound of his voice took her out of her thoughts and she looked at him again. "No idea at all?" she asked. She wanted to know, suddenly, urgently. He smiled, then, and despite the cooling water, she felt warmed.

"A fortnight, a few months, perhaps."

She shivered—how was she to find out if they could be friends, if he were to be gone that long?

"Cold, Catherine?"

She looked up at him—he had used her Christian name twice, but she didn't reprove him. Perhaps he, too, wished to be friends. But she said nothing of that, and nodded slowly. "Yes, the water is definitely cooling." She looked at her hands and grimaced. "And I am turning into a raisin—see?" She wiggled her fingers at him to show him the beginnings of wrinkles at the fingertips.

He stepped closer, a looming figure between her and the firelight, but she kept herself from flinching from him as he took her hand and examined her fingers. "Indeed," he said, and though his voice sounded solemn, an amused light grew in his eyes. "When I return, and when we duel for money, we can advertise you as the amazing dueling raisin woman. People will come to see you from all the provinces, and you shall be famous. We'll then be so exalted in wealth as to rival your king's court."

An odd feeling grew under Catherine's breastbone, a bubble of lightness. She felt her lips turning up, and then a laugh broke from her. It surprised her; she did not remember when she had last laughed. "I would like to see it happen," she said. "Except not the raisin woman part." She looked at the large towel Felice had left nearby and hesitated. The water was definitely cool now, and even if she asked Sir Jack to fetch Felice or a chambermaid, it would take a while before either of them came to help her. She would be cold again, and she despised being cold. She glanced at Sir Jack—there was nothing in his eyes but amusement. He did not find her attractive, she was sure. There could be no harm in having him give her the towel. "I would be pleased if you brought the towel to me, M. Sir Jack." Her nervousness forced the words out in a command.

His brows raised, but he bowed ironically deep. "I am only your lowly servant, mademoiselle," he said, and came forward, holding the cloth out to her. She took it and then looked at him again. His smile had an ironic cast, as if he expected some challenge, or was challenging her in some way. Rebellion rose in her; she admitted that she did not like that he thought her unattractive. Well, then! What did it matter if he looked at her or not?

She lifted her chin, brought the soft linen towel up between them, then rose from the water. Slowly she wrapped the towel around her, stepped out of the bath, then walked to the fireplace. She turned to look at Sir Jack, giving him just as much of an ironic smile as he had given her. "Well? You said you were my servant. Fetch my clothes—they are there on the bed." She knew she was being impertinent, knew she should remember to be grateful to him for all that he had given her, but she did not feel like being grateful to him. She felt she owed him something, and resented it. It put her into his power somehow, and she did not want to be in anyone's power.

"And what if I do not?" One corner of his lips lifted in a slight grin.

She bit her lip to still the sudden feeling of laughter again, for she wished to hold on to her resentment a little longer. She tried to look down her nose at him, which was difficult, she realized, because he was so much taller than she. "Well, then, you are not a very good servant."

A speculative expression came over his face. "A good servant needs to be paid, mademoiselle."

"I will pay you in coin after a while," she said. She turned away, facing the fire, suddenly conscious of her poverty. She had nothing but her rosary, her cross, and her dagger, and she did not want to part with those. She thought of the beads on her rosary... perhaps it might be possible to replace one or two of the beads with paste, and sell the stones for money. That was a possibility. She knew very well that she owed Sir Jack, Fichet, and Mme Felice a great deal.

A sound from him made Catherine look up, and she saw he was closer now, and his hands came up to her shoulders. She was proud of herself: She did not flinch at all this time, and the fear she felt at his touch was very, very slight and soon gone.

"There are other ways to pay," he said.

Her heart grew suddenly cold. She knew from her time in the alley of the ways women paid men. She had chosen to starve rather than pay for food that way; indeed, she had even approached a man once to sell her body but had vomited so badly when he agreed that he had left quickly. If she was going to vomit every time she sold herself, she had thought, she would starve faster than if she did not do it at all.

"I will not lie with you," she said bluntly. She felt

his hands move from her, then return, his finger under her chin to make her look at him.

His expression was kind, and he touched her cheek gently. "I am not asking for that, Catherine," he said. "Just a kiss. I am leaving soon, and would have something to remember you by."

She wet her lips nervously. A kiss, that was all. She suddenly remembered long ago that her mother had kissed her on the cheek—there could be nothing wrong with that. If that was payment, she could do it. She nodded and presented her cheek.

Jack's hands pulled her closer, and she stiffened—she could not help it—but he did not seem to mind, for he leaned down and kissed her cheek, a featherlight touch of lips to skin. He moved away, and she let out a breath she hadn't realized she was holding. She raised her gaze to his, and looked away from the warmth that was clearly there. "That... that was not so very bad," she said, and glanced at him again.

Amusement was clear in his eyes. "Thank you. I have been told in the past that my kisses are somewhat tolerable."

Obviously he had kissed other women... and, she suspected, not on the cheek. Her gaze lowered to his lips. She wondered... no. "When will you be leaving?" she asked instead.

"On the morrow—and don't tell Fichet or Mme Felice! They will no doubt nag me about something or other, and I would rather not have to deal with it."

She nodded, and crossed her fingers behind her back to negate her apparent agreement. She knew suddenly that she did not want to be left behind with the innkeeper or his wife, even though she was fairly sure by now that they would never complain of her presence.

They were... kind people, she realized with surprise. She did not remember meeting any such, but then, she remembered very little so far about her life before the alley. In fact, she felt reluctant to think at all, and had been content just to exist and survive these few weeks since the alley. She frowned. Weeks had passed, and she did not know how many.

"Are you displeased that I am leaving?"

Catherine looked up, startled out of her thoughts. There seemed a question in his eyes that made his words seem more than a trivial inquiry.

"A little," she replied, honestly but cautiously. "*You* promised to teach me fencing, not Fichet, and I assumed it would be only you and not anyone else. But a king's command is always his subject's duty."

He nodded, seeming both relieved and disappointed, but she looked away, not knowing how to respond. A chill draft drifted past her, and she shivered.

"I will need to dress now; will you ask Mme Felice to send up a maid?" She turned to her clothes set out on the bed. "I am still not used to dressing myself."

No sound came from behind her, however, and she glanced at Sir Jack. A frown creased his brow as he stared at her, and he stepped quickly toward her and seized her arm, too quickly for her to flinch or step away. Anger flared in her.

"Take your hands from me," she said between her teeth. Her hands turned into fists.

He did not; instead, he turned her so that she faced away from him. "Your back. Your weals are gone."

She twisted so that she could stare angrily at him. "What of it? I imagine I heal quickly."

His expression grew grim with suspicion. "No one recovers that quickly from such wounds. All you have left are pale stripes across your skin, scars older than those of a few weeks." He took one of her hands and turned them palm up. "There is no scarring there, either, though I know I saw bloody cuts on them when I found you."

She pulled away her hands and shrugged. "Perhaps you were mistaken in what you saw."

Indecision stayed a moment on Sir Jack's face, then disappeared. "Perhaps." He turned abruptly to the chamber door. "I will fetch Mme Felice . . . to help you dress." He strode to the door and left through it, closing it again with a decided slam.

Jack closed the door and leaned against it, breathing deeply and pulling as much control as he could gather through his heated body. Damn the inn-wife! She must have known Catherine was taking her bath, and had not told him, so that he'd get a good look at her without her clothes.

Very well. So he had not thought the woman—he could not deny she was a fully-formed woman any longer—was the sort he favored, and he was wrong. He had thought she was a skinny waif, but she had changed over the course of these weeks so that she had filled out, and her breasts had become full, her body lean but lithe. When she had leaned over the edge of the tub, her waist had curved in, then out to hint at trim hips, and the whole had stopped his steps toward her, stopped his very breath. It was worse when she had covered herself with the linen towel; it had covered everything, but the firelight had revealed a delectable silhouette that did nothing but bring him to wild imaginings.

He blew out a long breath. Very well. He was wrong. Catherine was indeed the sort of woman he liked; in fact, lusted after.

Then she had turned and gazed at him with her wary green eyes and he had felt . . . lost, as if he had mistaken his way after a long march and found another way to a new land. It had taken all his control not to seize her and make love to her right then and there.

But he remembered he was a gentleman, and hoped he sounded intelligent enough after his surprise to bid her a good farewell. He winced. Well, he had bid her a farewell all right, much more than he intended. But he could not at the end resist holding her, and thought he had done well only to kiss her cheek.

He pushed himself off the chamber door and went down the hall to his own room. He would not leave for Holland on the morrow, but tonight, for he was not sure if he could stand any more of Felice's machinations, or the chance that he might just see more of Catherine than he should.

It was just as well, however. He opened the door and entered his room, looking immediately for his knapsack. He would pack lightly for travel, and bring as much money as he could spare for the king and his cause. He'd bring his musket, as well, in case he'd be required to leave for England and fight for Charles's return.

It'd be a relief, truth to tell, for Catherine's fast-healing wounds disturbed him. He'd been well educated in the lives of the saints, and he remembered mention of such wounds on those holy folk. But the devil could also cause marvels to aid his sorcerers....

Jack shook his head. He did not believe in such things; he'd never seen any supernatural marvels that people had claimed to see, and what he had seen had clearly been the creation of disordered minds, or outright frauds. He'd grown from boy to man in the company of the king, and had seen for himself the very un-Christian strife such superstitious thinking had brought to both France and England. He was, in fact, not inclined to believe in the dogma of either the Roundheads or the Catholics. Give him the rationality of Sir Isaac Newton, or Galileo, over the ravings from the pulpits.

Surely there was a rational explanation for Catherine's wounds and quick healing; perhaps it was as she said, that she had healed quickly.

At any rate, Catherine and her problems were a moot point; he was leaving, and as soon as he was gone from Paris, he could focus on his true duty, his duty to his king.

Chapter 4

CATHERINE LOOKED AT HER HANDS, turning them slowly over. Her wounds...she had painful wounds, she remembered, but they were gone now. They were lean and smooth, with the beginnings of calluses on them, but no blood on them now, no wounds that slowly seeped red. Trembling seized her, and she sat slowly on the bed next to her clothes. Sir Jack would not hurt her...at least, she did not think so. But his words forced her to think, and memories rose inside...a whipping, an agonizing pain between her legs, and then blood, too much blood. She closed her eyes. Blood on the floor, blood on her hands, long ago, and again when she was the creature in the alley.

It was not a dream. She had hoped it was and had set aside the memory to the darkness in her mind, but Sir Jack had seen it, too.

She shivered again and let the linen towel around her drop while she reached for her shift. Quickly she pulled on the thin material, and covered herself with a blanket as she moved to the fireplace and sat on a stool in front of it. She stretched out her feet to the warmth and moved uncomfortably as a prickling went through them in response to warming past an icy cold.

She held out her hands to the fire, as well, and the light flickered over them, smooth and white. There was no mark on them, and she liked the way they looked now. A faint image came to her mind: at one time they had been plump hands. Now they seemed lithe and strong, well on their way to handling a sword—competently, she hoped. The wounds on them had appeared . . . twice, she believed. Once, long ago, and again in the alley—no more than twice in the alley. It had happened whenever she had seen someone abused, and would not stop until the abuse had passed.

She did not know what it meant. A word struggled to the forefront of her mind: stigmata. The word brought forth faint memories: lessons with nuns, the ritual of mass, of confession, of prayer, the lives of saints. However, she was sure she was no saint.

Perhaps it was a curse, a punishment for a crime. Fear formed a lump in her throat. She had caused some of the blood to flow in the time-long-ago, she realized. Surely this was a punishment.

A knock on the door made her jump, and she stood suddenly. She made herself relax. It was no doubt Mme Felice. *"Entré!"* she called.

The inn-wife smiled at her as she entered the room carrying a brush and comb. "M. Sir Jack said you were ready for your clothes." An amused, mischievous look entered her eyes.

Catherine frowned at her. "You knew he would find me in my bath," she stated.

Madame shrugged. "Perhaps, perhaps not." She held a bloused chemise out to her. "Here, put this on quickly so you will not become too chilled." A sudden billow of cotton went over Catherine's head, and she lifted her arms up to swim her way to sleeve and neckline. Mme Felice adjusted the drape with smart jerks here and there before she tossed the skirt over Catherine's head, as well.

"I think you mean to drown me in clothes madame!" Catherine protested.

The inn-wife grinned. "Eh, you have made a joke, mademoiselle! It is good to hear."

Catherine gazed at her, frowning. "Am I so somber, then, madame?"

Mme Felice smiled as she tied the skirt ribbons around Catherine's waist, and there was a great deal of understanding in her eyes. "Mademoiselle, if the scars you have had on your hands and your back were the story of your life, then you have a reason to be somber."

Fear seized Catherine, for she wondered if the inn-wife thought perhaps she had been at fault for her whipping, and she said nothing for a moment. But she looked again at Mme Felice and saw nothing but kindness.

"There . . . the wounds are not there any longer." She waited, wondering if Mme Felice would change and look at her with fear or hatred.

The inn-wife's hands only paused for a moment as she pulled the bodice around Catherine's torso and began to lace it. She sighed. "M. Sir Jack has told me what he saw; indeed, I have wondered at how quickly your wounds have healed. But I am only an inn-wife, mademoiselle, and though I can read and write and keep our inn's accounts, I am not a priest. I do not know what is a curse and what is a blessing, except what I know of my own life and my husband's. But I cannot think whatever has . . . happened to you is because you are a bad woman. What is it that our Lord has said of he who sacrifices his life for another? M. Sir Jack told me you almost sacrificed your life trying to save that girl. Surely such an impulse came from the goodness within you, and surely the Blessed Mother of our Lord would intercede for you for such a good act."

Catherine let out a deep breath, and her shoulders ached suddenly from the release of tension. "I have been afraid that I have been cursed, madame."

Felice smiled kindly and patted Catherine's shoulder. "Well, even if you were, did not M. Sir Jack bring you to us, and is that not a blessing? You have not the scars now, and you are looking very pretty." She grinned suddenly. "*En vrai,* I believe M. Sir Jack has noticed it, and if he has not, then he is surely blind."

A hot blush warmed Catherine's face, and she looked at Mme Felice accusingly. "You *did* know I was taking my bath when M. Sir Jack came up, and did not tell him!"

The inn-wife wrinkled her nose as she helped Catherine into a warm jacket. "Bah! What if I did?" She waved her hand dismissively. "The man is stubborn and would not see a dead herring in front of his face even if he were slapped with it, especially if he denied its existence at the start."

Catherine pressed her lips together to suppress a laugh. "I am not a dead herring, madame."

"*Dieu merci!*" the inn-wife said tartly. "Come,

turn and sit, mademoiselle, so that I may comb your hair." Catherine obediently turned and sat on the stool in front of the fire, and Mme Felice gave her a hand mirror, which she laid on her lap. She closed her eyes as the comb pulled through her hair, slowly and gently, with soothing strokes. "No, you are not a dead herring, but it is necessary to show M. Sir Jack the truth."

"I am glad you do not think me a dead herring," Catherine said, chuckling at last. "What truth does M. Sir Jack not wish to see?"

"That he is in love with you, mademoiselle."

All of Catherine's laughter stopped, and she drew in a deep, shuddering breath. Confusion gripped her—in love with her? She had not thought it; she had heard he preferred women who looked different from herself. And...she was not sure it was a good thing; she realized suddenly she did not know what love was like or even if it were real.

"You must be mistaken, madame. I have not seen it."

Catherine heard the sound of an impatient huff of breath behind her. "Then you are well matched with him, for it seems you are both blind to what is in front of you. *Tiens!* Did he not agree to teach you the swordfighting? He has taught others in the past, but never a woman. It is clear he can refuse you nothing. The man looks at you as if you were a feast and he a starving fool. He would gobble you up in a moment if you let him."

"First I am a dead herring, and now a platter of food—I suppose that is better," Catherine said, trying not to laugh. "But I do not wish to be gobbled up." The comb tugged suddenly at a tangle and she winced.

"Foolishness!" Mme Felice said as she worked at the tangle. "Of course you wish to be gobbled up, you simply do not know it."

Catherine frowned to keep back a laugh. "Madame, I have never wanted to be gobbled up in my life. *En fait,* I think it would be a frightening thing to be so consumed."

She felt Mme Felice's hand pause on her head, then resume the combing. A sentimental sigh came from the older woman. "Ahhh. To be consumed with love...so it is at first. But I tell you, you will not mind it with the right man...and I am sure you have not met the right man until now," she said confidently.

Catherine could not help chuckling at the woman's self-assurance. It was clear she was well matched with the very self-assured Fichet. "You are more sure than I...and should I not be more sure than you in these matters?"

"No," the inn-wife said bluntly. "For you are full of fear, mademoiselle. As is M. Sir Jack. Fear always obscures love—and most everything else of worth."

Catherine drew in a deep breath. It was true, she realized. She lived in fear as if it were a second skin, though she did her best not to show it. It was clear, however, that she did show it, for Mme Felice could see it. "Madame, I do not know if I understand love, or can feel it."

"Ah, that is a problem," Felice said, and moved around to gaze at her. She frowned critically as she used the brush here and there on Catherine's hair, then with a last tweak on an errant curl, nodded with satisfaction. "*La voilà! c'est bien.* You are a pretty lady, mademoiselle. I think, in time, you will understand what love is, and most certainly you have attracted it."

Fear grew in Catherine's belly at the thought of attracting a man's interest, but she remembered the inn-wife's words. She had very little in this world, but if fear did indeed obscure everything of worth, then she would have even less if she continued to fear. She took a deep breath and let it out. She would do her best not to be fearful.

She looked at Mme Felice gratefully. "Thank you, madame. You have been very kind. I will try not to be afraid."

Soft sympathy was in Mme Felice's smile, and she gently patted Catherine's cheek. "You are a brave lady, Mlle de la Fer. I know you will succeed." She lifted the hand mirror from Catherine's lap. "Now, look you—see, it is as I have said. You are a pretty lady, and it is no wonder M. Sir Jack has fallen in love with you."

Catherine smiled a little at the inn-wife's persistence, and shook her head, but picked up the mirror.

The mirror was not perfect, for it was old and had a few scratches in its polished metal. But it showed enough to make Catherine feel...odd, as if she looked on someone else's face that moved as she moved. Another image came to her mind, of what she had looked like before she had become the creature in the alley; except for the eyes, which were just as green and wide as they were before, and her nose, which was just as straight, everything had changed. She had had a round face before; now it was lean and heart-shaped. Her lips took on a severe line at rest; before they had turned down. She touched her throat—it was lean and long, not rounded and plump. Her hair, which she remembered had been short, now curled around her face in a fashionable masculine style.

She slowly handed the mirror to Mme Felice and shook her head. "I do not look like what I remember, madame."

The inn-wife nodded. "No, you would not. You were thin and starving when you first came to us. You have filled out, I believe."

It was not what Catherine had meant, but she let the matter rest; it was better than talking of love and fear and other uncomfortable things. Then, too, she felt pleased at her appearance; she looked different than she remembered, and therefore not easily recognized from before the days of the alley. It gave her a measure of protection... which would be lessened when Sir Jack left. She looked at the inn-wife. "M. Sir Jack is leaving tonight."

The older woman raised her brows. "Ah, so that is when. He would not tell us."

Catherine grinned. "Yes, I know." She paused, venturing cautiously in assessing her emotions. "Should I go with him, do you think?"

Mme Felice hesitated. "I... do not know, mademoiselle. Has he asked you?"

"No. But that does not mean I cannot go. He did not precisely say he forbids me."

Madame chuckled. "You are a clever one." She sobered again, however. "Do you know what is before you, mademoiselle? You will go through Normandy to Breda, where M. Sir Jack travels."

Normandy... fear rose again, but Catherine suppressed it. *I will not be afraid,* she told herself fiercely. It was not necessary that she come close to her home, after all.

"You are always welcome to stay with us of course; indeed, it is what M. Sir Jack wishes," Mme Felice continued.

Catherine bit her lip in indecision. It would be easy enough to stay where she was; there was no real reason why she should go or stay. She glanced at the inn-wife. "Perhaps I should do as M. Sir Jack wishes, and stay."

The older woman smiled, her eyes twinkling with delight. She nodded. "*C'est bien.* We shall be glad to have you." A clock tolled in the distance, and the woman looked up and out the window. "Ah. It is time I go."

Catherine thought of Sir Jack's imminent departure and felt suddenly as if she did not want to be alone. "May I go with you?"

Felice smiled. "I am going to Père Doré for my confession. If you wish to come with me, you may."

Catherine hesitated. She had not gone to confession or Mass since she had come to this inn; she knew there must be heavy sins on her soul if the images that came to her of her past were true. But there were her scars, and the bleeding that had come from them time and again. Fear rose, hard and sharp. Surely she was cursed. . . .

No. Fear again. She would not let herself be afraid. She lifted her chin and looked firmly at Mme Felice. "I will go with you.

The inn-wife patted her hand. "Very good. Let us go down, then."

Catherine nodded, pulled a shawl around her shoulders, and tucked her dagger in her pocket. Mme Felice frowned slightly at the inclusion of a weapon, but said nothing, merely leading Catherine down the stairs and out of the inn.

The late afternoon winter sky deepened the purple shadows between the buildings, giving them a bruised look, Catherine thought. It was as if winter had taken the city in a hard grip, leaving marks, and she saw it was indeed so as she passed streets where beggars shivered in corners. She regretted that she did not have money in her pockets to give any of them; she thought perhaps she would indeed take some of the small jewels in her rosary and replace them with paste.

She hunched her shoulders against a sudden chill, but a shivering took her nevertheless, raising the hairs on the back of her neck. She glanced behind her—there was no one.

"Is there something wrong?" Felice asked, her brows creasing in a frown.

Catherine shook her head. "No—my imagination, I am sure." And yet she still shivered, and a pain began to grow in the palms of her hands. Her shivering seemed not to have much to do with the winter air, for she was well clothed. But it seemed almost as if a dark mist seeped out from the corners of the street, and she was glad when their hastened steps brought them to a small church. She looked up at the spires that caught the brightness of the last few glimmers of the sun. It lifted her spirits somehow, and it was with a lighter heart that she climbed the steps to the church doors.

It was quiet inside, only the whispers of feet against stone, of cloth against cloth, as she and Mme Felice approached the font and crossed themselves with holy water.

It was not long before the priest came; he looked familiar, and Catherine recalled that this was the church she had come to for shelter when the alley had become too cold, and from which she had run away that day she had met Sir Jack. She had been afraid and ashamed, so much so that she had run when the priest had called to her. She wondered what would have happened had she stayed.... Her life would probably not be so confusing, she thought ruefully. On the other hand, she would not have saved the girl from her rapists, and she would have not met Mme Felice, Fichet, or Sir Jack. She could not regret any of that... except she was not sure about Sir Jack. She almost shook her head in wonder. How odd it was that a choice made in fear and shame should bring her to do something that was good, and to people who were kind. An unfamiliar feeling—a good feeling, she thought—flowed into her. She felt stronger... perhaps even more confident.

The priest frowned slightly when he gazed at her, as if he, too, were trying to recall who she was. But he shook his head as if to dispel a slight disturbance, and his smile was welcoming as Mme Felice introduced her. The inn-wife patted her hand. "Come, sit with me in the sanctuary. I will pray, then make my confession, and then you may go next, if you wish."

She nodded, and followed the older woman into the sanctuary.

Catherine hesitated at the door, once again feeling afraid, but she shook her head at herself. She had been in more dangerous places than this, surely, and there was no sense of... being watched, as she had felt outside the church. Still, there were the wounds that had been on her back and her hands, and the possibility that she was cursed.

No. She would not be afraid. She put her hand on the sanctuary door and pushed it open.

The door swung open to an arched ceiling, drawing her eyes to the altar and the cross above it. She swallowed, hesitating, then stepped within.

The slight pinprick of sensation on the palms of

her hands and on her back almost made her turn and run, but she gritted her teeth and made her feet move forward instead. She forced herself to look around the sanctuary as if it was usual for her to come here, as if she belonged. It was nearly empty, except for an old woman and a little girl who fidgeted at her side, and of course Mme Felice, who quickly entered a pew, knelt, and began to pray.

As Catherine kept her eyes on the cross above the altar, the prickling on her palms grew stronger. She pulled off her gloves and glanced down at her hands—they looked bruised, but did not bleed. She sighed; she could bear it, for the prickling was not much more than a strong tickle, and at least it did not seep blood.

She moved into the pew next to Mme Felice and closed her eyes, letting her shoulders relax. She should pray, but did not know what she should say; she felt she was at a crux in her life. Choices... she wondered if she was meant to do something other than merely survive, but what, she did not know.

A movement beside her made her glance up— Mme Felice had risen and, with a kind glance at Catherine, left for the confessional. Catherine thought of the inn-wife, and how she went about her business with a sense of purpose and satisfaction. She did not think that such a life was for her; she had tried to help with the work at the inn, but she was not good at it, for all that the inn-wife tolerated her unskilled help. She grimaced. Mme Felice even helped her dress, as if she, Catherine, was a lady of high estate. Well, she might have been, but she was not now. She shook her head at herself; the least she should do is learn how to dress herself. She glanced up at the cross again and sighed. It was good she had come here; a measure of clarity had come to her, and she felt less like the creature in the alley and a little more human. She sighed, giving up knowing how and what to pray for, and settled for the Lord's Prayer instead. She felt glad that she remembered it among the few things she did remember.

A lightness, a sense of optimism filled her as she finished the prayer. Her hands had ceased prickling, and a heat entered them instead, so much so that she left off the gloves she had worn and put them in her pocket instead. Another warmth seemed to center around her throat; frowning, she pulled out her crucifix and looked at it. It looked no different than it usually did, but it was as warm as if she had set it in front of a fire. She wondered what it meant; good, she hoped.

She sighed. Surely her life would become better after this; did she not have a place with the Fichets if she so chose, until Sir Jack returned? And then... well, she would not think what would happen then, but the more she thought of him, the more she believed he would do her no harm, none that he intended, anyway.

A rustling at her side made her look up to see Mme Felice smiling down at her. "I am done, mademoiselle. Shall we go?" Catherine nodded and rose to her feet, following the woman toward the church foyer.

As they stepped out of the sanctuary, Catherine glanced at the confessional; she could hear a stirring within and was sure the priest was still there. She hesitated, then briefly touched Mme Felice's arm.

"I...I have not been to confession in a while, madame. If you do not mind waiting..."

The older woman smiled. "No, not at all. I will

wait in the sanctuary; a few more prayers will surely be for my good."

Catherine nodded and went into the confessional, keeping enough control over her fears so that she did not flinch or hesitate before entering. She sat for a moment, savoring the silent anonymity, though she sensed that the priest was waiting. She took a deep breath. "Forgive me, Father, for I have sinned...." she said at last.

Her words, her fears, her feelings came tumbling forth, released by hope and the obscuring dark of the small room, the screen separating herself from the priest, and the sense that there was no judgment, only listening. Only once she hesitated, her hands clenching into fists, but remembered she would not fear, and told also of her affliction, of her wounds.

Her words faded into the silence of the room at last, and she felt drained and tired, as if she had just finished a long lesson in swordfighting. Her hands lay lax in her lap, and she waited.

A chuckle came from the other side of the screen. "Well, indeed, it seems you have not come to confession in a long time if all of this has happened since the last."

Catherine smiled. "Yes, I think it has been a while. I cannot remember the last time." She hesitated. "What must I do, *mon Père?*"

Silence, then: "I do not know, *ma fille.* For the sins I can clearly discern, ten Pater Nosters, and ten Marias. But all else..." She heard a rustling on the other side of the screen, the slight negative movement of his head's shadow. "What you say is remarkable, and though some would say your... condition is probably a good thing, I am no expert."

"Good?" Catherine grasped the word as a lifeline.

"What I have heard of stigmata—for that is what you have—has been borne mostly by those who are innocent, and pure in heart. But there are instances where it is not so, and I cannot tell the difference." He paused. "Do you see it as good, or evil?"

Catherine's lips turned down bitterly. "I know not. I only know I would be rid of it, and I do not know why I am so afflicted, for an affliction it is. If it is from God, I pray He removes it. If it is from the devil, then I pray I might receive whatever exorcism is needed to expel it."

"A practical answer, mademoiselle." A sigh sounded from behind the screen. "But not particularly religious. It would be best if this were investigated."

Impatience seized Catherine. "Can you not just perform an exorcism?"

"So you think it might be evil? But an exorcism will not work if it is from God... and I have not conclusive evidence either way whether it is from our Lord or from Satan. What if it is from God?"

Catherine groaned. "Then I wish *le bon Dieu* would tell me what I am to do with it. It is a most troublesome thing."

A chuckle emitted from behind the screen. "It is supposed to be a blessed sign if it is from God, but I myself have speculated that it would, indeed, be inconvenient." He sighed. "It is something the cardinal would understand better than I. With your permission, I will write to him and ask his advice."

Catherine gnawed her lower lip in thought. It would be good to know, and whatever the answer might be, she would be on her way to ridding herself of it. "Very well," she said. She paused, wondering about the good or evil of her condition. "If... I have been afraid, *mon Père,* that . . . that I myself might be a sorcerer because of my wounds." Fear rose sharply, but she suppressed it. It was out, at last, her great fear. She did not want to be a source of evil. "How may I know if I am or am not?"

"It is possible," the priest said, his voice taking a thoughtful tone. "There are various ways to find out, most of them unpleasant." He let out a snort of clear skepticism. "As far as I can tell, the methods are torture—which can easily force a confession from even the most innocent, as even the blessed Jehanne d'Arc has shown—or dunking in water, which would drown either the innocent or the guilty."

Catherine winced, seeing his point.

"I for one would not want the death of an innocent to stain my soul, mademoiselle!" he continued. "No, those methods are not exact at all for my satisfaction."

Catherine could not help grinning. "I do not blame you, *mon Père.*"

A chuckle sounded behind the screen. "I betray my enthusiasm, mademoiselle. I have long been dissatisfied with such methods, and would want better reasoned ways than those." He sighed. "The least harmful is to allow a sorcerer's victim to touch him, to see if the victim's curse or demonic possession ceases. It is said that aside from exorcism, the touch of the sorcerer will cure the victim of whatever afflicts him, if that affliction has come from the sorcerer himself."

Catherine shook her head. "I have not cursed anyone, *mon Père,* nor know of any who is possessed of a demon. If I am a source of evil, I can do nothing but ask for absolution, as I have already done here."

She hesitated. "Do you think . . . what do *you* think of my affliction? Good, or evil?"

A long silence came from the other side of the screen. "When I weigh your words and what I know, I can only say I do not know. But . . . in my heart, and in my hopes, mademoiselle, I think it is good."

Catherine sighed, and it seemed a weight came off her shoulders. But she shook her head at herself; regardless, it was a burden, and she would be well rid of it, she thought. "I thank you, *mon Père*," she said, nevertheless.

He blessed her, then she took her leave, and went to fetch Mme Felice.

The inn-wife looked searchingly at her when she found her in the sanctuary, then smiled. "You look well, mademoiselle."

Catherine nodded, wondering how much she should tell her. But the woman patted her arm. "You need not tell me. It is enough that you have some relief to your heart and your soul."

Catherine nodded again and smiled at her. She would tell Mme Felice later; it was enough for now to think about all she had told the priest and figure out what she must do with herself and her future.

The evening had fallen while they had been in the church, and Catherine felt a little guilty for delaying their return home, for she knew that if she had not decided to go to confession, there would have still been enough light with which to go home. Paris was dangerous enough during the day, and even more so at night. There were a few flickering lights that the linkboys had hurriedly lit on the streets, but the candles therein were thin and flickered in their lanterns. She hurried her steps in accordance with Mme Felice's; she was glad the inn was not too far away.

But it took only a few steps before the hair on Catherine's neck rose and a harsh prickling centered in her palms again.

Something was watching them.

Catherine swallowed and glanced at Mme Felice, who seemed untroubled. Perhaps it was her imagination? Surely that was all it was.

Her hands began to ache, and she remembered the dagger she had put in her pocket. She looked around her, then glanced behind. The dark mist she had thought she had seen earlier seemed to creep out from the corners of the street, a shadow against the night's dark. She wet her lips nervously. It reminded her of something, something from long ago. It... smelled of something she remembered, and it was not the usual smell of the streets or the alleyways. Her hand crept to her pocket, where her dagger was.

It came out from the darkest part of the shadowed mist, suddenly, like a bat from a disturbed crypt, but of a man's height, and misshapen. A scream struggled to release itself from Catherine's throat, but she could only seize Mme Felice's arm and push her toward the inn, barely visible from this distance. "Run, madame, run, hurry!" The inn-wife turned to protest, but caught sight of the dark figure that Catherine faced, and she paled, her hand fisted at her mouth. Catherine pushed her again. "Run! Go home, quickly!" Pain sliced her hands, and she gasped.

Mme Felice crossed herself and found her voice. "But what of you?" she asked, her voice trembling.

Catherine watched the monster as it weaved toward her, its movements quick and lithe. "Go! It will move quickly, and I can hold it until you leave, and then I will only have to defend myself, not both of us."

The older woman nodded. "I will get Robert," she said. "You cannot face this yourself." She ran before Catherine could protest.

It took only a moment's inattention as Catherine glanced back to see that Mme Felice had left safely. The creature struck, its claws glinting in the faint moonlight as it came down to seize her. She sidestepped the blow, angry that her skirts hampered her movements, and her hand came up, slicing with her dagger. The creature howled—she had cut it. Green oozed from the wound, and the smell that emitted from the monster was worse than the most rotten offal. She clenched her teeth against the vomit rising in her throat.

Another swipe, and she moved again to avoid it, whirling under its arm as she extended her arm to cut again at the creature. It hit something harder—bone, she thought—and the monster howled again.

The next attack did not come as quickly; either she had wounded the monster enough to slow it, or it was reconsidering its attack. She hoped it was the first; reconsideration meant that it had more intelligence to attack than she wished. A glance at what she thought might be its eyes showed nothing but twin pinpricks of red in the midst of blackness, reminding her of—

The thing lunged, and she jumped back, but it swiped not with its arm but with its leg, sweeping her feet from under her. Even she could hear her gasp of pain as her hip landed on the cobblestones, but she still had hold of her dagger. She rolled, slicing at the monster as it reached to grab her, but it knocked the dagger from her hand, slick with blood.

"Catherine!"

Sir Jack's voice. Relief and sudden strength surged into her. She rolled again away from the monster. Metal skittered on cobblestone, and she saw her sword inches from her hand. She grasped it and swung her arm upward.

The creature gave a cut-off howl and fell, and its severed head *thump*ed and rolled within inches of hers. Red light flashed in the darkness, searing her eyes for a moment.

Catherine gasped and moved hastily away, climbing at last to her feet. The monster's form before her seemed to melt, its flesh flowing outward to puddle on the street. She swallowed, and breathed deeply to slow her pounding heart.

The stench of the creature nearly choked her, and with it came a hard trembling. Terror and nausea struck her at once, and her knees became weak. She groaned.

A hand clasped her arm, holding her steady. She looked up. It was Sir Jack, disgust clear in his eyes as he glanced at the remains of the monster before them. He gazed at her, and his expression became concerned. "Catherine, are you well?"

She took in another breath, this time mindful of breathing through the cloth of her sleeve. "I think... I think so."

He looked at the pile of sludge before them. "What is that?"

She shook her head. "I don't know. I have never seen its like. It came out of the darkness to attack us."

He wrinkled his nose. "Faugh! It stinks worse than a latrine. Let us leave." She turned and stumbled, but his arm came up to steady her. He eyed her skeptically. "You are not well."

She shook her head and smiled slightly as the stench receded. "It is the smell of the . . . the creature. I have been too close to it for too long."

"Understandable."

She glanced at him, wondering what he was thinking, but the evening's shadows obscured his expression, showing only the sharp outline of his features.

She thought of the monster's actions, how it had attacked, and a slow realization took shape. She looked at Sir Jack again and savored his presence, for she suddenly understood she would soon never see him again. She took in a deep breath, glad that the creature's stench was behind her, and resolutely raised her chin.

"M. Sir Jack," she said. "I will need to leave you, Fichet, and Mme Felice. I believe the creature came not after us as defenseless women, but for me. It is best if I leave, so that I am sure to keep you all out of danger."

"Do you know why it came after you?" His words were sharp, abrupt, and she did not know whether it was from anger or urgency. She did not flinch from the sound, and realized that she did not fear any anger he might have.

"No . . ." She paused and remembered the creature, and the way it had red pinpricks of light for eyes. It reminded her of . . . of something, long ago, something terrible and painful. She swallowed down a residual nausea. "No. But it did not go after Mme Felice when she ran, and she had no weapon. And it reminds me of something long ago, and that is why I think it is after me."

"Of what does it remind you?" His voice was still stiff, still abrupt.

"I don't know...pain, fear. That is all I remember."

He said nothing, only nodded slightly, and she realized he had let go of her arm, and that she had clasped her hand at the crook of his arm. She released him, moving away a little. It was too late for such comforts. She had to leave quickly. She took a deep breath and let it out again. "You see, that is why I must go. There is something...wrong with me. I cannot let it affect those around me. I must leave so that no one else is harmed." Grief rose within her, hard and hot, and she closed her eyes. She had hoped...she had become fond of the Fichets and her life at the inn, and...and she had come to like Sir Jack, as well, for all that she had been frightened of him when they first met.

A soft warm light lit Sir Jack's face; they had come to the inn at last. But the light did nothing to soften the grim expression on his face. He looked at her, then nodded curtly before he opened the door.

"You are right," he said. "You must leave this place."

Grief threatened to overwhelm her, but she bit her lip and suppressed it. She nodded in return. "Yes. I will get my belongings and go now."

The door opened, and he waved her inside. The smells of food and wood polish came to her; and her heart twisted in her chest. This had been home to her for the last few weeks. It would be so no longer. She moved toward the stairs, but she felt his hand on her arm, and she turned to look at him.

His expression, if possible, was more grim than before. "No," he said. "You will not go now."

She looked a question at him.

"You will go in an hour, with me."

Chapter 5

❧ HE HAD NO CHOICE.

Jack gazed at the woman in front of him. Her red hair had come loose from its pins and ribbons, flying wildly around her face. A tear in her blouse exposed the top of a rounded breast, and a scratch on her neck bled. Dirt smudged her cheek.

But her eyes were hauntingly green, surrounded by thick, dark lashes, her figure lithe and sinuous when she had fought.

He wanted her as badly as he had when she had been unclothed, when he had seen her full breasts and slim waist. And in the moment when she had stiffened her back and gazed at him with resolution, telling him that she had to leave, he knew he could not let her leave alone . . . and that Fichet and Mme Felice were perhaps half right: he wanted Catherine de la Fer. Even now, as she looked at him, and her breath came quickly between her lips, he wanted to kiss her.

He forced himself to remember the blood that

had flowed from her hands and from her back. Her past was a mystery to her, what she could remember of it, and Fichet had spoken of a power in her family that the Marquis de Bauvin coveted.

A power that could perhaps call forth demons, a power that bewitched him. If anything should have turned him away from her, the sight of that demon should have, for it was evidence of witchcraft. But it had not, and he had given her sword to her instead.

He looked away from her, unable to bear her direct, lost gaze, then jerked his chin toward the stairs. "Go up and clean yourself off. You have dirt on your face and on your clothes. Then report to me in my chambers." He said it as if he were speaking to a raw recruit in the king's army. His words had the effect he wanted; instead of protesting his command to stay, anger replaced the grieving loss in her eyes, and she turned and stomped up the stairs.

He went to the taproom, where Mme Felice already had a mug of cider ready for him. She handed it to him in silence, merely looking her question at him. Fichet was with her, also silent, wiping mugs with a cloth and casting glances at him from time to time.

The inn was fairly quiet. Those who had come for their dinner were occupied with it; those who had come to stay for the night were mostly in their rooms. What talk there was in the common rooms was subdued, sleepy.

Jack looked about him. The guests were familiar, people he had seen before whenever he had stayed here. No strangers. For now, he supposed, they would be safe. But if what Catherine said was so, then it would serve none of them well if she remained.

"We will leave in the next hour," he said.

Fichet raised his brows, pausing over the next mug to clean, and Mme Felice frowned. "What? Now?" the inn-wife exclaimed.

"You saw what she fought."

She paled and clutched her husband's arm.

"'Tis sorcery." He lowered his voice, for such an accusation could cause an inquisition and a burning. "She has said that if she were to stay, she would endanger you. She is right."

"The sorcery is not from Mlle de la Fer," Mme Felice whispered fiercely. "She went with me to the church, and made her confession. She was sinless when the . . . the monster attacked."

The relief that came to Jack dissipated when he remembered that he did not believe in such superstitions, for he was of the same mind as his king: the differences in religion were nothing but trouble, and he could not see any more holiness in one than another. . . .

But then he himself had seen the monster. If such things existed, then perhaps . . .

Perhaps nothing. For all he knew, there were no rules that governed such creatures as he had seen but a few minutes ago. He shrugged.

"If it came not from her, then it came from someone who wishes her ill. In either case, if such a person has power enough to summon such evil, then it may well hurt those around her."

"It did not hurt me!" Mme Felice insisted.

Fichet laid a hand on her arm. "Peace, wife. It may not have hurt you because mademoiselle made you leave." He turned his gaze to Jack. "But what of you?"

Jack shrugged. "The creature was dispatched

with her sword. Both of us will have our own weapons. Therefore, we can dispatch any more that may come."

Fichet cocked his head in a considering manner. "And then where will you take her?"

He wanted to say away, where no one could find either of them. But instead he said, "Only one place will explain who and what she is: the home of the de la Fers. You yourself said there was a mystery, Fichet, and there she will find the answer."

"But the beatings—she must have received them at home, *la pauvre petite!*" Mme Felice protested. "You cannot wish to return her to that."

Fichet shook his head. "My wife is right, M. Sir Jack. It is not right that she be treated that way."

"I will not return her to abuse," Jack said. "I promise it." The couple before him relaxed. "It is on the way to Holland; if need be, I will leave her in Normandy, at her home"—Felice frowned—"if I am assured she will be well there," he continued. "If not, she will continue with me, to Holland."

"I am convinced it is not wise to leave now," Mme Felice said stubbornly. "Think, monsieur! Mademoiselle has been here these many weeks and has not left the inn yard until now, and that only during the day. The demon came after darkness fell. If you go out now, who knows, but that you might be attacked again? You will be traveling in the deepest of night."

Jack frowned. "There is something in what you say, but who is to say that she will not now be attacked here again, tonight?"

"You do not know, of course," Fichet said calmly. "Therefore, it is best that you keep guard over mademoiselle this night, and travel in the morning when it is light."

"No! That is, no," Jack said, lowering his voice after his first exclamation. "And if this is yet another of your machinations to get me to admit to Mlle de la Fer's attractions, M. and Mme Fichet, then it will not work."

Mme Felice brightened, then said, "I had not thought of that, but it would be interesting—"

Fichet chuckled and put his hand on his wife's arm. "Yes, *ma chou,* but that is not the intent." He turned to Jack. "Think, monsieur. My wife is in the right of it. Such creatures must be allied with the forces of darkness, and is it not fit that they then come out when darkness is in force? We have not seen any such thing during the day, and my dear wife has said that it could have come at any time before they entered the church. If it is an evil thing, would it not be stronger in the presence of those who are not yet shriven? And yet, it struck when these two women were in their purest state, after confession. Darkness, therefore, must be a condition of its existence. It is reasonable to assume that you would be most open to attack in the dark... and forgive me, monsieur, for saying it has probably been a while since you have been in a sinless state. Is it not reasonable to stay here while it is dark, and depart during the day?"

Jack gave him an ironic look. "But as you say, I am not in a sinless state, and if more monsters are to attack, then I might be vulnerable. What, did you think I would not be tempted to sin more if I were to guard Mlle de la Fer in her bed? Yes, I admit, she is a temptation; but the less temptation there is, the better. Furthermore, she killed the monster some distance from here. Whoever sent it might not yet know that we stay here. If that is so, then the sooner we leave, the less likely we will be found. If it is known that mademoiselle is here, then the faster we go, the sooner we will be away from another attack. Either way, both of us would be safer if we left tonight rather than tomorrow."

The couple's cheer at his admittance of attraction to Catherine disappeared at his determination. Mme Felice nodded reluctantly, and Fichet threw up his hands in a shrug.

"I cannot argue with you, M. Sir Jack," the innkeeper said. "Go, then, and with our blessings, and let us know what provisions you will need."

Jack nodded. "Food, of course. Bread, cheese, and dried fruit, if you would, my good madame. That should keep us until—what is the next good inn, Le Chat Gras?"

Fichet curled a lip in disdain. "Not as good as ours, but it will do. Make sure Titon does not cheat you out of a good meal, and let him know I will take it from his chary hide if he does so."

Jack grinned, and rose from his chair. "My thanks, Fichet and madame." He bowed and kissed the back of Mme Felice's hand. "I am fortunate indeed to have such good friends."

Fichet grinned, and Mme Felice beamed at him, then bustled off to get the provisions Jack had asked for.

He turned, and went up the inn steps two at a time. They needed to hurry. It would probably be best if they traveled during the night. If it was true that such creatures favored the night, it was best if they were awake to defend themselves. He did not relish being attacked in his bed. There were plenty of inns that would accommodate customers who required a bed during the day. He winced. It would look damned irregular, but there was no help for it. He came to his room and found Catherine standing, waiting for him.

She was, much to his relief, clothed in men's clothes; it meant they could leave quickly. She looked at him in her guarded way, and he regretted that he had been sharp with her. But he had been shaken by the appearance of the demon, something so outside of his experience, and he had no spare thought for careful words. Still, she should know by now that he wished her no harm. He wished she would not flinch when he came near her.

He approached her slowly now and kept his distance. "Come, we must go. Pack your things, please, if you have not already."

She looked at him steadily. "*I* must go. I will not endanger you or anyone else."

Irritation rose, but he squashed it. "Listen to me, Catherine," he said gently. "There is sorcery about; you must see that."

A cold chill crept up her spine, but she shook her head. She did not want it to be so . . . but she had seen for herself what had come after her.

She turned away from him, staring into the fire, swallowing down dread. The priest could be wrong; sorcery could explain her wounds and her bleeding. It might mean, then, that she was indeed cursed, not blessed. But surely not, for she had her sins forgiven and was in as pure a state as she could be when the demon attacked.

Discontent rose; she would never know if she did not go in search for the truth, and she would not find it here in Paris. She would have to go . . . home.

She turned to Sir Jack and nodded slowly. "Very well," she said. "I alone shall go."

"I cannot let you go alone. How will you defend yourself? I have not taught you everything you should know about swordfighting, after all."

She gazed at him, her eyes wide, and for a moment he thought her lower lip trembled. But she pressed her lips together in a straight line and shook her head. "You are very kind, M. Sir Jack. But if the creature was after me, then it is not inconceivable that more will come, and that will endanger any who accompany me."

"A creature that can be killed with a sword," Jack replied. "Does it not stand to reason that two with a sword against such a creature will be more successful than one? Then, too…" He hesitated, wondering how much he should reveal to her of her past, for it clearly frightened her. He looked at her, at how she bent a look of stubborn determination upon him, and smiled slightly. She had borne much already; she should be able to bear a few facts here and there. "Then, too," he continued, "does not your lack of memory trouble you? It frightens you, I know. Does it not stand to reason that there must be some answer to your affliction in Normandy, your home?"

A wild fear appeared in her eyes, and she said nothing for a moment, but then she nodded slowly. "I cannot hide from it forever," she said. "I think…I think if I kept hiding from my past, I would live in fear for the rest of my life." She gazed at him steadily. "Mme Felice said that fear obscures everything of worth in life, and since I have very little of worth, I cannot afford fear."

Admiration for her courage warmed him, and he smiled at her, taking her hand in his. He drew her fingers to his lips, and patted her hand. "You are a brave woman, Catherine de la Fer. I am honored that you consent to travel with me."

Her lips parted in a smile, a light came into her eyes, and he caught his breath, for she was beautiful. Silence reigned between them for a long moment, and then she sighed, an uncertain look coming into her eyes.

He released her hand, feeling awkward. He did not look forward to traveling with her. She was a temptation to him, and he could not give in to it. She was not his, but belonged to her family, and perhaps to the Marquis de Bauvin. Until he knew the truth about her, it was best if he kept his hands off her. "Go, pack what you have. We will leave as soon as you are done," he said, his voice sounding rough even to himself. She nodded and turned away.

He, too, had a few more things to pack. Stuffing the few remaining clothes he had into a saddlebag, the thought of a reward for his return of her came to him . . . there was that, too. Guilt accompanied the idea, but he put it off. Enough time to think of useless emotions later. If some sorcery existed in her, he would discover it as soon as they arrived at her home. And if it did . . .

He clenched his teeth. If it did, then he would be well rid of her, and no doubt it would be good for him to be rid of one who tempted him sorely, body and soul.

Catherine stretched out her arms as she stood in the stable yard, readying herself for the ride ahead. The men's clothes Mme Felice had given her during her stay were more comfortable and well made than the ones she had worn when she had first come to the inn, and for that she was thankful. She gazed at the horse she'd been provided—a gentle yet strong mare—and stuffed the clothes in which she usually practiced into one saddlebag, along with the packet of food the inn-wife had given her. There! She was done...except that when she turned around, Mme Felice held out yet another bag.

"It is a skirt and bodice, mademoiselle," she said in answer to Catherine's questioning look. She held up a hand as Catherine began to shake her head. "No, take it. There will be some time when you will need it, I think. You cannot always be a boy, but will need to be your true self."

Her true self...she smiled wryly at the inn-wife. "I do not know who my true self is, Mme Fichet."

Mme Felice smiled in return and put a brief, gentle hand on Catherine's cheek, reminding Catherine of a mother's touch. "You will find out, mademoiselle."

Tears threatened to burst from her at the inn-wife's kindness, but she bit her lower lip against them, then took the package. She gave the woman a wavering smile. "I thank you, madame. I...I will repay you some day, I promise it."

Felice glanced at her and hesitated. "There is something you may do...your wounds, mademoiselle—I do not think it is a curse or an illness. We... my sweet Robert and I...we have ached for children, but we have not been blessed with any. Give me a blessing before you leave, that we might have a child at last."

Alarm and embarrassment made Catherine blush and shake her head. "I have no special powers, madame, and am as bad a sinner as anyone, not worthy to give anyone a blessing."

Mme Felice smiled. "You have a good heart, mademoiselle. If you will not give me a blessing, then add your prayers to ours that we may have a child."

"That I can do, madame, and willingly, though I think you would be better prayed for by Père Doré."

Mme Felice pursed her lips skeptically. "Eh, he is a man, and dedicated to chastity at that. What would such a one ever know of bearing children?"

Catherine bit her lip again, this time to keep back a laugh at the woman's unconventional but practical perspective. "Well, let us both pray to the Blessed Mother of our Lord, for surely she knows what it is to bear a child."

Mme Felice nodded. "That will do." She cast a suddenly shy look at Catherine. "And…if you will allow it, mademoiselle, I would be pleased if you would call me Felice, and know I will be your friend if you need it."

Tears came to Catherine's eyes, unchecked now, at the inn-wife's kindness, and she took the woman's hands in hers. "Madame—Felice—I am honored that you wish me to be your friend. If it pleases you, you may call me Catherine." She turned to Fichet. "And you, too, Fichet." The man bowed and grinned.

Felice beamed. "There it is, then! We shall be friends, and surely the prayers of a friend are worth much."

A laugh bubbled out of Catherine at the inn-wife's clever argument. "Very well, Felice, I shall pray that you and Fichet have a child—children, yes?"

Felice shook her head. "I will not be greedy, mademoi—Catherine." She paused, seeming to take pleasure in saying her name. "No, if we have a healthy one, we shall count ourselves blessed."

"Very well." Catherine smiled, then before she could move, Felice gave her a brief and spontaneous hug.

"*Au revoir,* Catherine, and take care of M. Sir Jack, for I fear he will sacrifice much for his king, even his life."

Catherine nodded, then turned toward the horse, letting Fichet put his hand under her heel to hoist her up into the saddle. She did not know what she could do to protect Sir Jack, but if she saw he needed protecting, she would do it, if only for the sake of his friends, these two good people. She watched as Sir Jack strapped his saddlebags securely and mounted his gelding. She still believed she should be away from all of them, even Sir Jack, and she would make sure she'd leave him if another supernatural manifestation came after her again. But it was comforting to have his company for now, she admitted. She saw Sir Jack turn to look at her, but she could not discern his expression, for his face was in shadow. "Are you ready?" he asked. His voice was just as expressionless.

"Yes," she said. She did not know what else to say.

He gave a curt nod then, and turned his horse away, toward the road. Catherine sighed, shrugged, and with a last wave to Fichet and Felice, rode after him.

When the Marquis de Bauvin peered into the scrying hand mirror he held in front of him, it showed nothing but darkness. Slowly he put it down on the table next to him and sank back into his armchair, his fingers steepled as he gazed through them at the fireplace. For a while, he had found Catherine de la Fer. Paris, he thought, from what he could scrye in the mirror. He had caught a few glimpses in the past few weeks of her signature—a gleaming, feminine shape—in what seemed like an alley, or some place made of cobblestone and brick; any city might have such things. He had patience, however, and held his attention to her shape, hoping that there might come a time that the mirror would show her and where she was more clearly. He had even summoned a dark seeker to search for her and bring her back to him, though the effort had cost him much energy that he needed for healing.

It had been worth it, he thought. For at last he could see, through the eyes of the seeker, her gleaming form, shining more brightly than before, so that it illuminated her surroundings. She wore the dress of a common woman, and she had been accompanied by another woman also in common dress. She had come down the steps of a church, and as he pushed the seeker to seize her, he noted the surroundings—most definitely Paris.

But then she had fought the creature, and just as he thought he'd successfully retrieve her, the obsuring light had surrounded her, the hand mirror had darkened, and he knew that somehow the creature had been destroyed.

It was a disturbing development. The marquis frowned slightly. He knew the de la Fer women had some power, and indeed, Catherine had resisted him strongly when he had tried to take that power. However, she should not have had the strength to destroy the seeker; it would take at least the strength of a large man, if not two.

Perhaps she had had a helper. That was possible. Not that other woman—she had run off, from what he could tell. Someone else. The light around her had clouded everything, however, and he had not been able to see who.

The marquis rose again, careful not to turn too quickly, for his head still ached and he became too dizzy from time to time. Anger boiled again at the memory of Catherine de la Fer's resistance and defiance of him. He had managed to seize some of her power when he had taken her in her bedroom; but it had been temporary, for she had concealed a dagger from him and had stabbed him. The shock of pain and the flow of his blood had almost negated the power he had taken, but he had managed to retain a sliver of connection to her nevertheless and to strip what he could of her mind.

He would find her, and soon. He had made contact, and the next seeking would be faster, stronger. And he would not make the same mistake again.

He went to the fireplace, gazing into it for a moment before gathering a handful of herbs from a bowl on the mantelpiece. He made a few quick signs and cast the herbs into the fire. A thin grey smoke arose from the flames, and as he breathed in the fumes, he gazed through the hazy veil that rose up in front of the fire and saw a light, laughing face, crowned with golden hair. It was Blanche de la Fer, his bride-to-be. She was quite young, and therefore more malleable than her sister. He had not sensed as much power in her as he had Catherine, but it was there, little though it was. He'd be more careful about this girl, nevertheless. If he played his cards wisely, he'd have them both, and he'd have all that he'd need to have his vengeance.

Indeed, he'd been too hasty with Catherine. He had thought her easily led; he had been mistaken in thinking that her compliant manner had been natural instead of beaten into her. When he had found she'd been beaten into agreement, he had thought it would not matter. But perhaps the strength of her power had given her a strength of will that had enabled her to defy him. If that was the case, then he would be sure to be careful with Blanche.

It would be easy, he thought, easier than it had been with Catherine. He had made sure to cultivate Blanche's company and was glad that her father was no longer alive to make a blunder of the marriage arrangements. He had made sure of that, especially when he found the de la Fer *fils* to be more intelligent and yet more suggestible.

Blanche was not averse to the marriage. She had blushed charmingly, innocently, and had looked surprised and naively pleased when he had complimented her on her appearance. The marquis gazed at her in the shifting smoke of the herbs—she was running through a lighted garden. Her lips curled up in sheer happiness, so unlike what he remembered of her sullen sister. She stopped suddenly, and turned, her smile dropping from her, and de Bauvin saw that her brother approached. For one moment, he resented the Comte de la Fer for being the cause of Blanche's sudden gravity. But he passed his hand through the smoke, irritated that he had lost his focus from his purpose, and the vision disappeared.

He sat in his armchair again, frowning. He did not know why he could so easily see Blanche through such simple means as an herbal scrye, while Catherine was so hidden from him. It must be because of the strength of Catherine's power. It was imperative, then, that he find her as soon as he could. Such power allied with his would make him irresistible at King Louis's court, and then it would take just a few small moves until he had control of the throne...and Cardinal Mazarin's head.

He had to be careful, however. The king had never forgotten the incident of the Fronde, the uprising of the nobles, when he was a child; it was why Louis hated Paris and established his court at Versailles. And the last Marquis de Bauvin had been one of the nobles, and had been savagely executed.

De Bauvin had never forgotten it. He had been a lay brother at the time, and slated for the priesthood, for which he thought he was well suited. He had gone to Cardinal Mazarin himself to plead for his brother. However, the cardinal had promised nothing but soothing words.

When his brother's head was paraded on a pike, when his lands were stripped from him, de Bauvin had lost all faith, and knew there would be nothing left of his line if he did not act.

So he left the priesthood, and smiled and pandered to the king until it seemed he was at least not viewed with suspicion. He even managed to buy some of his lands back, through good means and ill, and found that the taste of power suited him well. And he watched the movements of the cardinal and the king, until he knew their habits as if they were his own.

He yawned and carefully stretched. It was the afternoon, and he would sleep for a while, for he had much to do in the evening, when his own powers were the greatest.

Some day, he would have control over those who betrayed him, but first he must cultivate control over those he could, to ensure his success...and that meant finding Catherine de la Fer and taking whatever he could from her, body and soul.

Chapter 6

THE NIGHT'S CHILL FROZE CATHERINE'S cheeks as she rode swiftly on her horse. She pulled the muffler that Felice had given her up over her nose, and gave a quick look over her shoulder for a dark, misshapen form. She could see nothing but the road, the moon, and the distance spinning it into a silver ribbon behind her. Shuddering, she clutched the reins tight, making her mare toss its head in protest.

She drew in a deep breath and let it out again, and the cold air in her lungs gave her a fresh, harsh clarity. She would not be afraid. She had promised Felice she would not, and she had promised herself, as well.

Still, she thought practically, it was not surprising that she had been afraid. She had never seen the likes of the creature that had attacked her. If it had been a man, she would be over her fear, she was sure, for she had dispatched men before. But this...She shuddered. This had been a creature from her darkest dreams.

What was worse, it was no nightmare, for both Felice and Sir Jack had seen it. She wondered again if she herself had been the cause of its manifestation, for was she not cursed with the bleeding from her hands and her back? But Felice had adamantly insisted that it was impossible, for she had just been to confession and had received absolution. The priest himself had thought that it might be more blessing than curse.

Catherine grimaced. He might think so, but he did not have to bear it. She would prefer to be rid of it, and she would work to have it stop as soon as she could. But it was something of a comfort that a priest thought it was not an evil thing. She sighed. It was too bad she could not stay in Paris to find out what the priest would discover from the cardinal.

They must be a few miles from Paris now, she thought, for they came upon fewer buildings along the road, and more trees darkened their path. She glanced to her side and saw that Sir Jack had slowed his horse to a walk. She did likewise. It was difficult to see his expression in the darkness, but the set of his body in his saddle was relaxed.

"That should have put some distance between us and…more of those creatures and whatever sent them. It's a good fifteen miles to the next inn, and at this pace, we'll be there in three hours or so."

"Three hours!" Fatigue that Catherine had held at bay so far threatened to wash over her.

"Three hours," Sir Jack said flatly. "I would be pleased if you kept yourself awake. My apologies, mademoiselle, but if such creatures you attract are active at night, I would prefer to be awake and ready to fight, rather than attacked while I sleep."

"You are right, of course," she replied. It only

made sense; she would not like to be taken unawares, either. "But how do you know I attract such creatures?"

He glanced at her, and even in the darkness she could tell it was an ironic look. "There is no one else I know whose bloody scars heal in less than half the time of anyone else's, and I think I can assume such a manifestation is supernatural. When a supernatural creature comes after a woman who has supernatural wounds, I think I can assume the two might be connected."

Catherine swallowed her disappointment—stupid disappointment, for though she had hoped he might have an argument she could counter, she also had come to the same conclusion. "I did say that I should leave alone," she said after a long silence. "Indeed, I still do not understand why you bother to travel with me."

There was an equally long pause, then he blew out an audible breath, as if he were a fighter readying himself for a struggle. "I will be frank with you—I was not going to reveal my motives for keeping your company before, but now...now things have changed. I will leave it up to you whether you wish to go farther with me." He took in another deep breath. "When I found you, I was ready to toss you a coin and leave you to go your own way. But when I saw you were well born, I saw an opportunity to further my king's cause."

She cast him a questioning glance.

"I thought to sell you back to your well-born family so that I could send those funds to my king. If not that, then if your family was favored at Louis's court, I would use their gratitude for your return and their favor to gain admittance to King Louis, and thus again procure funds for my king." He did not look at her, but ahead, his lips pressing together firmly again. "I thought to get you to better health first, so that you would...bring a higher price."

Catherine closed her eyes. Of course, it made sense. Why would a stranger take on a woman from the gutters? She clutched the reins in despair and her horse stopped. She was not worth much except what price she could bring to Sir Jack's cause, it seemed, regardless of what Felice had thought.

Sir Jack's mare took a few steps forward before he also reined it in and turned toward her. "I will not lie to you—I still intend to collect what money I can for your return. I have vowed loyalty to my king, and will not have anything else turn me from that vow. In addition, a woman belongs with her husband, and if she has not that, then her family. Even you must agree this is so."

Catherine nodded slowly and they continued on. In the normal course of life, it was right. She would have felt the same if she had been in his place. "I understand." She looked at him, but after a quick glance at her, he said nothing further. She looked away from him at the lacy silhouettes of trees against the full-moon night, and tried not to feel alone and lost. She would just have to find her own way after they parted...for she felt sure that she would not like what she would find at her home. Yet she knew it was important, at least, to find out more about who she was and why she had come to the alley in Paris, starving and without her memories.

"So," he said in a conversational tone. "Are you a witch?"

She jerked in her saddle, and fear rose in her. It was a serious query. She had heard rumors of witches being burned or hanged, and it was a question that had skirted the borders of her mind even now, even after her talk with Père Doré. She looked at him, wishing she could discern his expression. He turned and looked ahead of him, but all she could tell from his profile was that he had closed his mouth firmly and set his jaw.

"I do not know," she blurted. "I assume not, since the priest said he thought my...unusualness was not a curse."

He looked at her, and the moonlight caught his raised brows. "But I am not a Catholic, so the words of a priest hold little weight with me."

She gazed at him, startled. She hadn't thought that he might not believe as she did, for he was exiled from his very Protestant country. "Are you a Huguenot, then?"

A slight smile crossed his lips. "No. Let us just say that I have seen enough of un-Christian fighting between various believers that I have become...skeptical of their claims to holiness. It has certainly done my king and my country no good. I have seen how the Scottish Presbyters have held the hammer of religion over His Majesty's head instead of giving freely what is a king's right and privilege. And your king is known as a devout man." Sir Jack's voice held an ironic note. "For all that he has his mistresses."

"And your king has not any?" Catherine asked, irritated.

Sir Jack laughed. "Aye, that he does, but at least he does not pretend to piety."

"At least our king is absolved of his sins," she retorted.

He chuckled. "Until the next time he decides to sin again with his mistresses."

"Perhaps they are very tempting to him," she said, wanting to somehow disprove his argument. "Perhaps they use wiles that he cannot resist."

"Like sorcery?"

The words hung between them for a moment, but Catherine pressed her lips together briefly, refusing to be afraid. "Like sorcery," she said firmly. "King Louis cannot be held responsible if his will is taken from him."

This time Sir Jack's glance was clearly skeptical. "If his will has been so taken, then I would think your country would be less well run than it is, for I hear your king personally oversees every detail of government. Still," he admitted, "a woman might use her wiles, sorcerous or not, to claim the attention of the king. And there is his habit of postponing his decisions on matters of state and policy forever. Certainly his delays have plagued me more than any sorcery could."

Catherine stared at him, realization slowly dawning. "You do not take witchcraft seriously."

"I . . . have not." There was a pause. "I have seen nothing but harmless old men and women persecuted for their senility, or the accusations of an envious neighbor. No witchery there but accusers who care nothing for breaking more than a few commandments."

She nodded, feeling relieved.

"But," he continued, "if I find that you are indeed a sorceress and have had dealings with poisons and forcing people to do evil, then I will feel obliged to hand you over to the authorities. And if I find you applying any of that to me, I shall have to kill you."

A chill fell over Catherine, but she lifted her chin and stared hard at him. "If you suspect me of such things, then I wonder that you wish to have me along at all. It would be best to leave me with whatever dark creature might decide to have me."

"You have a point," he said. Her words seemed not to affect him. "But remember that I am, in general, skeptical of such things, and still think there may be some other explanation than sorcery. Then, too, there is the much-needed money I wish to get from your family." He turned to her and drew his horse to a stop, and she did the same. "So, now we have our cards on the table, and you may stay with me on my travels until we come to your home, and then you may stay with them until I collect my money. After that, you may do whatever you choose. Or, you may leave now . . . but be sure that I shall find you and collect what I'm owed."

"Why do you tell me this now?"

Sir Jack hesitated. "I thought it best to bring you away from danger first, or if you are indeed a sorceress, bring you away from my friends. I want you to hold no illusions about me, mademoiselle. What I do, I do out of necessity and loyalty to my king. If you think I will be as loyal to you, you are mistaken."

"You do not give me much reason to stay."

He looked away from her. "I know. Except . . ." He stared at her, and his face was in shadow. "Do you know the Marquis de Bauvin?"

She shook her head slowly, searching her feelings. There was a blank, as if a portion of her had been rubbed out . . . but if she had no memory of the man, it meant nothing. She had lost memory of many things.

"I have heard you were betrothed to him."

She shook her head again. "If I was, I do not remember it."

Jack gazed at her, wondering if she told the truth. It did not worry him, however; he felt that she did, and he believed he was a good judge of whether a man or woman lied. "Then do you not think it best to discover whether it is true? Perhaps you were stolen from your family and managed to escape your captors, but because you lost your memory, you did not know until now where you belonged." It was a plausible reason for her being in Paris, he thought.

She nodded slowly. "That is possible. And if I have agreed to marry the marquis, then it would be wrong not to honor that promise."

A part of him wished she had not come to that conclusion, or that he had even mentioned the marquis. But it nevertheless fell in with his own plans, and he could not wish anything better than that.

"Come, then, and let us watch out for dark creatures as we travel."

She nodded, frowning at the thought of the monster she had encountered in Paris, and nudged her horse forward with her knees. "I think perhaps there will not be any tonight," she said slowly.

He turned to look at her. "How do you know?"

She transferred her reins to one hand and pulled off her glove, turning her hand from one side to the other. The moonlight showed pale, smooth skin. "I ... I feel a pricking in my hands, even pain, whenever evil is near. I felt it in the alley when the men attacked the girl, and my hands even bled then. I felt the same pain when the monster appeared, and again my hands bled. I feel nothing now."

"A handy measure of danger," he said, "if it is true." But his shoulders relaxed, and she thought perhaps he did believe her. "Very well. Tell me when your hands pain you again." He sighed. "I will be glad

of a slower pace, and I am sure our horses will, too."
He jerked his chin forward. "Onward, then, *ma chère*."
He spurred his horse, and once Catherine pulled on
her glove again, she did likewise.

It seemed like forever before a pinprick of light in the
darkness told Catherine that there were other human beings in front of them instead of the silent
cold night. She urged her horse faster toward the
faint light, but the horse, too, was tired and could
only manage a halfhearted canter before it subsided
back into a slow walk. She could not blame the poor
thing, for it had worked hard and faithfully. She
looked up at the candlelight that illuminated the
windows of the inn before them, and it acted like a
sleeping potion upon her. Wary tension fell from her
aching shoulders and back, and she slumped in her
saddle.

    She gazed wearily at Sir Jack next to her; he sat as
steadily as he had for the last six hours. They had
stopped at Le Chat Gras for only a few hours; there,
Sir Jack had allowed her to sleep for a while before
they departed again. They had not even stopped to
partake of any large meal, but had eaten only what
Felice had provided. Catherine could not help feeling
some resentment; it was one thing for a soldier to
ride steadily for more than six hours, but it was
something else entirely for someone who was not
trained for it. But she forced her back to straighten
and lifted her chin nevertheless; she was, in a way, a
soldier in training, and she would not complain.

    He glanced at her, then said, "Only a few more
minutes, and then you may rest."

    "I am not that tired, M. Sir Jack."

She could see his grin now, for the moon had set, and the early dawn cast its faint light on his face. "Don't lie. You were slumping in your saddle just now, and I am sure if I had not spoken, you would have nodded off. You are not used to such travel, at least not lately."

A slight embarrassment made her say roughly, "I did not want to be a burden to you."

Silence, and he turned away from her so that she could not see his expression. "You are not a burden, and you are only human, mademoiselle," he said at last. "Besides, I feel much better that you *are* tired; I am, and would welcome some rest, and would hold a grudge against you if you insisted we not stop at the inn to take in food and sleep."

There was a teasing note in his voice, and her heart lightened, especially at the idea that he did not think her a burden. She remembered, too, that he had not slept, but had sat guard at her door as she did. She was grateful for that.

But she wished to hold her own in whatever relationship there was between them, and...yes, even that he should get his due for his care of her. It was only right, after all. After the initial terror of facing the monster and riding in the night, she had forced calm and logic on her mind, and thought more about what was owed to whom. If she was indeed betrothed to the Marquis de Bauvin, then it was only reasonable that she return to him and to her family.

A flicker of fear came to her, and she remembered that she had thought she had run away from them; but there was no logical evidence of this, and the scars on her back could have come from her kidnappers, or perhaps were supernatural in origin after all. In truth, she knew very little of her past, only her name and where she came from. Her fears, she felt, were as instinctive as her fear that she must have as much food as possible in case what she had would be taken away. All of that could have come from her time in the alley. Food... Her stomach grumbled.

"It will be good to eat again," she said, and urged her horse into a faster walk toward the inn.

Sir Jack chuckled. "I have never seen anyone eat so much or so often," he said. "I am surprised you have not become as round as a ball by now."

She grinned. "I am not fat because you are as bad as a slave master, the way you make me work and work at fighting with the sword. I must eat to keep up my strength."

"Well, it is working," he said, and there was a note of approval in his voice. "You are much stronger than I would have expected, and have progressed very quickly."

His approval warmed her, and she held herself straighter in her saddle. "Thank you," she said.

"Not that you don't have much to improve," he said, deflating her spirits a little. "But you are a quick student."

She did not mind the check on her optimism; that she had much to learn was truth, after all. She only nodded, however, for they had come to the inn at last, and the early morning scents of baking bread seeped from behind the door, making her mouth water. She had partaken of the cheese and bread earlier, but it had not been enough, and the scent of warm bread made her stomach groan with anticipation.

They went around to the stables, and she was glad when Sir Jack helped her down, for her legs trembled with fatigue and were sore from the long ride.

"Walk around the yard for a bit and stretch your legs," he said. "I am afraid you will be extremely sore after you rest, but it's better that you rest than not."

She did as he said, as he took the horses to the stable, and could already feel how her legs and buttocks ached. But she ignored it for now; there was promise of food, and she almost ran for the inn when he came out of the stable at last.

The smell of baking bread was stronger once Jack pushed open the door and held it open for her. The inn was quiet, for what few guests were in the common room slept on their benches near the fire, and the servants at their duties moved sleepily around them. The most activity seemed to be at the kitchens; voices came from there, as well as the sound of clanking pots and the smell of food.

Catherine almost groaned at the scent, and her mouth watered. Another chuckle sounded behind her. "Patience, mademoiselle. You will eat soon enough. We must get our rooms first."

She nodded, but she could not help looking toward what must be the kitchen and the source of the mouthwatering scents. There was bread most prominent, but then could there be?...Yes, she could smell a ham, and perhaps a roast chicken. She inched closer to the smells, glancing at Sir Jack arguing with the innkeeper. She would not actually go into the kitchen, of course, but certainly Sir Jack would not mind if she went closer. She slipped past Sir Jack and the innkeeper, and would have gone much closer to the kitchen and its wonderful smells, but Jack's and the innkeeper's voices rose, and she caught the words "your wife."

She whirled and stared at Sir Jack, and noticed that the innkeeper gave her a curious look, taking in her male clothing. Her gaze shifted to Jack, and he gave her an apologetic glance and a lifted hand to halt her when she opened her mouth to protest. She shut her mouth, the kitchen suddenly without interest for her, and focused her attention on the two men.

"Well, if that is the case," the innkeeper was saying, "then you may have the room. You are lucky; it is one of our best rooms, and the only one left, for as you see, we are on the road from Rouen to Paris and it is rare that we have any rooms left at all."

She looked from the innkeeper to Sir Jack, and saw Jack's frustrated look. It must have been that he had asked for two rooms, but was refused, and then claimed they were husband and wife so that they might have the one left. She looked about the room and noticed it was a fairly prosperous inn, and thought perhaps the owners could afford to be virtuous, and she nodded slightly at Jack to acknowledge that he had wished to protect her reputation. A relieved expression came over his face, and he nodded to the stairs. "Let us go up, then," he said, and took the key from the innkeeper.

He hefted their saddlebags as if he had not been traveling for so long, but a glance at his face in the growing light revealed red, tired eyes and weary creases around his mouth. Guilt crept into Catherine's heart. He had not slept at all this long night, and she knew his day had been occupied with training her as well as writing letters to various court officials for entrée to King Louis. She pressed her lips together in determination. She would make sure he would sleep in the bed this time; she was tougher than he thought, and had been used to sleeping in a cold, dirty alley before this, after all. Sleeping on a blanket next to the fireplace would be a luxury in comparison.

He unlocked the door and opened it with a kick, hauling their belongings within. Catherine looked around the room, pleased. The room was well lit with sunlight through the clear windows, and the bed looked clean and lofty with comforters and pillows. Weariness struck her like a hammer at the sight of such comfort, and she could not help a small groan as her body relaxed into a small chair. But she forced herself from the chair again and took a pillow and a spare blanket from the bed, then set them next to the fire. She sighed as she sank down on the blanket and set her head on the pillow.

"*What* are you doing?"

She turned over to face Sir Jack, who had a frown on his face. She lifted her brows. "I am going to sleep, monsieur."

His frown deepened and he pointed to the bed. "There is a bed. You will sleep on it."

She shook her head. "No, monsieur, *you* will sleep on it. You have not slept at all this night, and I have already slept on a bed. It is your turn now, and besides, I have slept in less accommodating places than on a blanket near a fire."

His look softened somewhat, but he still frowned. "No, Catherine," he said more gently. "The bed is for you. I, too, have learned to sleep on hard ground, and you have lately been ill and need to gain more strength."

Her heart warmed at his consideration for her, but again she shook her head. "I am strong already, M. Sir Jack, stronger than I look. And..." She hesitated to bring up the subject. "And you yourself said that my wounds have already healed."

She wondered if he would withdraw from her at mention of her wounds, but he did not; a thoughtful look came over his face and he nodded slowly.

"It is true," he said. "Very well, you may sleep by the fireplace."

She could not help looking at him suspiciously, for he gave in to her argument all too easily for such a stubborn man, but his expression held no hint of anything but bland innocence. She gave him one last wary glance and then turned her back and lay on the blanket.

The warmth of the fire soothed her aching limbs, and she sank into the soft pillow and cocooned herself into the comforting blanket. Her stomach growled, but it could not rouse her; food later, she thought. She would eat later.

Jack watched as Catherine's body sank into relaxation next to the fire, and his heart also sank... into the realization that his feelings for the girl were becoming too complex, too... concerned. It was not a good time for amorous entanglements, and he was not all that sure he was the type to be trusted with an affair lasting more than a month. He was too fickle, too used to travel and fighting for this or that.

This or that... it did not sound like a dedicated man. The thought niggled at him; he had dedicated himself to the cause of his king, did he not? That was something, at least.

But weariness pulled at him, and he glanced at the bed, and then to Catherine. Foolish woman... but one with a good heart, he thought. She had clearly seen his fatigue, though he had done his best to conceal it from her. A slight snore came from her, and he grinned. Stubborn woman, as well. She had not even taken off her boots before she fell asleep, as if she were a well-seasoned soldier on the march.

But they could afford a little relaxation now. He had seen no sight of any monster or other supernatural thing, and surely they were far enough away from Paris by now that Catherine's enemy had lost their scent. He had made sure that they had gone by a circuitous route—longer, unfortunately, but not one easily traced. And chances were good that they would not be attacked during the day.

His shoulders ached and he rotated them, working out the kinks and the stiffness. Another glance at the bed brought further weariness to the fore, and he sat on the edge of it, slowly pulling off his clothes. Damned if he would sleep in them—after all these hours on horseback, he deserved the feel of soft clean sheets.

A cold basin of water and towels sat on a table near the fireplace, and he liberally splashed himself with it and washed off the grime of travel. He gave a glance at Catherine, and a short, soft snore from her made him grin. He warmed the towel near the fire, then went to her. Her face was dirty.

Gently he wiped her face, and when she did not awaken, drew away the blanket. Taking off her boots and jacket, he lifted her up and took her to the bed. For one moment she turned her face toward him, snuggling into the crook of his shoulder, and a painful ache touched his heart; in that moment, her face was unguarded, and she was vulnerable to him. But he shook off the feeling as he lay her on the bed and pulled the covers over her.

He looked at the blanket and pillow near the fireplace and shook his head. Damned if he was going to sleep on hard stone when there was a bed big enough to accommodate both of them. A wry smile twisted his lips. She was safe from him for now; weariness sat on him like a large stone, and he doubted he'd have the energy to do anything but sleep. He was tired to death; propriety was suddenly of little importance in comparison.

He slipped into the bed and pulled the covers over his shoulders, his body aching as it relaxed into the soft mattress. God's blood, but he needed this. He often felt that he had never quite relaxed in all the years he'd been exiled with King Charles. He'd always looked back over his shoulder for Cromwell's spies, or forward toward whatever opportunity he could find to scratch out a living and gain funds for the king. He'd done well for himself, come to that. He had built up a good sum in the French banks, and had siphoned off enough for the king from time to time, as well. But all that was nothing compared to what he might be able to get from King Louis . . . if he could get the French king's ear, that is.

A slight sound next to him made him turn and look at Catherine, still asleep. She frowned for a moment, and he wondered of what she dreamed. Something unpleasant, no doubt. He thought of the quickly disappearing wounds on her back and on her hands, wounds that seemed to appear and then disappear. He had seen blood on her hands as she had fought the monster, and it had not been the creature's blood, for green slime had flowed from it when Catherine had cut off its head. A soft feeling—pity, he thought—entered his heart. Whatever her wounds meant, he was sure she had suffered greatly and had fought as bravely as any man might. He propped himself up on his elbow and gazed at her, her profile now serene in deep sleep. Her features were delicate, almost fragile for a woman of clearly great strength of body and heart. It made him sorry that duty made it necessary for him to return her to her family.

She turned, then, and her hand fell on his chest. Gently he took it and kissed her fingers, then gathered her into his arms. Surely it would not hurt to do this, to give some comfort and take some, even in sleep. He let himself relax into the bed, and settled his head on the pillow. Surely she would not mind. . . . He grinned before sleep took him. Well, she might mind, but he could argue her out of her irritation, he was sure.

Catherine let the fog over her mind and body persist, for it was warm and comfortable, and warmth and comfort were worth jewels to her after her long sojourn in the alley. Except for the cold air that chilled her face, she was surrounded in the soft heat; below, around, behind—

Behind was not so soft, though it was warmer than anything else. It was a hard warmth, in fact, and if she was not mistaken, it extended around her waist and cupped her breast in what felt like a very large hand.

She opened her eyes, the unfamiliar surroundings at first disorienting her, then the memory of the night's travels flooded into her mind. She raised her shoulders, retreating from the dreadful images of dark and monstrous, and her back met the hard warmth again. Slowly, she turned and her gaze met the sleeping face of Sir Jack. She remembered where she had lain down to sleep, and how Sir Jack had argued with her, and now . . .

And now, here she was in bed with him.

Panic seized her and she froze, then frantically pushed herself away, breathing in short, gasping breaths, waiting for anger and pain and—

His arm fell from her, lax in sleep. He rolled to his back, and a slight snore came from his open mouth. He closed it again and rolled on his side again toward her, but did not wake.

She slowed her breathing and gathered up the scrambled thoughts in her head. He was only asleep...in this bed. He had agreed they would sleep apart. Her cheeks flared with anger and embarrassment, and she put her hands on his chest to push him off the bed, but noticed that she was still clothed—indeed, she was fully clothed in the shirt and trousers she had worn on their journey.

So, he had done nothing but sleep next to her. She bit her lower lip in thought. He had taken off her jacket and boots, and obviously carried her to the bed, and she had been so tired and so deeply asleep that it had not awakened her. He could have taken off more, and she was sure she would not have noticed.

She was suddenly conscious that her hand was still on his chest, and that her fingers had threaded through the slight furring of hair there. She quickly pulled back her hand, watching him to see if he would wake.

He did not. He slept with one hand under his head, the other lax on the bed where she had been. She remembered how she had been pressed against him and how his hand had cupped her breast. It had been very comfortable, she admitted to herself, warmer and softer than huddling next to a fireplace, for a fireplace only gave heat to one side of her, and hard stone to the other, while she had felt comfort and warmth all over when next to Sir Jack. All this was not to be scorned, not after the freezing cold she had lived with every day and night in the alley. Indeed, the part of her that was still the creature in the alley felt it would be good to settle into him to sleep a little more.

But curiosity stirred in her, something that had not had much play in her mind, she realized, for she had been occupied thinking mostly of food and warmth for so long. She wanted to know more of Sir Jack.

She stared at him, at how he breathed deeply and how his relaxed face looked very young, as if he were less than her own age instead of four years older. The scar that had made him look dangerous when he was awake seemed only a slight crease down his cheek rather than a reminder that he had faced death. Her gaze went from his face down to his neck and chest again—he was obviously not much clothed, she thought belatedly, and shook her head at herself. She had thought of warmth and comfort, rather than propriety. But she could not help looking at him, at how the slope of his neck met his shoulder, firm with muscle even in sleep, at how his skin molded around a chest both deep and hard—hard, she knew, for her hand had moved as if on its own and touched him there again. The hair on his chest was soft, and she could see it flowed down to his belly, and she wondered if it was just as soft there. She glanced at his face again—he was still asleep, his breathing slow and regular. He had traveled long and hard, with no rest until now. She doubted he would wake. Her hand moved a little lower....

And was caught in a hard grip. Her eyes flew up to gaze at Sir Jack, and saw that his face was grim.

"There is only so much, mademoiselle, that a man can stand," he said. "Touch me further and there *will* be consequences."

Fear lanced through her, and she strained against his hold. "Will you hurt me, then?"

His expression softened, and he released her. She lay still, suspended between primitive fear and the hope that his changed expression meant he would not hurt her. He lifted his hand, and she could not help flinching.

Pained disappointment flickered over his face. "Don't be afraid, Catherine." His voice was low, almost a whisper. "I would never hurt you."

She nodded slowly, letting out a deep breath, determined to keep to her vow to not give in to fear. She made herself lie still, instead of jumping out of bed, and then closed her eyes when his hand descended to touch her cheek.

His touch was soft, a caress, and there was no hurt in it, said the creature-in-the-alley part of her. She let out another slow breath and let the tension flow out of her as she opened her eyes and looked at him.

He gazed at her, his head propped up on his hand, studying her intently as if she were a book he needed to memorize. Again his hand came up, but this time he touched her with only a finger, from her temple down to her cheek, then slowly, slowly over her lips. It soothed her, and she let her body relax more, and let out another sigh.

"Will you let me kiss you, Catherine?" he asked.

She gazed at him, his eyes still intent, and thought of how he had kissed her before on the cheek, and how it had been very gentle. She would not mind it, if it would be like that, soft and comfortable and warm. She nodded, not trusting to speak.

He came nearer, and she did not flinch, but put her hand to his cheek. His face felt rough—he had not shaved, of course—and it felt interestingly different from the soft hairs on his chest. She felt his arms come around her, gently, slowly, as if he were a hearth-heated blanket. And then his lips came down, not to her cheek, but upon her mouth.

She could not help giving a gasp of fear, but the fear was quickly gone, for the touch of his lips was featherlight, a summer breeze, no more than that. *Warmth,* said the creature-in-the-alley part of her. *Heat.* She moved closer, and shifted her hand from his cheek to behind his neck.

Again he kissed her, and again it was light and warm and lasted longer. His arms drew her closer to him, and she did not mind it, for it made her even warmer. His lips released hers then, and she felt a . . . disappointment, for he drew away and there was less warmth. But when she looked cautiously up at him, he only stroked her cheek, a considering look on his face, and she thought he might not mind it if she lay her head upon his chest.

Carefully, she leaned against him and snuggled close, and for a moment thought his body stiffened before he put his arms around her. She sighed, and smiled when she felt the beat of his heart against her cheek. The beat was strong and slow, and lulled her into drowsiness again, and she felt as if he were rocking her, as if she were a child. She closed her eyes and put her hand on his chest, sighing again, and just before she fell asleep, whispered, "Thank you."

* * *

"You're welcome," Jack said, and felt a tearing in his gut, as if he were being torn in two. He closed his eyes, holding Catherine close, rocking her, feeling her body, breast to chest, hip to hip against him. It hurt, this tearing—he wanted her, more than wanted her. He was hot and hard against her body, but held her as if he were holding a baby, and knew that all he could do for now was hold her and kiss her. It was enough; he had seen how she had looked at him, her gaze that of a wild animal fearful of pain. He hated that look. It brought back memories of leaving England, of betrayal and loss.

She sighed again, and the movement of her breasts against him became long and regular; she was falling asleep again. His heart lifted—it meant, possibly, that she trusted him, and God help him, he wanted that trust.

He wanted more than that—he wanted all of her. He had known it the day she had opened her eyes and looked at him with her impossibly deep green eyes, so full of fear. But she had lifted her chin and clearly pulled all her resolution about her, as if she were facing an army and readying herself for battle, and—he smiled ruefully at himself, for Fichet and Mme Felice were right—he had fallen in love with her.

It was not something he could tell her. She was not his; she belonged to her family, and was fiancée to the Marquis de Bauvin. He sighed and stroked her hair. It was ever thus, and the saying that "all is fair in love and war" was quite wrong: it was never fair. He had little but honor left, however, and at least he could keep to that. He would do what he could to return Catherine to her true state, and then leave her to his duty, ever his duty.

Jack rose and gently covered Catherine with the bedclothes, then pulled on his clothes that he had set near the fire. He shivered, for the heat from the fire hadn't penetrated through his shirt and trousers, and they chilled him. He would get food—he smiled at the thought of how Catherine would welcome the sight of a meal—and prepare for their journey. With one last look at the sleeping woman, he shook his head at himself and his very tangled emotions, and left the room.

Chapter 7

❧ CATHERINE WOKE TO FIND HERSELF alone in bed, only an indentation on the mattress beside her to show that Sir Jack had been there at all. She passed her hand over the bedsheet—there was not even any warmth left, so he must have left quite a while ago. She could not help feeling some disappointment; she would have liked to have talked to him for a little, although what she would have said to him, she did not know. His presence would have been . . . comforting, at least.

Comforting. She was not afraid of him. Her heart lightened—there, that was one less thing she feared. He was an honorable man, she thought, despite his warnings to her. Indeed, he could have taken advantage of her, but he had not. She wondered why he thought he might betray her—he had spoken nothing but the truth to her so far, after all. Had he betrayed someone in the past, then? If so, he clearly regretted it, or else he would not warn her.

She sat up and gazed around the brightly decorated room. They would eat—her stomach growled at the thought—and then they would go to her home. She would meet again this Marquis de Bauvin, and perhaps be married to him.

Rebellion rose in her; she felt very much like a cow taken to market. She did not remember the marquis, so did not know if she would like him, or if she ever had. She thought of Sir Jack again, and thought she would like to be as free as he was, to come and go as she liked and marry whom she liked. But then, there was her family, and there was duty. She did not remember who they were, only that they lived in Normandy. But if she was indeed taken from them, then it was only right that she return.

Fear again rose, but she squashed it. It must be fear of the unknown, the fear of other, less pleasant possibilities. But it would do her no good to think of what may or may not be, but to face what truly existed.

And once she did, then she could make whatever determination she wished. Surely if she did not like this marquis, she could refuse to marry him, and perhaps do something else, such as marry someone else, or enter a convent.

The thought of these two options for her future depressed her. She had seen already that she had not any skills—except for the swordfighting Sir Jack was teaching her—she could employ for money. But perhaps, perhaps it might not be an impossible thing from which to earn money.

Her stomach growled again, and she moved off the bed—then gasped in pain. Her body ached, and her legs felt as if they had been beaten with sticks. She was horribly stiff and sore from riding all night, which was most definitely not something she was used to. She sat on the bed again, and a knock sounded on the door.

"Entré!" she called out, and winced from her muscle aches as she tried to stand.

It was Sir Jack, and her mouth watered when she saw the large tray of food he brought in and set on a table. She surged forward and seized a piece of bread and stuffed it in her mouth, ignoring her protesting muscles, focusing only on the taste and texture of bread, how the crust crunched beneath her teeth and how the spongy center filled her mouth and went down her throat to a very empty stomach. She closed her eyes and groaned as she took another piece of bread between her teeth.

A chuckle sounded from across the table and she looked up at Sir Jack's grinning face. "What is it?" she asked.

"You, *ma chère*. You eat as much as the biggest trencherman I have known."

She shrugged. "It was a long ride, and I am sure I have used up a great deal of energy. Also, I am very sore, so I do not think I will wish to ride tonight."

He lifted an eyebrow. "You will, nevertheless, or at least for the next few nights until we are sure we will not be attacked again."

Catherine groaned, this time from the thought of traveling so hard and fast once more, but she felt a smile form on her lips nevertheless. She did not mind it, she realized. The aches would pass after a while, she was sure, just as the aches of sword practice passed after she became used to it. She sighed. "What will we do until then?"

He smiled and took a piece of dried apple. "Practice swordfighting," he said, and popped the apple into his mouth.

This time Catherine's groan was heartfelt. "You are a slave driver! I ache from head to foot, and now I am to work even harder."

His grin grew wider. "But think, *ma chère*, afterward you will have more food. Practice well, and I swear you will have a hot bath, too."

Catherine nearly melted at the thought of a hot bath—she had come to like them very well. She nodded, only half reluctant, then fell to the rest of her meal. She would do the best she could at practice, especially for a meal and a hot bath. Surely he would not be as stringent a taskmaster after their ride.

She was quite wrong.

Sir Jack gave her only enough time for the food in her stomach to settle, then he ordered her out into the chilly courtyard.

"No, no, no! You hold the sword like a broom. *This* is the way you do it."

Jack—Catherine let herself call him that in her thoughts, for they were pretending to be man and wife, after all—roughly took her hand and curved it around the haft of the sword just under the guard. She did not mind; his touch was impersonal, instructive, and she knew now that she did not have anything to fear from him, and in fact, after sleeping in the same bed with him—

"Your mind is wandering. God's blood, girl, keep your attention on the moment! Do you think your opponent will wait until you finish your woolgathering?"

"*Non*, M. Sir Jack." Catherine pulled her attention back to the lesson. "I will do as you say."

"Good—and damme, stand straight, knees slightly flexed. I'm teaching you to fence, not curtsy."

She grinned. "It would not be a good curtsy,

either, and what can you expect after our hard ride last night?"

"As you say." His expression remained stern, but she could see amusement in his eyes. "A more graceless scamp I have never seen. I wonder that I had seen the gentlewoman in you."

"Perhaps you were wrong," Catherine replied, even though she knew he was not, and however much she avoided probing the past. His demeanor did not change. Instead, he moved away and jerked his chin at her.

"Go through your exercises. I wish to see if you have remembered them."

She obediently positioned her feet and hands in prime, then moved into the intricate pattern of defense and attack. "I am not wrong," Jack continued. "There is no use trying to make me think you are anything else. Everything about you cries out 'gentlewoman.' I am surprised your sex and station were not discovered earlier."

She turned to him. "Perhaps I am more clever than you think."

"Your exercises, girl! Pay attention." His voice was sharp, forcing her back into thrusting and parrying against a phantom opponent. Irritation flared, but she was glad of it—it reminded her of her purpose, and that discipline was part regular practice and part attention to the smallest detail. She imagined a shadowy figure before her, then remembered the monster she had faced before, and parried as if she were still fighting for her life. She would remember that, for as long as she lived, she was sure. It was necessary to fight so as to survive.

But her muscles screamed fatigue and ached horribly, and her breath labored. She glanced at Jack. He merely watched her and said nothing. Surely he must have noticed that she was breathing heavily by now? He said nothing, and she came to the end of her exercises, but since he still said nothing, she went through them again, for she had learned that if he did not command her to stop, she was not to stop.

Sweat poured from her brow, even though the inn's courtyard was coated with frost. Her heated breath blew in clouds in front of her, but still Jack said nothing.

Her lungs hurt now, and her legs pained her even more. She glanced at Jack, but he seemed to be examining his fingernails rather than looking at her. Impatience grew into anger, and she glanced at the empty space in front of her, where her imagined opponent should be. She was tired, her breath came in gasps, and she had had enough.

"Ha!" she cried, and lunged forward. She leaped back, sheathed her rapier, and then turned to Jack.

He looked up from his fingernails and frowned. "Why are you still? Fight on."

Catherine lifted her chin defiantly, then put her hands on her hips. "I cannot, monsieur. My enemy is dead."

Jack peered at the empty space where her opponent was supposed to be. "It is merely a flesh wound; continue."

Catherine pressed her lips together for a moment, suppressing a grin. "No, you are mistaken, M. Sir Jack. Did you not hear me say 'Ha!' very loudly? It signified a death thrust."

"Was that what it was? I thought the sound was a burp, or perhaps your stomach growling again, for it's a devilish appetite you have for food, *ma chère*."

A laugh sounded from behind her, and she

whirled around. A number of the inn's guests had gathered in the courtyard, and were grinning. Her sword practice had attracted some notice, and her shoulders went up for a moment, wishing she could disappear in embarrassment. But she remembered that she would not be afraid, and that she had promised Jack she'd pay him back in some way, and if she were to fight for money, then of course she would have an audience.

She turned to Jack and shook her head. "If I have an appetite, monsieur, it is only for fighting." She looked at the small crowd in the courtyard, smiled, and bowed.

Jack's grin grew wider, and he waggled his eyebrows in an exaggerated leer. "*Ma chère,* I know you have an appetite for... more than that."

The crowd laughed, and she could feel her cheeks grow warm. But she could give as good as she got, she thought. "Why, monsieur, I do not know what you mean. All you have done is teach me about swords, but I have never seen you employ yours."

The onlookers roared with laughter. She could see Jack's lips press firmly together as if offended, but his eyes twinkled and she knew he understood her implied insult to his manhood.

He spread his hands out and appealed to the growing audience now watching eagerly. "How can I answer that? She has insulted my honor. How am I to deal with her?"

Various lewd suggestions came forth, making Catherine's cheeks grow even warmer, but she lifted her chin and eyed Jack with mock sternness. "You may try... but I will bet that you cannot."

Jack's expression was amused, but he turned a look of pretended horror on the courtyard's crowd.

"She is a difficult wench! Shall I teach her a lesson?" Shouts of approval came from the crowd, but Catherine held up her hand.

"But think, all of you! You have just watched me practice. Do you think I would be defeated that easily?" Some of the inn's patrons began to look dubious. "What would you wager against me?"

The sound of a coin tinkled against the stones of the courtyard. "I would wager at least that—and a *private* lesson in what I can do with my sword." Jack winked at the crowd, drawing more laughter. More coins followed as he swaggered in front of them. Catherine bit her lip to keep down her laughter—he acted for all the world as if he were a mustachioed villain in a play. He turned to her. "I see you have very little confidence in yourself; you have not put down any money to wager."

A challenge: of course, he knew she had no money. Catherine looked at him and his gaze flickered to her lips. She remembered the night before, and how he had asked for a kiss, as if that simple act had some worth to him. Well, she could afford that, certainly.

She turned to the crowd and sighed sadly. "I am but a poor maiden, alas! The only thing I can wager is ... a kiss."

"A kiss!" Jack snorted in disbelief. "A paltry wager."

"Three kisses, then," Catherine said boldly. The crowd roared its approval, and she bowed in acknowledgment, then turned to Jack. "Your sword, monsieur! *En garde!*"

But then a derisive voice came out of the crowd. "I'll not wager a settled game." It came from a burly, coarse-looking man who bore a sword at his side.

"Look you, they must be master and whore—a win for one would mean a win for the other."

Catherine could feel her cheeks burn with insult as she watched the crowd make dubious noises and withdraw their wagers. "I am no whore, monsieur, and will prove my honor by the sword—if you dare."

The crowd grew silent in clear anticipation. "Excellent," Jack whispered in her ear. "Speak on, *ma chère*; this is better than I had hoped."

Her heart lightened at his encouragement, and she continued. "Three livres," she called out boldly. "Three livres that I win." Three livres of Jack's money, but perhaps he would not mind.

"Five livres," he called out. "I have trained her well." He winked lasciviously at the inn-yard crowd and they laughed.

She drew in a deep, shaky breath. Obviously he did not mind, and thought she could indeed win. She would do her best, then.

The burly man grinned and spat on the ground. "Six livres that I win."

"Done!" said Jack. "First blood, and it's finished."

She looked her opponent up and down—they were of the same height and so perhaps their reach would be equal. His clothes were not of the best, but if he was willing to wager so much, either he was very sure of himself, or he had more money than he was willing to spend on his attire. She pressed her lips together grimly. The man before her was also heavier and probably stronger than she, and she had just finished a tiring practice. Her fatigue would diminish her agility, she was sure. She glanced at Jack, but he merely met her look and nodded encouragingly. She closed her eyes, for she still felt unready for her first true duel, and as she took out her cross and kissed it, prayed for success. She took a deep breath, let it out, and stared at her opponent. Very well.

She took up her sword and placed herself in front of the man. *"En garde!"* she said.

She put her sword up in position, but it was soon clear the man would not attack until he had got her measure. She relaxed, and a strange calm came over her, a detachment. She let down her sword as she circled him, allowing him—she hoped—to think she was more fatigued than she was.

It worked. He lunged forward, but her sword hand came up as if it had a life of its own and deflected his thrust neatly. He grunted, clearly disappointed, but thrust again at her, which she parried easily.

The man frowned and stepped back, clearly reassessing his opinion of her. The man leaped forward and engaged, sooner than she had thought he would, and almost touched the cloth of her sleeve, but she parried in time. The man grinned, clearly encouraged, and he struck at her again. But she countered easily, and once more. She raised her brows. She had sparred only a little with Jack, but never seriously. And yet, even after her strenuous practice, this fight was less difficult than a session with Jack.

The man began to frown as he tried to pierce her guard but could not.

It began to be a game. Defense came surprisingly easy, she realized with that detached part of her mind, even as she could feel the strain of the fight. What of attack? She watched for an opening.

The man's breath came more heavily than before, and for one moment his sword dropped. She lunged forward, shoving aside his arm as she neatly pierced his shoulder. She leaped back and put up her sword. *"Touché!"* she said. The crowd cheered and clapped and money began to change hands.

A surprised look crossed the man's face as he brought his hand up to his shoulder, then his face reddened. "A trick!" he cried, and lifted his sword again.

Anger quickened in Catherine's gut, and her hand tightened around the haft of her rapier. "What trick?" She turned to the inn-yard crowd. "You have seen me practice—did you see me employ any sleight of hand? Did you see anything but work?"

Some of the people in the crowd jeered at her opponent, which only made the man's face grow redder. He spat behind his back at them, and turned to Catherine. "Witch! No doubt you employed sorcerous powers to win."

Fear sliced through her stomach, but she pressed her lips together and gathered up her courage. She would not let such an accusation stand. "It is a coward and a poor loser who would use such an excuse to defeat another fighter instead of skill and strength," she called out. "Yet you have my leave to bring me a priest to examine me…but I think he would say that a fighter who prays to the Holy Mother of God for success would not use sorcery but would fight fairly." She seized her cross and held it up, glinting in the winter sun, to the crowd.

A murmur of approval moved through the spectators, and the man snarled. "I will not lose to a woman," he said, and leaped forward with his sword.

Catherine put up her rapier, deflecting the slash of the man's attack, countered it with another thrust past his defense, and slashed his other sleeve. Anger made her push him back and back until he was almost pressed against the bystanders, who scattered as the fighters drew near. She stared into his eyes, discerning his intent as he shifted his gaze here and there, looking for an opening in her defense. There was fear in him, she could see it, smell it. All her senses came to the fore; she could see the gleam of sweat on his brow, the smell of his sweat, the shouted encouragement of the betting audience . . . and something, something buzzing through her fury, as if a fly came near her ear, a buzzing that became a roar—

"I said *stop*!" A bright flash came between them, and the man's sword flew from his hand as a sharp shock and then brief sizzling numbness shook her arm as her rapier fell to the ground. She whirled toward the interruption, her hands curled into claws, ready to jump and attack.

"Damn the both of you!" Jack roared, and kicked away their swords. "We agreed to first blood, not a duel to the death." He pointed to Catherine. "You! Go over there." He swerved his finger toward a far corner of the inn yard. Catherine crossed her arms and stood where she was, gritting her teeth at Jack's interference. "I said *go,* or you will know the feel of my hand, my lady," he said, his voice lowered, but more threatening nevertheless. He gazed at her steadily, and she managed to put aside her anger enough to see there was another emotion behind his irritation. She nodded curtly, and walked as slowly and insolently as she could to the corner he had pointed to.

"And you!" Jack turned and snapped at the man. "By our Lady, you go too far! I tolerated the insult to my wife—yes, my *wife*—since she could well prove her honor, but now you cast aspersions on her honor to account for your own failure." He spat on the ground. "Coward! Lose to a woman? You would lose to a goose with one leg and claim it was the Devil's work."

The crowd laughed, and the man growled in clear anger. He stooped to pick up his sword, but found Jack's own sword at his throat. "Don't, monsieur. If you think my wife has any skill at all, it is nothing compared to mine."

Catherine gazed at Jack, her anger dropping from her. He had changed; his voice was soft, but his face had turned cold, and his eyes, chill. She thought if the man did engage in a duel with him, it would be to the death indeed, and not Jack who would fall.

The man slowly rose, and Jack lowered the point of his sword. He grinned and gave the man an apparently friendly *thump* on the back. "There's a good sport. Now, distribute your money to these good folk, and be on your way," he said heartily, as if there had been no altercation at all.

The man edged away and thrust his hand in his pocket, withdrawing a purse and tossing some coins onto the ground with the rest of the wagers. Jack's brows rose. "You put in five livres—not six." He gazed at the man coolly. "You agreed on six." Catherine's opponent muttered a curse and threw another coin to the ground, then stalked away. The crowd surged forward to collect their gains, and Jack stooped to pick up the livres the man had thrown down.

He glanced at her and jerked his head toward the inn. "I'll see you in our room. Go."

Rebellion and irritation at his interference rose again and she stood her ground, staring at him. "Not until I get my share," she said. It was not what she wanted to say, but it reflected her irritation that he did not think enough of her skill to have let her continue fighting.

His gaze grew cool, though not as chill as when he had stared down her opponent. "You do not trust me, I see. Very well." He counted out three livres and held them out to her. "Half of whatever comes in—fair enough?"

She nodded, but did not take the coins right away, only stared at them for a moment before she slowly put out her hand. He dropped the coins in her palm, and she closed her fingers around them.

The metal was warm from his touch, and she remembered the warmth this morning as they lay together in their bed, how he had draped his arm around her, and the comfort of it after her initial panic. Her irritation fell from her, and she looked at him, nodding. "Thank you," she said. She smiled a little. "It is the very first money I have earned, I believe."

The coolness of his expression evaporated and he grinned. "It's a novelty that does not wear off, I assure you," he said. "With luck, we'll earn more." He squinted at the sun creeping toward midheaven and motioned to the inn door. "Go now—I'll be in shortly."

She nodded and turned away. She could feel the grime and sweat of last night's travel on her, combined with the dirt of today's practice and duel, and she wanted her promised bath and the cleanliness the time in hot water offered. Jack had said she might bathe once she was done with her practice, and she had practiced, and more. Her heart swelled with joy and pride, and she grinned—she had done well, she thought, and deserved a reward. As she entered the inn, she called to a chambermaid for a bath to be brought up, then almost skipped up the steps to her room.

She had pinked the man and had won the fight. She had earned good money for it, and might even had won a duel to the death had Jack not interfered. The disgruntlement she felt at his interference was brief, however. She knew despite his insistence that he was merely interested in returning her to her family for a price, that it was a surface protest covering what she knew was kindness. Nothing said he had to agree to teach her to fight, after all, and nothing said he had to provide good clothes or bountiful food for her. She did not know if it was true that he was in love with her as Felice and Fichet had insisted; she was not certain what love was like, or if she could return it. She did know Jack was, at least, as kind as they had been to her.

He did not even have to split their winnings evenly between them; he could have rightfully claimed the whole amount as payment for what he had expended on her. But he had given half to her, and had not grudged it, and had smiled when she had told him it was the very first time she had earned money.

Two chambermaids came up with buckets of hot and cool water, and poured it into the tin bath that sat by the fireplace. Catherine sighed, anticipating the warmth and cleanliness. She could sit in a bath forever if it did not cool. She thought of Jack again, of the warmth he had given her at night and in the morning, and how he had been quite generous. She should, in truth, pay for what he had given her. Granted, he would be paid when she returned to her family. . . . A shiver went through her. The sooner she got into the bath, she thought, the warmer she would be, and waited impatiently for the maids to finish pouring the water.

No, she needed to pay Jack herself. He had been generous to her, for her sake, she was certain of it. She thought of the livres she had earned. At least she could give him some of it. She dug into her pockets and pulled out the money. She would give him two of the livres and keep one herself. And if she were to fight in another duel, she would do this again until she had paid him back for what he had given her, including the fencing lessons.

But the thought came to her that he might refuse payment. She frowned. For all that he insisted that he kept her by his side so that he could return her to her family for money, she felt he would not like it if she offered to pay him for her tutoring or the food and shelter he had given her. If he had truly thought he should have been paid for it, he would have taken all of the wager they had won, not split it with her. She was his apprentice, and a master did not give anything to an apprentice but food, shelter, and clothing until the apprentice achieved journeyman status. She knew that, at least.

She drew in a deep breath and closed her eyes against the pressure she felt under her breastbone, as if birds fluttered frantically against her rib cage, yearning for flight and freedom. She wanted to be free, and she could not be if she owed   so much.

A kiss.

Catherine opened her eyes, remembering that it had been part of their original wager, before her opponent had come to challenge her. He valued kisses, and she was sure he would accept them if she offered. She remembered also the way he had looked at her when she had been in her bath—as odd as it seemed, she thought perhaps he desired her.

Carefully she weighed the thought, testing it in her mind for fear or threat. There was a little fear, but she had pledged she would conquer fear whenever she felt it. The idea came to her that perhaps she was moving away from the grace she had acquired after her confession. A rebellion rose in her at the thought, however, for she also remembered that the priest had said her stigmata was probably a blessed thing. Well, she did not want it. If kissing Jack meant she would be rid of the affliction, she would be glad.

A weight came off her heart, and she felt suddenly free. Quickly she took off her clothes, readying herself for her bath. A movement in the mirror nearby caught her gaze; it was herself, moving toward the tub. She gazed at her reflection for a moment, startled, for she had not really ever gazed at herself unclothed.

She was different, she thought, than what she had been. Not fashionably plump, but her form, she thought, was not unpleasant. She could see muscles in her shoulders, and her skin smoothly covered more of them from chest to stomach to hips. A pleased feeling came over her; she looked strong and sleek, like a cat. She liked the thought of being cat-like; they were clever animals, and knew how to survive.

But she was more than that. She was her own woman, someone who could earn her own money and not be obligated to anyone. She sighed happily. Jack had given her this opportunity, and she was grateful. He had been the source of warmth and food, and yes, gentleness. She had not minded, after a while, the way he had held her without threat or trying to use her. She nodded to herself in satisfaction. When he came up, she would make sure he knew how grateful she was.

Jack watched Catherine, how she walked with more confidence now, and grinned. She had done well, but he was glad he had stopped the fight before it had gone further. He could not afford to have her injured before he returned her to her family.

He winced inwardly at his old reasoning. The truth: he wanted to the kill the man himself for insulting Catherine and for pushing the fight further than they had agreed. Though she was strong and had a great deal of endurance, no one could be expected to bear up under a death-duel after such a practice as he had imposed on her. And . . . he could not bear to see her hurt.

An impractical feeling; she would be hurt even in sword practice. An image of her strong, straight body, the way she pressed her lips together as she fought, came to him, and his lips turned up in a rueful smile. He doubted she would listen to him in the future. She was not afraid of fighting, he realized. Perhaps he should not be afraid for her

Yet she was still very capable of being hurt. He remembered how she had touched him this morning and how she had let him kiss her—tentatively, her eyes wide and vulnerable. She had not understood when he had ordered her away; his voice had been harsh and impatient, but it came from his fear for her.

An eagerness to tell her this, to tell her that what he wanted for her seized him, and the sound of coins jingling in his pockets was the sound of optimism as he strode across the courtyard and up to the room.

He made sure to knock on the door this time, in case she needed her privacy. Despite her willingness to kiss him this morning, and that she did not seem to mind that they had slept in the same bed, she seemed somehow virginal, untouched.

And yet, when he opened the door at her call of "*Entré!*" she was not dressed.

Catherine looked at him as he entered, a linen towel held up to her breasts as she stood by the bath newly drawn and still steaming in the cold air. The steam curled up around her, tendrils caressing her body, and the firelight behind her painted red lights and dark shadows on her skin.

He could only stare at her. She seemed like an elfin woman, made of fire and air, half insubstantial. He shut the door. He managed to do that, at least.

She glanced away, then stepped into the bath, discreetly holding the towel high until she was submerged, then letting it drop down to the floor. "I owe you money," she said. She frowned for a moment, as if discontented with the way she had spoken. She cleared her throat and looked at him again, and reached out her hand to the table next to the bath. A *clink* of coins sounded as she opened her hand to him. She cleared her throat, then looked away.

"You have clothed and fed me," she said. "And you have given me a way of earning a living." She glanced at him, her expression uncertain. "You did not have to do that. I am grateful, and know that I should reimburse you for your expenses."

A brief anger flitted through him. "I don't want your money," he said. "I have plenty of it, I assure you."

Her lips pressed together in clear discontent. "That does not matter," she said. "I will not be beholden to you, M. Sir Jack."

Irritation grew. "As far as I am concerned, you are my guest. You need not pay me.... Besides, I will be paid once you are returned to your family."

She turned then and looked at him earnestly. "But there is no guarantee they will pay you, *hein*? And what you have done, you have done for *me*. I am ... grateful. I wish to give something back to you, and all I have is the money I have earned, which I would not have earned had you not taught me to duel."

He did not want her gratitude, he realized. She continued to stare at him in silence, as if willing her determination to pay him into his brain, then turned away and took up a sponge, dipping it into the water and washing her face. He watched as the sponge came down from her face, at how her eyes were closed in sheer pleasure when she applied it to her neck and shoulders. His loins stirred, and he made himself sit in a nearby chair and cross his legs. He looked toward the door. He should leave; she was too much of a temptation to him. But she looked at him again with her eyes so impossibly green, and he thought perhaps it would not hurt to stay a little longer.

He cleared his throat and looked away for a moment as she rose a little from the bath and moved the sponge downward. "It amused me to teach you. And you are a good student. Any teacher would find it agreeable to teach one who learns quickly." A wide smile lit her face, and he could not help staring. He didn't remember seeing her smile so—and she was lovely when she did.

"I'm glad you approve," she said, then sighed. "I am done with my bath now. Will you give me the towel?"

He looked at her, suspicion rising. The towel was well within reach if she moved out of the bath—she need only tell him to turn away while she picked it up. Her gaze was wide and innocent—too innocent, he thought. His loins grew hot with sudden realization: she was trying to seduce him.

It was not right, of course; she belonged to the Marquis de Bauvin. He thought of the money she had offered him... well, that was it. She wanted to repay him and, because he had refused money, offered seduction.

He lowered his eyes for a moment, hiding anger. If she thought to pay him by offering her body, he did not want it. He wanted more than that. His heart suddenly felt squeezed tightly to the point of pain, and for a moment he closed his eyes. *Damme, damme, thrice dammed.* He wanted all of her, body, heart, and soul. Anger at her, at himself, swelled inside of him. He should never have let himself come to this point. He should have contacted her family immediately, whatever state she had been in, and taken the money right away. Stupid, stupid of him.

He bent, then, and picked up the towel, looking down at her as he held it out to her. "I know what you are doing," he said. She took the towel and put it between them, rising out of the water, then wrapping it securely around her. She did not look at him, and if she had not pressed her lips together in a stubborn expression, he would have thought she had not heard him. "Look at me, Catherine." She turned and gazed at him, her face showing a wary vulnerability.

He cleared his throat. "I will not take your body as payment."

She lifted her chin and a slight blush came to her face. "I thought perhaps you might accept a kiss, and since I am not comely, I thought you might be persuaded if you saw me in my bath." She stepped out of the tub and moved closer to him, close enough for him to smell the scent of soap she had used. She put her arms around his neck. "You have asked me to kiss you before. You cannot object now. A kiss would be payment, would it not?"

He looked down at her, at the way she stared at him in determination, at how her lips were very close to his. He did not know whether to laugh at her stubbornness or push her angrily away. "You belong to the Marquis de Bauvin," he said instead.

Anger flared. "I belong to no one," she whispered fiercely. "I remember nothing of my family, of the marquis, of my home. I remember nothing but the alley, the dirt, and cold hunger. Nothing but hiding from whores and their masters, from thieves and beggars. No one came for me, until you. Until *you*."

Catherine closed her eyes briefly. It was true; Jack was the source of all the good that had come to her. He had given her food and warmth, even the warmth of his body. The air around her chilled her skin, but where she was pressed against him, she was warm. She belonged to no one, and she was glad; those who survived best in the alley chose whom they belonged to, and the idea that she belonged to someone she did not know or choose made her feel trapped. She opened her eyes and stared at Jack. "I will choose whom I belong to. *I* will choose. I will choose who to kiss, or who will look at me."

Desperation seized her as she gazed at him, as he

shook his head. "It is not as simple as that. I will not dishonor you or my word—" he began, but she put her hand over his mouth.

"Shut up!" she cried. "Shut up!" She drew down his head and kissed him.

He groaned, his arms came around her, and he pressed his lips hard upon hers. For one moment, a faint unease made her pause. She withdrew a little, gazing at his eyes, and wondered at the look of sorrow and loss that flitted across his face. But a soft heat grew in her heart, and she wished suddenly to erase the grief that seemed to live in his eyes, and she drew even closer to him, moving her hands inside his jacket and onto his chest. "Don't be sad," she said. "Kiss me." Surely kisses would remove the sadness.

He said nothing, only brought his lips down to hers again, and she felt the towel come undone, until she was bare. She shivered at the chill air on her back, and she nestled closer to him, putting her arms around him. "I am cold," she said. "Make me warm."

He gave a groaning laugh then and took her to the bed, lifting her gently onto it, then pulling off his jacket and kicking off his boots before he followed her onto the sheets. More clothes came off Jack as he kissed her, and then his hands touched her breasts.

His hands were gentle. "Mmmm. More," she said, and kissed him again. But his lips left hers, trailing down her neck and one shoulder, making shiver. She shifted toward him, closing her eyes so she could better feel the heat of his body. She wanted to be closer to him, close enough to feel the source of the heat he put on her with his hands and his mouth. His lips were at her belly now, making her shiver more, and she cautiously touched his hair. Her fingers threaded through the surprisingly soft locks, soft like feathers, and then she clutched at them, for his lips touched her secret places, making her eyes open with surprise and her breath come fast.

No heat now, but fire, and she twisted beneath his hands that held her gently down to the bed. She felt his fingers on her, moving where the heat was, and then they moved *inside*, an odd, familiar sensation—

Fear struck like a knife and she twisted away, kicking her feet on the bed.

"No. No!" she cried. She closed her thighs, closed her eyes, and it seemed her lungs closed and she could not breathe. "No, stop, stop, stop, stop!" She twisted away from him, curling up into the mattress, her hands clawing the bedclothes into a shroud over her head. The dark comforted her, and she felt she was safe, as if in the alley hidden from everyone.

Silence. She could hear the crackling of the fire, and breathing—her own, a gasping, shaking breath—and then another, heavier and regular, from outside the bedclothes. She wished she had her dagger. The mattress beside her sank—slowly, so she managed not to flinch from the sensation.

"Catherine." It was Jack. She remembered he had taken her from the alley, and he had given her warmth and food. "Catherine." His voice was gentle. Her shoulders relaxed.

The sheet over her head came down slowly, and Jack's face appeared above it. His brows came together in a frown, but she thought perhaps he was not angry, for his eyes held concern, as well. He looked puzzled, she realized. She let out another long, shuddering breath and let herself relax. He came closer, moving slowly, and though she flinched when he touched her, she allowed him to turn her on her side. She felt the mattress move behind her, and then there was his warmth again, his body strong underneath his skin, smooth along the length of her back.

His arm came around her, slowly, as if he were moving around a wild creature, and settled on the bed in front of her. She tried to make herself relax, but the effort made her tremble instead.

"Hush, *ma chère,* hush." Jack's voice was soothing, and his breath brushed her hair by her ear. "I will do nothing you dislike, and will not hurt you."

She closed her eyes, nodding slowly in acknowledgment. A mist obscured her mind, and beyond it was terror, confusion, a memory out of her reach, thankfully out of her reach.

I will not be afraid. I have vowed not to be afraid. This was Jack, and he would not hurt her. She let out a deep breath, and her body relaxed.

She felt his hand on her waist, and she managed not to flinch, though she knew she tensed. But he did nothing but stroke her waist, a soothing sensation, and she relaxed again. His hand went up to her breast—he had done this before and she had not minded it, she remembered. More stroking, and his thumb came up over her nipple, moving across the tip slowly.

She moved back against him, for his warmth meant safety to her, and he was the source of it. A hardness moved against her buttocks, and she thought perhaps it was his manhood, for she had seen men's privates as they worked on the prostitutes in the alley. She did not want to see it, though; it was enough that he stroked her breasts and her belly, and that his body against her back was very warm.

He kissed her neck, and his breath was soft on her skin. "That does not hurt, does it?"

"No," she breathed.

"How does it feel?"

"Good."

He kissed her just under her ear, and his hand moved from her breast to her belly. "And this?" His hand stroked in a circle on her stomach, massaging gently.

"Good."

Jack let out his breath, controlled the heat in his loins, making himself touch Catherine's skin and run his hand over her body as if she were not a woman he wanted desperately, but a wild creature needing to be gentled.

He did not know what else to do. She had seemed willing, had wanted him to kiss her, and had not protested when he began to make love to her. She had even seemed pleasured as he began to touch her woman's parts . . . but then she had cried out not in passion, but in terror.

He knew terror. He had heard its cries on the battlefield . . . and heard it as Cromwell's soldiers had invaded that most sanctified of all places to him—invaded his home. He had heard terror in the cries of his mother and sister. He remembered it like an old knife wound with bits of splintered steel still inside of him, knowing he had led the soldiers to them.

He closed his eyes. The memories took the lust from his body; he touched her now for comfort, for him and, he hoped, for her.

She moved closer to him, her back pressing into his chest, and she gave a shuddering sigh, as if a long bout of weeping had shaken her. He brushed her face gently with the tips of his fingers and felt no tears. He remembered he had never seen her weep.

Her breath continued to shudder, but he moved his hand over her waist to her stomach, rubbing his fingers gently over the muscles of her belly, moving up to her breasts and down again in a widening circle. He did nothing else, only brushing the soft hairs at the base of her belly, going no farther. Her chest's rise and fall became regular, and the shuddering became the smooth and even flow of breath. The tension in her body seemed to fall away as she relaxed into his chest and stomach.

His touch must have given her some comfort, but there was none yet for himself. He smoothed his hand across her belly again, then cupped her breast. Catherine did not tense this time, but let out a deep breath.

"This does not hurt, does it?" he said again.

"No," she said. She drew in a deep breath and let it out again. "It feels . . . pleasant."

Pleasant. Hope allowed a chuckle to escape him. "Good," he said. "But before I do anything else, you must tell me what frightened you." Perhaps she was indeed a virgin . . . but he remembered the terror in her cries for him to stop. A virgin might be fearful, but the few virgins he had known had been more curious than fearful at the threshold of pleasure. The liquid heat he had felt inside of her told him she had begun to feel at least some pleasure.

"I wasn't—"

"Shhh!" he said. "Don't lie. You were terrified." He let his hand drift down from her breast to her belly, circling her navel with gentle fingers. "Did I hurt you?"

"I . . . no." Her voice sounded puzzled. "I thought

I remembered..." A hint of fear sounded underneath the puzzlement.

"Did someone hurt you before, down here?" His fingers slipped among the fine curls below her belly, caressing with a light touch. He stilled his hand, moving no farther, for tension hardened her body against his. Her skin was soft and warm against him, but her fear dampened his desire. He did not want her afraid; he wanted her to want him. She had come willingly to him so far, and lay with him now, not rejecting him. He wanted more.

He heard her release another long breath. "I don't know...but I am afraid, Jack." Catherine turned slightly toward him, a little on her back, so that she could look at him. Sorrow clearly lived in her eyes, and it struck him hard. "I think I am not a virgin, and am afraid this will hurt," she said.

He kissed her gently, hopeful that she was not a virgin, and angry that she had suffered. "If you are not a virgin, *ma chère,* then it will not hurt. I will make sure of it." He shifted himself lower, watching his own hands move over her body and gentling it until she relaxed again. She closed her eyes, and he did not ask her to open them, for he feared seeing the sorrow and terror there.

Instead, he kissed her belly, then the indentation of her navel, then lower, beginning again where he had left off when she had cried out in fear.

I will not stop him this time, Catherine thought. *I choose this, not anyone else. I choose.* Not memory, not fear—*nothing* would choose for her.

She let him kiss her breasts and belly; she let him kiss her woman's parts, and then she gasped and opened her eyes, for again there was the heat when she felt the movement of his tongue upon her. She trembled, but this time it was not from fear but an odd tension that she had not felt before. Again, his fingers slid between her thighs. She tightened her legs together.

"Shh, *ma chère,* open for me." His breath brushed her hips like a breeze. Cautiously Catherine moved her legs apart. His hand was hot between her thighs, moving slickly between them, making her twist against them and breathe a soft moan. This was not so terrible, Catherine thought. She was not certain why she had been so frightened or thought it would hurt. But Jack's hand slipped inside again, and all thought fled.

Instead there was the heat and the smoothness and an ache that was all yearning, not pain. A cool draft wafted over her skin, and she shivered, but she was not sure whether it was because of the chill or the sensations Jack was making in her body.

But he rose up next to her, and all was well; he turned her on her side, facing him, as he pulled her hips toward him while he kissed her and caressed her waist. She tensed once more when his hardness moved between her thighs, but he did nothing but what his hand had done, gently sliding back and forth until she could not help moving with him.

His kisses heated, insisting that she open her mouth to him, but she did not mind. She felt as if she had no mind at all, but was all sensation as she moved upon him—feeling, tasting, hearing his quickened breath, the heat, the tension, and then, then the bright unbearable flash, making her cry out.

She shuddered again and again against him, and he smoothed his hands over her skin, holding her close, until she breathed evenly and the shuddering stopped.   •

Her body grew lax in his arms then, and Jack opened his eyes and gazed at her. Her eyes were closed. He could feel his lips twist in a wry smile. He had not allowed himself to enter her, but had taken his satisfaction between her thighs instead; he would not risk giving her a child when she could still belong to another. But he doubted Catherine appreciated his efforts, for she clearly slept.

And he would let her. He had worked her hard—he grinned at the thought—in more ways than one, and she deserved rest.

He gazed at her again, at how her face softened in sleep, no longer guarded or wary. He wished suddenly he could banish the habitual caution in her eyes, or at least when she looked at him. Perhaps if he continued his lessons in swordfighting, and taught her all he knew, she would trust him.

He grimaced. He had told her more than once that she should not trust him—and now, he wanted otherwise?

He bit back a groan. He was an idiot. He needed no such commitment. Catherine had been betrothed to the Marquis de Bauvin, and for all he knew, the marquis would wish her to be his wife once she returned.

God knew he would.

So he wished. Jack closed his eyes. It ever came to that, wishing and hoping and building castles in the sky, and furnishing them with elaborate plans to regain his estate and be wealthy once again—all pretense. He lived in a play of his own making; even claiming that Catherine was his wife was as much a dream as protecting her reputation.

She deserved more than a vagabond whose future

was uncertain. Until he could claim his due, he could not ask her to marry him.

He ran a finger across her cheek....She was so fast asleep that she did not move. Hope drained from him. Even if he did regain his estates, it would mean very little; if they had not been ravaged by war, they would have fallen into neglect. He had not even the deed to the land, for he had had to escape as soon as he could when he was a boy. It would take the return of his king to give him even a little chance at it.

In short, he had nothing to offer her.

Nothing but this comfort, this closeness, and whatever aid he could think of.

It was little enough. He pulled Catherine closer to him, letting his cheek rub against the soft curls of her hair. But perhaps for now it would be enough, and perhaps he could find some other way to aid her, for whatever her situation at home, she had suffered grievously.

He smiled wryly. Damn his charitable instincts. Even his mother had complained that he had brought home too many mongrels, too many stray cats—

He turned away from the memory, focusing on the sensation of Catherine sleeping next to him.

He grew hard at the feeling of her soft skin, the heat of her buttocks against his loins, but he forced himself to move away. It was too soon, and she was clearly too recently scarred for him to press more of his attentions on her.

Better that he prepare for the journey ahead. He'd let her sleep, for she'd earned it, and then he'd waken her for a meal. He smiled slightly. She would welcome a meal once she awoke, he was sure.

Carefully he disentangled his legs from hers and rolled from the bed to his feet. He looked at her; she barely moved, only leaning slightly more into the mattress than she had before, and breathing in long, slow breaths. She had, indeed, earned her sleep, as any trooper might. She would make a good soldier, he thought.

She would make a good soldier's wife, came the next thought.

He let out a quick, impatient breath at himself, found his scattered clothes, and quickly put them on. He looked about, found Catherine's clothes, and draped them on the foot of the bed so that she'd be able to dress quickly once she woke. He was an impractical fool, but not that much of a fool to dwell on useless thoughts. They would move quickly on to Normandy, finding other opportunities for bringing in funds as they could. Once they arrived at the de la Fer estate, he would collect his reward and go on to Breda. It was for the best.

He took one more look at Catherine sleeping. Even she agreed that it was necessary that she return home to understand what had happened to her. No doubt all would be revealed to her satisfaction, and she would be welcomed with open arms. It was, at least, what he hoped for her.

Enough. Enough of pondering and wishing. Jack opened the door and, with a last sigh, gently closed it behind him before he went down to order a meal.

Chapter 8

CATHERINE AWOKE WITH A START. THE room was cold, as were her shoulders, which were naked above the sheets and blankets of the bed. She pulled up the sheets and attempted to find more warmth for a while, but restlessness made her thrust away the bedcovers and pull on the clothes she found at the foot of the bed. Jack must have put them there, she realized. As far as she remembered, they had fallen to the floor as they had . . .

As they had made love.

Warmth flooded her, and she was not certain whether it was embarrassment or the remembrance of pleasure and comfort. Remembrance, perhaps, because she could feel a smile moving her lips upward.

Except for that one instance of unreasoning terror, she had felt comfortable, warm, and oddly secure. She frowned a moment as she pulled on her shirt and trousers. "Secure" was not the right word. She had felt vulnerable and exposed, and there was nothing secure in that. She picked up a hairbrush and made a face at it. She hoped she could untangle her hair as well as Felice had done.

She sighed, remembering the warmth of Jack's arms around her, the heat of his body, the strange, soothing excitement of his kisses and touch. She had not minded any of it; she had, after a while, sought it.

Trust. The word came to her, and a part of her recoiled—she trusted nobody. But Jack . . . she did trust him, at least with her body. He had fed her and taken care of her, and then had pleasured her.

She caught sight of her hands in the small wall mirror as she clumsily brushed her hair. She put down the brush and looked at the palms of her hands, then turned them over. There were no marks on them, and even better, they looked strong and competent.

A defiant glee made her grin. Well, she had no doubt sinned in laying with Jack, and if Père Doré was right that her stigmata was a holy thing, then it would surely not return. Good. She was better off without it, and she could not see what purpose it had other than to give her pain. She wrinkled her nose in disgruntlement. If God had wanted to give her a blessing, she did not know why it was not something more useful, such as healing powers or the ability to lead armies to victory. Certainly King Louis's armies could use some help, and it was not as if God hadn't used a woman to lead the armies of France before. And if the stigmata was some kind of punishment, it made no sense that God would keep her from remembering what sin she had done to warrant such a punishment. If she did not remember the sin, she would very likely repeat it, after all. She shook her head. No, it made no sense at all.

Her stomach growled loudly, and she put her

hand over it. She was hungry. Now, this was something that made sense. If one was hungry, one ate, and then one was filled and that was the end of it. She would go down to the common room below and see if Jack had ordered a meal.

She sighed happily to find that Jack had indeed ordered food, and that one of the inn's maids was just putting it on the table in front of him. This was another thing she liked about him—he never stinted on food, despite his teasing about her appetite.

The look he gave her when she sat across from him seemed tentative; it sat oddly on his face, she thought, for he had normally a determined expression when at repose. But the look disappeared when she sighed, surveying the food before her—a roasted capon, buttered bread, dried fruit, cheeses, and wine—and amusement replaced it. The amusement became a chuckle when she bit into the capon leg and moaned as the salty and herbed juices burst on her tongue and she swallowed the tender meat.

"Hush, *ma chère,* the other guests will think we are in the throes of lovemaking with the sounds you make over your food."

Catherine drew in an indignant breath, intending some sharp words, but she choked instead and began to cough. Jack rose, thumped her back until she regained her breath, and then gave her a glass of wine. "I did not moan," she said at last.

"Yes, you did." He picked up the other capon leg and bit into it, chewing thoughtfully as he gazed at her. "You moaned as if you were at the height of pleasure. I should know, since I—"

She hastily put her hand over his mouth. "*Tiens!* Very well, I did moan." His eyes twinkled above her hand, and she moved it away. "You are teasing me," she said, but could not help smiling a little.

"Yes," he said. He nodded toward the food, then moved closer to her, his voice lowering. "Do continue to eat. I find I like hearing you moan—"

She stuffed a piece of dried apple into his mouth. "Eat," she said, feeling her cheeks heat. "Or else I shall have all of it, and you shall have none."

"True," Jack said, after he had swallowed the apple. He glanced down at the food he had put on his plate and then back at her, the uncertain look again in his eyes. "We should not have done it, Catherine."

A sinking feeling made her lower her eyes to the chunk of bread she had broken off the loaf. She gnawed at her lip and tore small pieces off the bread onto her plate, trying to gather her thoughts and emotions together, trying to identify them. Did he not like what they had done? He had protested only a little at first, then had gathered her up in his arms and had pleasured her until she had cried out helplessly from the sensations he had made in her. Surely he would not have done it if he had not wanted to?

She looked at him squarely. "Perhaps," she said. "But I wanted to. If you did not like it, you should have said so."

"Of course I liked—" He stopped and winced. "That is, it was not right."

Her heart lightened, and she grinned. "I am glad you liked it, for I did, very much. And if it was not right, then I am still glad, for Père Doré said that the wounds that appear on my hands and my back are most probably a holy thing, and I would much rather not have them, for they are a painful nuisance. So, it is reasonable, is it not, that if I do what is not

right, then the holiness will leave me, and I will not
have the wounds?"

Jack opened his mouth and shut it again. A disgruntled expression crossed his face. "Is that the only
reason you wanted to do it?"

Catherine gazed at him uncertainly. What did he
want of her? First he said they should not have done
it, and now he looked discontented when she told
him a very practical reason why she had. She shook
her head slowly, trying to think over her reasons, her
emotions. It was difficult; she was used to thinking
of sheer survival, and she had only recently been focused on conquering fear—successfully so far, she
thought. Had she not continued to allow Jack to
make love to her, even after she had become terrified?
And there were other feelings . . . she frowned fiercely,
shaking her head again.

"I . . . wanted not to be afraid," she said. She
looked at him, and the irritation on his face faded a
little. "I was not afraid, by the end. And I felt . . . I felt
I wanted to give something back to you."

The irritation returned. "I have told you I do not
want your gratitude."

Frustration seized her. "You have it, nevertheless," she said sharply. "I have told you my reasons,
and look you, they are reasonable. Why do you say we
should not have done it?"

His lips pressed together in clear frustration. "It
was not honorable. You belong to another, the Marquis de Bauvin. Even if not that, you belong to your
family, and they are the ones who are to say who you
may bed."

Anger made her clench her hands. "Honor. Bah!
Worse than that, I now have a sin on my soul, but do
I care?"

He said nothing, but raised an eyebrow at her and tapped his fingers on the table, impatiently waiting for her to answer her rhetorical question.

She hunched her shoulders in irritation. "Very well, I care, a little, and will confess it when I go to a priest the next time, but I will no doubt want to do it again if it means that my wounds will not return. I would rather do something pleasant than bear something that gives me pain. And..." She stopped, hesitating, struggling for words. "And...*I* want to choose. I wish to choose with whom I stay or give my body or—or even my heart."

Felice's words came to her suddenly, that Jack had fallen in love with her. She gazed at him, searching for any sign of that love, hoping she would recognize it if she saw it. But he looked away, and she saw only frustration instead.

Felice must be wrong, Catherine thought. For all that she did not remember much before her life in the alley, and had thought only of finding food and shelter, she had managed to observe a few things while there. Even among the whores and the people of the streets she had seen something that could have been love on their faces.

She was not certain that she had seen it on Jack's face, or that what she had seen he felt only for her. She made herself shrug, as if she did not care. She knew he was her friend, however, and that was more than she had had before in her life; she would be content with that...make herself content with it.

His expression did hold some sympathy, though, when he replied, "I understand, *ma chère*. Who would not wish the freedom to choose what they will? But that is not the way of the world." He took her hand in his, rubbing her palm with his thumb for a moment, before moving back and sighing. She gazed at him—he seemed suddenly much older than his twenty-four years, the scar on his cheek deeper, etching his face with weariness. "Our obligations . . . give us a home in ourselves to return to, when we have no other. Honor gives us an anchor when the storms of war and loss toss us beyond endurance." He gazed at her steadily. "This is what I have learned since boyhood, Catherine. This is what I live by. That, and hope."

She nodded slowly, realizing that she knew little of Jack, other than he was a soldier and he had left his family behind in England to fight for his king. She felt a little ashamed she had not been more curious about him; he had been very much her enefactor, after all, and she was most certainly obligated to him.

Obligation . . . he had said obligations acted as a home to him, and suddenly she understood. She wished freedom from obligation to him, of course. But it was also something that tied her to him, and she was not sure she wanted totally to undo that tie. The thought of it was like traveling the path to a home where friendship lived.

She nodded, taking his hand and squeezing it briefly. "I understand. I do not like to be obligated to you at all, which is why I wish to pay you back in some way. But it is an obligation that reminds me that you are also my friend, and I cannot regret it."

He looked at her then, gazing long into her eyes, and seemed about to speak. But his lips pressed together again, almost grimly, and he gave a brisk nod. "Good," he said. "Then we understand each other." He jerked his head toward the door. "The evening darkens. We will travel again this night, and if we are not attacked, then I think we can be more at ease that another such creature as we saw in Paris will not come after us. We may then travel during the day, as normal folk might." His smile was wry, as if he did not quite believe in the word "normal." He rose. "Come, let us leave. I have ordered fresh horses. We will not need to travel as far and fast this time." He grinned suddenly. "You will be glad of that, I think."

Her spirits had fallen when he seemed not to respond to her mention of friendship, but lifted again at his grin. It mattered not what he said about their relationship, she thought. It was enough for now that there was understanding between them and that he perceived her moods and thoughts quite clearly. Surely such understanding existed among friends, whether the word "friendship" was spoken or not.

She rolled her eyes at him. "See, this is why I must eat as much as I do! You would work me to the ground, and I must have a great deal of food to sustain me."

He laughed and waved his hand at the still-laden plates. "Go ask the innkeeper to pack it up so that we may take it with us. I cannot have you fainting from hunger in the middle of the road." He turned and strode out the inn door.

Catherine grinned, feeling relieved and lighter of heart. Surely once she returned home, her family would allow Jack to visit from time to time. Her thoughts lit on her former betrothed, the Marquis de Bauvin, but flitted away again. Time enough to think of such things once she returned home. For now, she would seize what joy she could of Jack's company, and leave tomorrow's troubles for tomorrow.

* * *

No natural or supernatural attacks came that night, much to Jack's relief. He and Catherine rode steadily under the moonlit sky, their collars, scarves, and hats close around their faces for warmth. No movement disturbed their travel except for the flit of owls across moon-illuminated clouds and through the silhouette of barren trees. If they heard a lone wolf howl, it was a problem easily rid of with sword or musket—much easier than some hell-born demon.

He glanced at Catherine, who rode at his side. He could see nothing of her face except for the occasional cast of moonlight on the tip of her nose. She had been silent since they left the inn; he wondered what she was thinking.

He scowled. No, he did not want to know what she thought. It was clear she sought his attentions as a means to an end. At best, she sought his friendship. Her reasons were practical; he could see her point of view and if he were in her place, he'd seek to rid himself of the affliction of the stigmata.

His scowl turned into a reluctant smile. He had to admit, she was a determined wench, and he doubted she would allow anything to get in her way once she set her mind on having it. If she was determined to rid herself of the nuisance of a so-called blessing, she would clearly do it as quickly as possible.

His grin turned wry. That he had refrained from entering her and putting his seed into her was but a weak concession to honor. The truth was, he'd been more than willing to help her, and his protests had been weak at best. But the other side of that truth was that he was torn between seizing what he could of her body and heart in the short time they had left together and wanting what was best for her—returning her to her family in as whole and untouched condition as he could.

It was a damnable thing, and ever the tale of his dog-spewn life, panting after what he could not have and losing what he held dear. He rolled his shoulders around in a shrug, trying to loosen the tension. He glanced at Catherine, who kept her attention to the road ahead. He'd miss her when they parted, he knew. She was not like any woman he had ever met, and he was certain he would not find another that would suit him so well.

He shrugged his shoulders again. It was just as well, therefore, that affinity for one's spouse was not required for a marriage, but practical considerations were. And, except for his damnable loyalty to his king and his wish to keep Catherine by his side, he was in essence a practical man. It was best that he keep his mind on what was useful, not on anything else. He looked into the darkness of the road ahead of them, hoping for some flicker of light that might indicate the existence of an inn or farmhouse. They must have traveled a good forty miles by now; another ten would bring them to Rouen, not far from Catherine's home. Since there had been no attack so far—supernatural or otherwise—it might be best to rest and return her in as fresh a condition as possible. They would procure a coach, and travel the last ten miles or so in comfort—and God knew he could use some comfort himself—so her family would see that he had taken care of her as well as anyone might. It would go far in convincing them to pay him for her return...and perhaps allow him to visit her again at some time in the future. He rolled his shoulders again, trying to shake the ache from them. If, of course, she was not then married to the Marquis de Bauvin, and if the marquis had not taken her away to his own estates.

He wondered about the secrecy that surrounded the marquis—even Fichet had not been able to discern rumor from truth, and gathering intelligence was the innkeeper's foremost talent. Could the demon have come from the marquis? Fichet did say that the marquis sought some power in the de la Fer family. Other than having some little influence at court, he could see no advantage for the marquis in marrying into the family except for the usual breeding of heirs. The man by all accounts was rich and influential all on his own.

Jack let out a short, harsh laugh. Aye, there it was: now he was looking for any evil there might be in the marquis, so that he might have the excuse to keep Catherine for himself. Any objective mind would come to the opposite assertion: that the demon came from Catherine herself, or from her influence. He had seen the stigmata himself, and the demon had appeared in her presence, not in any other wise. He had no such evidence regarding the marquis.

He caught Catherine gazing at him, her head cocked in a questioning manner. "Did you say anything, Jack?" she asked.

He shook his head. "No, nothing, *ma chère*. Merely reflecting on my faults and foolishness."

The moonlight lit one corner of her upturned mouth. "Ah. I wondered why you were silent for so long."

This time Jack's laugh burst from him unwillingly. "Minx! It's a miracle my self-worth hasn't been stripped from me long before now, with your sharp tongue."

"Perhaps it would take a miracle to do it, then." Her voice was sly.

He laughed again. "No doubt, for we Marstones are damnably full of pride."

"Then it is good I am your friend, Jack, for think how much more troubled you would be if I were not as sharp of tongue as you say I am."

He grinned, but sobered at the thought of how her presence had changed his life. " 'More troubled' or less? I tell you, *ma chère,* I do not know if I would have been as troubled if I had not met you."

He regretted his words immediately, though he had meant it only as a joke, for she said nothing, and he could see her body hunch in the saddle for a moment, as if warding off a hurt.

He sighed. "Ah, Catherine, never fear, you are worth all the trouble in the world."

She straightened then in her saddle, and he regretted his words again, for he could see her eyes widen in gladness in the light of the moon, and he had already determined that they would part into their own lives once she returned home. Saying such things would only make parting more difficult.

"Perhaps we'll have another duel at some time," he made himself say. "With some word of mouth, we could raise a little more money—you'd like that, wouldn't you?" It was not what he meant, but it'd make the sting of his leaving less.

He could feel her gaze on him, and when he glanced at her, she seemed neither offended nor put off, but thoughtful.

"Indeed" was all she said in reply.

Again he wondered what she thought—but no,

he'd not go that way again. He turned his attention to the road and shut his mouth on any other unfortunate words he might say.

Catherine allowed the silence between them to lengthen until she was forced to contemplate her own thoughts. Clearly honor kept Jack from spiriting her away from her home, that and her wish that she recover her memory and learn once again what it was to be Catherine de la Fer of the noble de la Fer family. She would ignore the first and pursue him shamelessly, for she did not entirely see much practicality in his honor. But the closer she came to her home, the more her curiosity and the need to know herself, her own true self, strengthened. She had been the creature of the alley forever, it seemed, and then something that felt neither human nor animal, but something in between. And now... now she had known Jack's gentle, heated touch, and she felt she had gone beyond that in-between state into... something very close to human. All that she needed now was to remember.

She looked at the road in front of them with eagerness. Not long, now, before they came to Rouen, and Jack had told her that her home was not far from that. The road seemed a milky stream in front of them, as if some heavenly milkmaid had spilled her bucket on the way to her home. She grinned at the image that came to her mind—Jack was right that food still occupied her thoughts more than it should.

The road seemed to widen a little ahead of them, and she breathed a sigh of relief, for it meant that a town was sure to be near, and then they could rest.

This night's journey had not been as hard or as long as their first, thank God. But she was chilled to the bone and wished for a good soft bed, and—Catherine could feel a determined smile form on her lips—she would make sure Jack would be in the bed with her. She had been successful the night before; she felt she could be just as successful this time, too. She would seize what she could of their time together—if she had not learned anything else from her time in the alley, she had learned that if she did not seize what she could, she would have nothing at all.

She looked forward, then, to the end of this part of their journey, and urged her horse forward a little faster on the road.

The silence between them relaxed and became companionable, partly from fatigue, partly because ... she felt it was from their friendship. For all the tension that existed between them, regardless of anything Jack said, she knew in her heart they were friends. She looked at the moon, frowning a little. A dimness seemed to cast itself across the light—thin clouds, she thought, but if they grew thicker, it would be too easy to lose their way and take the wrong road. She looked at Jack, who seemed to be lost in his own thoughts. Perhaps she should alert him; indeed, the scene ahead of them seemed to shift, for a mist seemed to arise from the dirt and cobbles, blurring the outlines of the road with the trees to either side. Her frown grew deeper. The mist hung low, curling forward toward their horses' feet like beckoning hands, and then rose like slow, cold flames along their legs. Her mare flicked her ears forward and gave a concerned snort, and Jack's gelding tossed its head nervously. Catherine could see Jack's hand tighten on his reins. Clearly he, too, felt uneasy.

She cast a quick look behind her, and dread grew in the pit of her stomach. She could not see the road behind them; the moonlight should have illuminated it as clearly as it did the road before them.

She turned her attention to the road in front of them—no, that was not clear any longer, either. The mist had risen higher, up to the horses' knees, and she could feel a chill touch her feet from time to time. She halted her horse as Jack drew his to a stop.

"God's blood, this is a nuisance," he said, clearly disgusted. Catherine nearly laughed at his pragmatic tone, but a finger of mist crawled up to twine around her ankle, and a stab of ice pierced her foot, making her jerk in her saddle. She swallowed.

"We must leave here, Jack," she said.

"Certainly," he replied, his voice ironic. "Where would you suggest we go?" He nodded toward where she thought the road must go. "If you can find the way out, lead on!"

"This way," she said, jerking her chin in the way they had been going...or as much as she could determine the way. The mist rose higher, and snaked along her leg, and another lance of pain pierced her calf. She gasped. "We must go, quickly!"

Jack stared at her. "What is it?"

She looked wildly around her—a faint, sweet, familiar scent came to her, and her hands began to prickle with imminent pain. Despair seized her as the mist crept higher, and her back began to ache. She felt as if she could not move.

"Catherine, speak to me. What is wrong?"

Jack's firm, patient voice roused her out of the fear that had numbed her muscles. She nudged her horse forward. "We must go. There is...there is evil here," she said between gritted teeth, for icy pain seethed up the skin along her spine.

Jack muttered something in English—she thought it might have been a curse—and he moved his horse forward. The gelding tossed its head again and pranced about nervously; Catherine was glad she had a more placid mount, for her mare only flicked her ears forward again.

The mist rose higher, and Catherine swallowed bile. The familiar sweet scent grew stronger—she glanced at Jack, the sight of him dimmed by an occasional rise of mist—did he not smell it?

She wet her lips, and made herself breathe long and slow. She would not be afraid. She had vowed it. She lifted her chin and encouraged her horse forward a little faster.

"Damned fog."

A lift of mist obscured Jack from her sight for a moment, making her heart hammer quickly.

"I thought I'd left fog like this behind when I left London," he continued in a conversational tone. "But the devil would have it I'd be plagued with it in France, as well."

A bubble of laughter escaped her. Despite the threat she felt around her, the aggrieved note in his voice at the contrary nature of France's climate pierced her fear and made her heart feel lighter.

"We have more fog than you English think," she said, trying for an equally casual tone. "Such as... such as this, for example." She glanced at him, and caught the glimpse of an encouraging smile.

"Eh, this, a fog?" He gave a skeptical snort. "This is nothing compared to what we have in England. This is the sun at noontime, *ma chère*! Why, if you were to have a real English fog, you'd swear you were fighting your way through a bale of wet Suffolk wool."

She grinned, but shuddered when the mist rose thickly between them as if to defy Jack's words, chilling her so that she could hardly feel the reins in her hands. The cold crept up from her spine to her neck and seemed to creep up to her face. Her chest felt stiff, and she took in a slight, moaning breath.

"Catherine." Jack's voice held concern, an edge of urgency. "What is it?"

She forced her attention on him beside her, and her leg bumped against his. She looked up—he had moved his horse closer to hers. Warmth spread from where they touched, and moved over her heart; a heat grew there, and the prickling in her hands receded. She put her hand over her heart and felt the cross underneath. *"Jesu, Marie,"* she breathed in relief.

She looked ahead of them and saw nothing but dark blankness—no moonlight or shadow, only a deep formless grey. "Do...do you see anything, Jack?" she asked. She cleared her throat, for her voice had come out a whisper. "It looks...like nothing," she said, forcing her voice out louder. "It is as cold as a grave."

"No..." Jack's voice sounded thoughtful. "No, I've been in a grave, and even this is a damned sight warmer, I give you my word."

His words startled a laugh from her, and the chill retreated until her hands unstiffened on the reins.

He let out a long breath. "But I'll admit, it's as bad as the worst fog I've seen, and I've seen the worst."

"It chills me to the bone, Jack, but we can't go back or stay here."

He looked at her, but she could not discern his expression, for the darkness obscured his face. "I should say not," he said. "I'll not sit in the middle of wet Suffolk wool." She could see his hand gesture in front of them. "But damned if I can tell whether forward is any different than backward."

She took in a deep breath that came more easily to her now, and summoned up a smile. She nodded in the direction at which he had waved. "That must be the way; we have not turned one way or another, and if we leave the road, we'll know by the sound of the hooves on grass instead of dirt and stone."

He nodded, and they moved forward.

She could see nothing, only a dark, grey, formlessness in front of her. She felt for the chain around her neck and pulled out her cross, holding it tightly in her hand. It gave her comfort, and the prickling in her hands and the pain across her back receded. She sighed. At least she had not bled again. She noticed that Jack had brought out his sword. He, too, must have felt the strangeness of the mist.

She was not sure how long they rode through the thick fog; she was only aware of how fingers of mist would catch at her legs with a freezing grasp. But she noticed that as long as she kept near Jack and kept her hand on her cross, the paralyzing chill would go no farther than her leg.

It was an evil thing, this mist. It reminded her somewhat of the monster she had faced in Paris, though she was not sure exactly how. Perhaps it was the cold, or that elusive scent—and yet, the monster had certainly not smelled the same as what she was sensing.

Dread tried to force its way up from her gut, but she tamped it down. This was no time to give in to her fears. But she could not help thinking that Père Doré was wrong; here she felt the signs of the stigmata she bore, and if it were true that it was a holy thing, then surely she would not feel it after having lain with Jack.

It was all of a piece; the stigmata had come in the presence of evil, regardless of the state of her soul. It had nothing to do with whether or not she was in a state of grace, but in the presence of evil. It must mean, therefore, that the stigmata was more a curse than a holy thing.

She briefly closed her eyes and swallowed down despair. It was just as well that she return to her home and that Jack go on to Breda. If she was cursed, she did not want to endanger him any more. Even if they were not attacked, manifestations of her curse would certainly delay them. Indeed, even if Jack did not feel this mist as painfully as she did, it was nevertheless an obstacle.

She would show him, once she returned home, that she was content to stay there, and then she would seek a convent or find a way to travel on her own, perhaps even fight duels for money once she regained some knowledge of who she was. She had shown she was capable of winning one so far; surely there were others she could win.

"There, it seems we are out." She heard a clear sigh of relief from Jack. She looked up from her thoughts; stars shimmered in the dark night sky where the moonlight did not overpower them, and behind them the trailing mist seemed to curl into itself and fade away. She let out a long, shuddering breath; her hands and her back ceased to hurt. Cautiously she released her cross and glanced back again... the mist was still gone. "Yes," she said. "It's disappeared, and the evil with it, *Dieu merci*."

"Are you well? Damned if you didn't seem about to faint, *ma chère*." His teasing voice held a note of rough concern. It made her smile a little, for he sounded as if he talked to a fellow soldier, and she realized she had done well. Many other women would indeed have fainted or screamed.

"Not I!" she said firmly. "Did I not cut off the head of a demon? What is a little mist to me?"

Jack chuckled. "Little fire-eater. If you could, you'd fight the Dev—"

"Shh, shhh!" Catherine said hastily. "Do not tempt fate, Jack! Did you not feel the evil in the mist? It crept up my legs like a viper and froze me with its bite, I tell you." She gazed at him, hoping he would understand, that he would not think she had gone mad, for no mist was like the one she described.

He was silent for a moment. "It was the damndest thing, Cat." He took in a deep breath. "When I was a boy, I attended a hanging. The man deserved it—he'd... he'd done a foul thing to two little girls in the village near my home, and then killed them. The whole village came out to watch and throw offal at him; God knows he deserved it. I never thought about evil until then—hell, I was just a boy, and if you'd asked if I believed in it, I might have had my doubts before then." He fell silent again and drew in a deep breath. "But just before they pulled his neck, the man looked around, grinning as if he were at a wedding instead of being measured for his own funeral. And I swear, if I didn't believe evil existed before this, I believed it then, for the man looked me straight in the eyes and he had nothing behind his own except the cold soul of the Devil himself." He let out a long breath and shook his head. "I doubt I felt all the things you did, *ma chère,* for you're a sensitive thing, but I felt as if that man were staring at me the whole damned time we were in that mist, and that I was going to my own hanging." She shuddered, for she could understand the sensation. "If I ever complain about wet English Suffolk wool fog again, *ma chère,* slap me. I'd much prefer it than…*that.*" He jerked a thumb behind him.

He hesitated, and she saw him glance at her. "I'm of half a mind not to return you to your home, Cat, for if you've got this kind of thing so near it, it can't mean any good."

She thought the same thing, but she shrugged. "Or it could be merely the consequences of being with me, Jack. No—" She held up her hand at his imminent protest. "You cannot say you haven't thought it, for certainly I have. And this…" She jerked her head toward the road behind them. "This shows me I must find out all I can before I go anywhere else."

"Hmph." The sound was disgruntled, as if Jack could not find words to protest. He shook his head. "But—"

"And what is this 'Cat' you called me?" she interrupted. She did not want to talk more of the mist or her fate, for she feared she'd break down and agree with him and avoid returning home altogether.

He chuckled. "'Cat' is 'le chat' in English, *ma chère.* It's often what we English call women named Catherine, and it fits you, for considering all you've gone through, I think you've got more lives than a cat."

She smiled, for the thought pleased her. She liked cats; they were one of the best survivors on the streets and were good at ridding houses and alleys of vermin. She, also, had rid the alleys of human vermin . . . and with God's and the Holy Mother's help, she'd survive whatever she encountered. She nodded. "You may call me Cat, then. It is a good name."

"I thank you. I shall," Jack said, and there was laughter under his words. He gestured at the sword at her side. "Heaven knows you can scratch as well as a cat."

" 'Scratch'!" Catherine made her voice sound insulted. "I do more than scratch! I can fight even an accomplished swordfighter—you have seen that yourself."

" 'Fight'!" he said, and snorted in apparent disbelief. " 'Scratch,' that's all, *ma chère*. With a bit more training, I *might* say you could fight—"

"*Might!*" she cried in protest. "I have had plenty of training!"

"Not in my opinion," Jack said firmly. "Next inn we find, we rest, then you train again."

"Jack—!"

But it was a weak protest. She was glad they argued as friends, and if it meant she'd train to fatigue later this day, she did not mind, for it meant they could, for now, put the thought of the mist, evil, and her future aside.

For now. She closed her eyes briefly. I do not want to think any further than that, *Dieu me sauve,* she thought. Tomorrow, she would return to her home, but before that, she would make love to him one more time if she could. She would focus only on that . . . just for now.

Chapter 9

❧ CATHERINE MANAGED ONCE MORE— after sleeping, then her sword practice, after winning another fight with a cocky musketeer and gaining more livres than she had at the first fight—to lure Jack into the bath with her after they came to an inn just outside of the city of Rouen.

Catherine had seemed to withdraw from him after their night in the mist. She was friendly, she was cheerful, and though she practiced her fencing exercises in excellent, amazingly expert form, she seemed distant from him until they entered their room at the inn again.

He protested very little, less than he had before. They had only a short time together; if his kisses had an edge of desperation, if he allowed her to kiss and touch him more boldly than she had when they had first made love, if it meant he had abandoned all honor, he cared not any longer. He said nothing as she moved her hand down his belly and grasped his manhood, only groaned and slipped his hand between her legs in return. *I am a weak fool,* he thought. *A greedy fool. Most definitely a fool.*

He did not care any longer. She would be gone from him this day, and he had nothing else to offer her but this worship of her with his body. He could feel her knees become lax and she shook with sudden heat when his fingers reached her woman's parts. She would not protest if he took her fully, he was certain. He lifted her suddenly from the bath they stood in, the wet chilling his skin on the way to the bed.

He lay her gently on it, and followed her more quickly and held her more tightly than before, wanting to meld his body into hers. He kissed her mouth, her throat, her breasts, and spread her legs, pressing his hips against her, hard.

This time she did not pull away or cry out in fear. She even allowed him to lay atop her, and she gasped when he entered her.

"You did not do this before," she whispered.

"I know," Jack said. "Dear God, I know."

He closed his eyes and slowly moved upon her, and he felt her tightness around him in his retreat and return. His actions drew out the exquisite sensations she'd begun in him earlier, and she twisted her body against him, clutching the small of his back with her hands, drawing him close.

"Come to me," he whispered in her ear. "Come, Cat. My Cat, my Catherine." It was a chant, a prayer, holding hopeless wishes as he touched her and moved in her deeply, wanting to weep with longing and impending loss. He gritted his teeth instead, and thrust hard.

She stiffened suddenly, and he thought she might have done so in fear, but she let out a cry of pleasure instead, and his manhood was squeezed tight. He almost spilled into her, but managed to remember he would not put a child in her, and pulled out, pouring his seed on her belly instead.

He fell, gasping, beside her, and held her close and tightly. He heard her sigh, and felt her stroke his hair, then heard her make a disgusted sound. He looked up to see her expression marred by a wrinkled brow and a puzzled frown.

"What is this?" She pointed to the seed he had spilled on her. She stared at him a moment, then realization cleared her face. "Was this supposed to go inside of me?"

Laughter bubbled up inside of him, and came out in a chuckle. "I am sorry, *ma chère*, but I thought it best if I did not." He rose from the bed and picked up the rough towel draped across the back of the tin bath. Carefully he wiped her belly.

"I might have had a child if you had," she said thoughtfully. "I . . . would not have minded it."

Frustration twisted inside of him and turned to anger. He threw the towel into the tub and moved quickly away from her, dragging on the clothes he had dropped on the floor.

"I have managed," he said through gritted teeth, "to retain just a small shred of honor, *ma chère*." Almost none, he thought. "You know my thoughts on this—I have already mentioned them. I will not go any further and ruin you totally by putting a child in you. I barely had the presence of mind to withdraw in time as it was. Thank God I did—at least I thought of the possible consequences, if you did not."

His anger did not seem to have an effect on her except to make her smile smugly, and he snarled in frustration. "Put on your dress this time—I will not have you look like a ragamuffin when I return you to

your family. Be ready in an hour. We will leave then."
He thrust his feet into his boots and, with one last
yank to tighten his belt, slammed the chamber door
shut.

Catherine's smile faded slowly as she sat on the
bed, and she sighed wistfully. She was glad she had
seduced Jack this one last time. Of course, she knew
it would be disastrous if she bore a child—her family
was a noble one, and most likely she'd be cast off.
She would not even be able to support herself by
fighting duels for money.

But a primal, unreasoning part of her had
wanted a child from him, and the discovery that she
was not a virgin—she had felt no pain when he entered her, and there had been no blood—half pleased
her and half worried her. Pleased her because their
lovemaking had not been hampered, and it gave her
one more clue to her past. Worried her because that
clue did not speak well of either her, or what had
happened to her.

Slowly she rose and unpacked the dress that Felice had given her, smoothing out the wrinkles as
best she could. She put on her shift, opened the
door, and called out to a chambermaid who had
passed the room, and asked her to iron the dress.

She shoved her feet into her stockings, meanwhile, then climbed into the bed again, pulling the
bedcovers over her shoulders for warmth. She
smoothed her hand over the indentation in the mattress where Jack had lain. This was the last time they
lay together, warm and comfortable. She had savored every minute of it, taken in every bit of heat
she could, and hoped she had given as much to him.
She would remember it, remember her time with
him for the rest of her life, she knew.

A knock sounded on the door; it was the chambermaid with the ironed dress. Catherine thanked and paid the girl, who curtsied and left hurriedly to do her other duties after she helped Catherine to put on and lace her dress.

She looked at herself in the mirror and pushed aside the curling hair from her face. She looked different from what she remembered from before her time in the alley. She looked thinner and stronger. Perhaps her family would not recognize her, and perhaps then she could travel with Jack.

She bit her lip—it was a useless hope. Even if they did not recognize her, she knew she should not go with Jack, for she would not impose whatever curse she had on her on him, especially with his important duties to his king. She was obligated enough to him as it was, without putting more of a burden on him, whatever he might say.

A distant church bell tolled the hour. She should leave now. She stuffed her trousers and the rest of her belongings into the saddlebag, and left the room.

The coach Jack had procured for them was a good one, possibly the best the inn had to offer. He helped her into it, glancing at her only once, then climbed in, as well, after tossing her saddlebag within. He said little in what must have been at least an hour and a half in the carriage.

It did not matter. She had no words now, and could only take comfort in his presence. She looked down at the coach seat between them; his hand lay lax at his side. Perhaps Jack would not mind it if she put her hand in his.

He only sighed and looked at her with the loneliness she had seen before in his eyes. She grasped his hand and looked away, for looking at him would surely make her weep, and she would not let herself weaken in these last few moments with him. She gazed out at the soft hills near the Seine River instead, not truly seeing them, but too, too conscious of Jack's hand covering hers.

The carriage took a slight turn to a narrower road, and soon they came to an iron gate that seemed vaguely familiar. The coach stopped for a moment as the coachman called out to the gatekeeper, who opened wide the gates.

She could not see forward, and she did not want to lean out of the window to look at their destination. It was enough to gaze out at the frosted green grass and the somewhat ill-kept grounds. She frowned. She had noted that the gatekeeper had not been well dressed, even for a gatekeeper, and the gatehouse was in some disrepair. She wondered if her family was either negligent of their tenants or not as well off as they should be for what was clearly a large estate.

The coach came to a halt at last, the wheels crunching over the gravel at the foot of the mansion's stairs. Jack stepped out, then handed her down.

Catherine looked up—it was more chateau than mansion. It seemed a combination of an old Norman chateau and a later Gothic addition, and a web of ivy vines wove their way up a part of it, giving it a neglected air. The coachman knocked on the door, and when it opened he stepped back and climbed up on the coach again. The butler looked curiously at her and at Jack.

"Sir John Marstone," Jack said. "And Mlle Catherine de la Fer."

The butler's eyes widened, and he stared at her,

searching her face. "Mlle Catherine?" he whispered. He smiled. "Yes, I think I can see—" He stopped suddenly, his face taking on a respectful look. He bowed formally and moved from the door. "The Comte de la Fer awaits you." Catherine glanced at Jack. Clearly he had sent word of their arrival from the inn.

Jack did not look at her; he merely bowed and indicated she was to go before him. She sighed, and stepped past the door.

She felt suddenly as if she could not breathe. The hall was covered in heavy dark draperies—obviously to help keep out the cold, but the effect was oppressive. It dimmed what light came into the room, and the fire that flickered fitfully in the hearth nearby only increased the impression.

She pulled her cross from her bodice and clasped it tightly, forcing a deep breath into her lungs. The feeling of oppression faded.

She glanced at Jack. Still he did not look at her, but followed the butler, his back straight and his steps firm, as if he were ready to march into battle.

The butler led them up a staircase and opened a door. "Sir John Marstone. Mlle Catherine de la Fer."

This room was better. The afternoon light shone through open windows and the draperies had been drawn aside. A rustle drew her eyes to a corner of the room. A young, blond-haired man sat on a chair, turning the pages of a book. He looked up. He could not be much more than eighteen or nineteen, Catherine thought, and had a studious look about him. He looked tired and a little pale, but he rose from his chair and came forward, smiling and holding out his hands to her. He was well dressed, his hair well styled, and he was a good six inches taller than she. She could see the family resemblance in the shape of the eyes and the stubborn chin. His eyes were a deep blue, however, while her own were green.

"Catherine? Is it truly you?"

She did feel a nudge of recognition as he took her hand and gave an exquisite bow over it. His name...it started with an "A." Antonine? Adrian? She sank into a formal curtsy, trying desperately to remember, feeling despair that memory seemed just beyond her grasp. "I...I am sorry," she murmured. "I remember you...my brother, I think. Your name begins with an 'A.'" She could feel her face heat with embarrassment.

"Adrian, and yes, I am your brother." He glanced at Jack. "It is true, then, what M. Marstone wrote to me—that you do not remember much of your life beyond perhaps the last six or seven months."

She nodded mutely, glancing at Jack, as well. He stood stiffly, formally in front of her brother, and for a long moment, an awkward silence sat in the room.

"I am much obliged to M. Marstone," Catherine said. Her voice sounded small, even to her own ears. "I was starving and near death when he rescued me from vile men who sought to kill me. If he had not done so, surely I would be dead by now." At the very least, she thought, Jack should be paid for what he expended on her, if not more. "*En vrai*, he has brought me back to health and provided me with clothes."

The comte raised his brows. "A veritable good Samaritan," he said, and smiled.

Catherine thought Jack had made a sound as if beginning to speak, but when she looked at him, his lips were set firmly together.

"As soon as I heard you had run away, I left the

university and searched for you, Catherine," her brother continued, his voice softening. He looked away, as if ashamed, then brought his gaze back to her, his expression hesitant. "Our father..." His face darkened for a moment. "After our father died, I sent our servants to search for you, as well."

He did not like our father, Catherine thought, and wondered if she had. A flash of memory came to her—she had not, either, though she did not know why. The thought both encouraged and depressed her. She was glad she had regained another memory, but had hoped for pleasant ones. "What happened to you? What did you—" Her brother—she must remember to think of him as Adrian now—stopped his eager questioning and shook his head, smiling ruefully. "I am being a bad host. You are clearly tired. We will speak of this later."

Catherine managed not to sigh with relief. His questions would be awkward to answer. She did not know how to tell him everything she had experienced without seeming half mad. If she had not Jack to confirm what she had seen and done, she would not have believed it herself. She had much for which to be grateful to him.

She smiled at Adrian. "You are kind. I am tired, indeed, and would be worse off if it had not been for M. Marstone." She gave a quick smile to Jack, but he merely nodded gravely. "I would like to see him well rewarded, brother, for my safe return."

The comte nodded and waved his hand in a genial manner. "Of course, of course. I will arrange it." He smiled.

He smiled. "Meanwhile, stay and have dinner with us. We will have guests—let us make it a celebration of my dear sister's return." He looked at Catherine up and down. "I think your old dresses will not fit you, but perhaps one of the maids will be able to fix one of them in time." He turned to Jack. "Monsieur, if you wish, you may refresh yourself in one of the bedroom I will have reserved for you."

"I am afraid I cannot stay," Jack said suddenly. "I have an errand to run for my king."

The comte raised his brows, then smiled. "Understandable, but surely you can stay to sup, at least? I imagine you would have to do so anyway." Jack hesitated, and the comte turned to Catherine. "Sister, perhaps you can persuade him."

She smiled a little. "My brother is right that you will need to eat soon, Monsieur—Marstone, so I will add my pleas to his." Her words were formal, but she gazed at Jack and put all the hope she had within her into her look, for she wished to hold him to her for at least a little longer. She returned her gaze to her brother, who looked from her to Jack and back again, as if trying to discern the quality of their relationship. She lowered her eyes to her folded hands in front of her. She felt, suddenly, that she should seem as indifferent as possible, other than having gratitude for her safe return to her family. She made herself shrug carelessly. "However, I doubt I can persuade him to anything, since he is a very stubborn man."

"I thank you," Jack replied, bowing. "I will partake of your hospitality, my lord, but will need to leave soon afterward." His smile had a grim edge. "Duty calls, after all."

The comte bowed again, formally. "I am glad." He turned to Catherine. "Do show M. Marstone to the Blue Room—ah! My apologies, sister, you would not remember which room it is, I assume?"

Catherine shook her head slightly.

"Very well, I will have the butler escort you to your respective rooms." He smiled at her. "We have kept your room very much like it was when you left. You will be pleased, I think."

He summoned the butler and, after giving instructions to the servant, bowed them formally from the room.

Jack had become as formal as any French nobleman, she noted, as he bowed, said nothing still, and left for the room to which the butler led him. She did not like it, but she did understand; he was probably preparing himself to part from her, and wished her to do the same.

She would comply—for now. For now, she needed to find out who and what she was, and then find a way to see him again. She was determined on it. Their parting would not be forever.

The butler opened the door for her, and she stepped into a room of pale yellow walls and pastel green draperies. It was pleasant, she thought, surprised, and then wondered at her surprise. Why would not her own room be pleasant? The wardrobe was well made and richly scrolled, the escritoire dainty, and the papers and pens on it neatly laid out. The bed—

Bile flooded her throat and she wanted to vomit.

Catherine groped for the chair at the escritoire and sat before her weakened knees made her fall to the floor. She closed her eyes and took in a deep breath, calming her stomach and wildly beating heart.

She was being stupid. There was no reason for

her feeling like this. The bed was just as pretty and well made as the rest of the room, and she felt certain it was indeed her room. She felt this way, no doubt, because her return home was overwhelming to her, such grandeur after living in the alley and then at various inns. That must be it—certainly she felt intimidated when she first entered this house.

She made herself walk to the bed, though she could not help touching the bedpost cautiously, as if it might have teeth and might bite her. It did nothing, of course. She made herself sit on the bed itself. The mattress was soft and the bedsheets fine; anyone would be glad of such comfort at night.

At night...she was not certain she'd like sleeping here at night, but that, too, was nonsense. She had made do with sleeping on cobblestones in the alley in Paris; she had slept under church pews; and she had slept on the floor and a good bed in the Fichets' inn. This bed was finer than any of them. She would get used to it, she was sure.

A knock on the door roused her from her thoughts. *"Entré!"* she called out.

A maid entered and curtsied. "Mademoiselle, I have been sent to dress you."

"What is your name?" Catherine smiled at her, half in apology, half in embarrassment. "I have lost my memory of much of my life, you see."

The girl's eyes held sympathy, and she smiled shyly. "I am new, mademoiselle. My name is Marie, and I have been told I am to be your maid." She gestured to the wardrobe. "Your dresses do not fit you any longer, I hear, so I am to fit one to you as best as I can so you may go down to your dinner."

Catherine let out a deep breath. This she understood and had dealt with before. She nodded, rose, and opened the wardrobe doors, which contained dresses that seemed familiar and whose colors suited her. She thought of the male clothes she still had... she would have to get them washed soon. Pushing aside one dress after another, she chose one that was of dark green wool and looked warm. The fabric was soft, not scratchy like the wool she had worn so far, and was delicately embroidered in silk along the edges. It looked simple enough so that it would not be difficult to alter.

The girl was quick with the needle, and the dress had a separate bodice and skirt, so it did not take long before it was ready to put on. Marie brought out a corset, and for one moment Catherine felt her back tense before she put it on, but the girl's hands were gentle and she did not pull the lacings tight at all. It was only enough to keep Catherine's posture straight and push her breasts up higher than she was used to.

A distant clock tolled the hour, and Marie moved more quickly. The maid pulled a light linen chemise over Catherine's head, and then the skirt, then the bodice of the dress, again lacing the bodice lightly. A small lace fichu was tucked at the edge of the bodice, and Catherine thought it did less to cover her décolletage and more to enhance it and her bared shoulders. She wondered how highborn ladies managed to survive the winter, showing such expanse of flesh, but since her maid looked on the whole with approval, it was no doubt the usual thing for noblewomen to wear.

Marie was also deft with styling her hair and pulled most of it to the back in a knot, letting the rest fall in curls about Catherine's face. A quick glance in the mirror showed a stranger, and made her shake her head at herself. Only her face was familiar, the rest... the rest belonged to someone else. Someone who was called Catherine de la Fer and whose family lived in this estate. Someone she did not know.

Her spirits lowered, but she turned and made herself smile at her maid. "You have done well, Marie. I thank you. You may go until it is time to let me know when to come down to dinner." The maid grinned and curtsied, and curtsied once again at the door before she left.

Catherine wandered about her room again, looking at the china figurines on the mantelpiece above the fireplace, a needlework sampler above it, as well as a watercolor painting. She supposed she might have stitched and painted them, since her name was at one corner of each. She did not feel much connection to them.

She made a complete circuit around the room before she found she avoided the bed. She went toward it again, and again she felt nauseated. But she gritted her teeth and went to it once more, sitting gingerly on the edge of it.

Nothing. Nothing happened to her when she sat on it. Not even the prickling of her hands or an ache to her back. There was no evil, then, that existed here. But she wondered if something happened here that made her feel ill.

She remembered that she was not a virgin, and dread crept up from her belly. Perhaps whoever kidnapped her from this place had taken her virginity, and perhaps that was why she had been so afraid the first time she and Jack had made love. She thought of her betrothed—her former betrothed—the Marquis de Bauvin. Would he still wish to marry her if he knew she was not a virgin? Many men would not. Her heart grew lighter at the thought. If he did not, then she could persuade her brother as head of the household to let her marry Jack.

She loved him. Catherine let out a deep breath. He was not just a friend to her. She had thought she did not want to marry anyone, or that she would not know what love was. But she knew she wanted to be with him always and have children with him, if he wanted her.

She smiled a little. He did want her. For all his protests, he had made love with her, and still tried to preserve her reputation by pretending to be her husband during their travels. Perhaps even if the marquis still wanted to marry her, she could refuse and persuade her brother to let her marry Jack, if he would have her.

A knock sounded at her door again—it was her maid. She rose from the bed, smoothed down her dress, and walked out the door and down the stairs to where her maid led her.

She could smell the food, and her mouth watered. She hadn't eaten for quite a while, and hoped somehow she would remember the manners she had probably been taught from childhood, and not disgrace herself. She shrugged. If she forgot, she'd watch the other guests and do as they did.

The guests had not yet been seated, but the scents of chicken and savory beef almost made her weak in the knees as she entered the room. It managed somewhat to assuage her uncertainty at the unfamiliar faces of the people there, until she saw her brother smile at her, and then saw Jack, resplendent in an obviously borrowed and fashionably beribboned suit of clothes. He stared at her, then quickly looked away, and she lowered her eyes, feeling a blush come over her face, especially after the voices of the dinner guests had quieted. Her brother held out his hand to her and took hers in his, leading her near a seat beside him.

"May I present my dear, long-lost sister, Mlle Catherine de la Fer."

She glanced up at the guests and saw clear curiosity and speculation in their gazes. It felt oppressive, but she lifted her chin and smiled at them, for she would not show her uncertainty. Anyone would feel curious about someone who disappeared and was returned to her family again.

Her brother lifted a glass of wine. "Let us drink to honor her safe return, and"—he gestured the glass toward Jack—"to her rescuer, Sir John Marstone." The guests raised their glasses and gave the toast, and Catherine noted, with a small pang of jealousy, how the ladies looked admiringly at Jack.

She felt a touch on her sleeve, and she looked up at Adrian. "You will sit by me, sister, and beside you"—he smiled widely—"is one you knew once, and who is my friend."

She turned to gaze up at a tall, handsome man. His brows were even, his eyes large, and a thin line of mustache lay just above his well-formed lips. His nose was neither too large nor too small, and his face was an even oval beneath the curls of his well-ordered formal wig. She did not recognize him, but she smiled warmly at him, for he was, after all, her brother's friend. A look of surprise sat on his face, then quickly disappeared, his expression turning smooth and congenial.

"Catherine, I present the Marquis de Bauvin. Marquis de Bauvin, may I present my sister, Mlle

Catherine de la Fer." He gave an apologetic smile to the marquis. "My apologies for my sister; she has been ill during her absence and remembers nothing of her life here."

A small shock went through her—this, then, was her former betrothed. She cast a look at Jack from under her eyelashes. He only glanced briefly at her, then returned to conversing with the lady who stood beside him. She looked again at the marquis and sank low in a formal curtsy.

"I am pleased to meet you again, monsieur, and am sorry that my late illness prevents me from remembering you as I should."

He gave an elegant and precise bow. "And I look forward to reacquainting myself with you," he said. His voice was deep, musical, and pleasant. He seemed about to say something more, but her brother gestured to the table and bade the guests to sit and eat.

Catherine sat with relief, a little too quickly perhaps, for she almost bumped into the marquis in her haste, but managed to move so that only the sleeve of her dress brushed his arm. She gave him an apologetic smile, then frowned as she turned to her plate and picked up her knife and fork.

Her hands felt odd and achy, and then began to prickle. She looked about her, but felt no other sensation of evil, not as she had felt in the alley, or just outside the church when the demon had attacked her and Felice.

Her brother leaned toward her, his expression both shy and curious. "I hope I do not cause pain when I ask—that is, I cannot help wondering why you disappeared. I had thought—" He glanced briefly at the marquis who sat on her other side. "I thought perhaps you had run away because you did not wish to marry. That is what our father said. But I cannot think it was for that reason, for de Bauvin is an exceptional man, as you can see." He lowered his voice so that only she could hear under the other guests' conversation. "I had thought it was because our father..." He gave her an apologetic look. "Because he mistreated you."

Affection for her brother filled Catherine's heart; he had cared for her—still cared for her. She felt at last that this was indeed her home, now that she knew she had someone in her family who was concerned for her welfare. She looked at Adrian's pale, tired face and thought he had probably worked very hard to be the Comte de la Fer. She squeezed his hand.

"I do not know why I left, Adrian," she said softly. "I do not remember. I assumed I had been kidnapped, for I cannot remember how I came to be in Paris, so far away from home."

Sympathy and guilt showed in his eyes, and he squeezed her hand in return. "I wish...I wish I had been at home. I wish I could have protected you. I tried to find out what had happened to you, but our father—" A look of frustration crossed his face. "He told me it was none of my business." Adrian looked earnestly at her. "It is my business now, however. I promise you, I shall do everything I can to restore our estate, and make sure you and Blanche marry well."

"I am certain you will," Catherine said, smiling.

He gave her another shy, eager look. "Are you glad to be back? I hope you are."

She smiled at him. "I believe I am. Certainly I have not seen food like this while I was gone. It is pleasant to find I have a brother, and a generous one at that." She indicated the dinner utensils. "You have provided forks and knives for all your guests."

He grinned. "It's the fashion at court. The king has done it, and has said that all his nobles must do the same. Isn't that so, de Bauvin?" He looked across her to the marquis.

"Quite so," the marquis said, and delicately pierced a piece of beef with his fork. "Do you remember going to court, mademoiselle?" He kept his attention on the slice of meat he was cutting, merely glancing once at her, but Catherine felt he was somehow testing her. Did he not believe she had lost her memory?

"No," she said. "I have no idea if I have or not." She turned to Adrian. "Have I, brother?"

He shook his head slightly. "No, you have not, nor Blanche."

Blanche. She frowned; he had said the name before. It meant something to her. "She must be related to us, I think? Our cousin—or no, sister?"

Adrian beamed at her. "Yes, that is right." He turned to the marquis. "We should all go to Versailles—what say you, de Bauvin?"

The marquis paused for a moment in cutting the piece of beef on his plate before answering. "I see no reason why you should not. It would be well, I think, if both your sisters and you were presented at court. Our king prefers to have his nobles close by."

Catherine glanced at the marquis again, then at her brother. Adrian's expression was eager, and it was clear he sought the older man's approval. *How much control does the marquis have over my brother?*

The thought startled her. There was no reason to think that de Bauvin had any control over Adrian, though clearly her brother looked to the man for guidance and approval. And if the man did have influence over Adrian, then there was no reason for her to think that it would be anything but benign. The man had a cultured voice, though he said little so far, and he was well mannered. Indeed, that he questioned her about her memory could mean he doubted her identity, and if he was at all concerned about her brother, he would naturally wish to know if she were an impostor. Except perhaps for her hair and eyes, she had changed a great deal, she thought, for she did remember a little of what she had looked like before she had come to Paris. It would not be surprising for anyone to question even a little.

Adrian nodded and grinned at Catherine. "Yes, but now we have a dilemma." His voice turned teasing. "The marquis was your betrothed, and then he became Blanche's betrothed when you disappeared. Now that you have returned, I wonder if he will still choose Blanche, or decide to become your fiancé again."

She could feel her face become warm and lowered her eyes; she hoped that the guests—and the marquis—would think she had become embarrassed at the teasing. She was, but it was overpowered by anger. She felt, suddenly, as if she were a broodmare put up for auction.

She glanced up and caught Jack's gaze for a moment before he turned away. Anger lit his eyes for a moment, before a bland, cordial smile replaced it. She smiled at him; he did not like that the marquis might have a claim on her, whatever he might have said before. He need not fear; she would be quite content to have her younger sister marry de Bauvin....
She remembered then her resolution to let Jack go

on his way, so that she would not be a danger to him, and looked away. She glanced quickly up and down the dinner table.

"Where is my sister?"

Adrian grinned. "She was to arrive before dinner from the convent, but no doubt she was delayed. I have noticed that girls are often late for their appointments." He winked at a very pretty girl who sat across from him, and whose parents sat on either side of her. The girl blushed and smiled, and her mother looked smug. No doubt the girl's parents thought to make a match with Adrian, Catherine thought, amused.

Dinner was soon over, and though the meal was delicious, Catherine was glad. She found she was not good at company talk, or at least not at this time, for she kept most of her attention on her manners. She was used to inn company, not nobility.

The party removed themselves to the drawing room, and more lavish refreshments were offered. Catherine wondered at it; the dinner utensils had been new and well made, and these refreshments could not be inexpensive. And yet she had seen for herself that the estate was not in good repair when she traveled through it. Had her brother come into money, then? She tried to remember what it had been like before she had left her home, but it seemed as if she tried to pierce a mist in her mind that refused to recede.

The mist she and Jack had gone through came back to her memory and she shuddered.

"Is there anything the matter, mademoiselle?"

It was the marquis. He looked down at her coolly, and she wondered if he had truly had any affection for her. It was not as if all or even most marriages were contracted out of love, of course, but she had hoped that the marquis had been the sort who would.

"No...I was very ill when I lived in Paris, and though I am much stronger now, I still feel the cold more acutely than most, I think." She looked into his eyes and felt uneasy, for his expression did not change. She wondered if he cared for anyone at all.

A light, high voice sounded near the door of the drawing room, and a flustered and apologetic footman followed a small whirlwind into the room. "Oh, hush, Henri the Footman, it is well. I am in my own home, so it does not matter. Go, you, to your duties."

The girl could not have been much more than fourteen, for her figure was still more straight than curved. But her eyes were a large, merry blue, her curling hair the color of golden wheat, and her cheeks pink with cold. She was still dressed for travel in a deep red cloak, but she looked about her at the guests and then let out a happy cry. "Adrian! See, I said I would be home today!" She ran to her brother and would have hugged him had he not laughed and held her off.

"Blanche, behave! We have guests!"

The girl looked about her and her expression became apologetic. The expressions on the faces of the guests were indulgent; clearly the girl had charm, and her good nature shone clearly in her countenance. She was a sort who would be forgiven easily for her errors. She made numerous small, hasty curtsies to them all, the way an errant schoolgirl might, and then turned back to her brother. "You must tell me, where is our sister? She is here at last, is she not? I must see her—it has been so long, and I have been so afraid for her!"

Adrian laughed again and turned to Catherine. "Here she is, Blanche. She is changed, but you might still recognize her."

Blanche looked at Catherine uncertainly, clearly searching her face. A smile dawned, and she held out her hands to her. "Catherine...oh, Catherine, I *do* recognize you! And, oh—" Her lips turned down and trembled, and tears formed in her eyes. "Oh, I have missed you so much!" She ran to Catherine and threw her arms around her.

The guests sighed sentimentally, and Catherine pressed her lips together to keep back her own tears. The mist in her mind parted just a little, and she thought she did indeed recognize this girl. A fleeting memory came to Catherine of a small blonde girl sitting in her lap as she told a story....It must have been this girl, when she was younger. Her heart melted, and she dropped all formality, hugging Blanche close.

"I am glad to be back," she whispered. "Glad that you remember me." She wished she could remember everything, for surely the memories of being with her sister had to have been pleasant.

They parted, and Blanche searched her face again. "You have changed—you are so thin, Catherine! Have you been ill?"

Catherine wondered how much Blanche knew... possibly very little, since it seemed she had spent much of her time at a convent. She smiled at her and merely said, "Yes. Very ill. It has affected my memory, you see, and so I must work to remember as much as I can of my life before I...disappeared."

Dismay was clear on Blanche's face, but a resolute look quickly replaced it. "I will help you, you shall see! You may go about with me in our house and on our lands, and I will tell you everything."

Catherine smiled. "I shall be very pleased if you would, thank you." She looked about her at the guests—Jack, who still refused to look at her, at the marquis, at her brother—and put a wider smile on her face. This was as good a time as any to leave and repair to her room; she was tired, and did not really wish to have more company. She glanced at Jack again; it seemed his expression had slowly turned to stone over the course of this afternoon. "Indeed, I am very tired from my own journey. If you all will excuse me, I think I shall rest for a while."

Some of the guests looked disappointed, for curiosity had been rampant on their faces for the whole course of the meal. But she had not the stomach for questions, or for watching how Jack avoided her.

Her brother bowed elegantly, though he also looked disappointed. "Of course, I understand. M. Marstone did tell me you had been very ill. Go, then, and if Blanche wishes to go with you"—he nodded at his youngest sister—"she may, although you must let her know if she chatters too much at you." He gave Blanche a wide grin.

The girl wrinkled her nose at him. "I shall not talk too much, for I can see for myself that Catherine is tired." She gave another quick series of schoolgirl curtsies to the guests, then turned to her sister. "Come, let us go. I have much to tell you, and you must tell me everything about your adventures." Catherine smiled and turned to follow.

"Mlle de la Fer." It was Jack. He took her hand and bowed formally over it. "I am afraid I, too, must leave."

Her heart sank. She had hoped that perhaps he

might stay the night. But his mouth pressed together in a firm line, and she knew he would not.

"I have many miles to go before I reach Breda, and my king is impatient." He hesitated. "I hope ... I hope I might visit your family again at some time."

He still held her hand—it was firm and warm, and she closed her eyes to memorize the sensation. She wanted to remember everything about him; for all that she was returned to her family and welcomed warmly, her life would be colder for the lack of his presence. She swallowed, and nodded, then sank into a curtsy.

"I am grateful for all that you have done for me, M. Marstone," she said. *Jack. Jack.* She would never forget him.

He bowed once more and released her hand, and for a moment her hand seemed frozen in the air, half reaching for him. But she dropped her hand to her side and turned to her sister, who was watching with great curiosity. She heard Jack's footsteps behind her as he walked down the stairs to the hall, and the doors to the mansion seemed to boom hollowly as the footmen closed them behind him.

"I, too, must leave."

She looked up to see the marquis, who had moved toward the door, as well. He had little expression on his face, but she felt somehow that he was watching her.

"I shall return on the morrow, however, to see how you"—he bowed toward Blanche—"and your sister fare."

Blanche smiled uncertainly, but gave a deep curtsy. He held out his hand to Catherine, and she placed hers in his as he bowed over it in farewell.

Blackness rolled over her mind and thundered in

her ears. For one moment it seemed she was encased in the creeping fog she had encountered but hours before when she traveled with Jack, and pain pierced her, freezing her bones. She fought it, pulling in a deep breath against a force that seemed to squeeze her chest.

"Catherine, are you well?"

It was her sister, calling to her. She opened her eyes.

She was in her home, the home of the de la Fers. She was at the threshold of the drawing room. Her sister Blanche looked at her, worry clear in her eyes.

Catherine looked up. She still held the hand of the marquis. Slowly she curtsied low, as was proper for one in her station to one who was higher, and released his hand. Slowly she rose again, putting all the control she had in the precise rise from bent knee to a steady stance. She put a polite smile on her face and nodded cordially.

"I am well, Blanche," she said, and was glad that her voice was steady and even. "I still feel ill from time to time, though you must not worry, for I grow stronger every day." Blanche's face cleared, though she still wore a small frown of worry.

"I will most certainly visit again, then," the marquis said. "I will wish to see if you have fully recovered."

She looked up at him—did he know? Did he know the effect of his touch on her? His face was just as smooth and uninterested as before; there was nothing in his expression to suggest he had noticed anything. She suppressed a sigh of relief. He must not know. He must not know until she was ready for him to know.

"Thank you," she managed to say, and her voice

even sounded pleased. "I shall look forward to your visit." She turned to her sister and made herself smile. "Don't worry, sister. I shall be well with some rest, and I am sure you will need to rest as well after your journey."

Blanche nodded and, with a last curtsy to the marquis, led the way to their rooms.

Jesu, Marie, Catherine prayed silently. *Help me bear this, for Blanche's sake.*

They came to her room, and Catherine thought she must have looked pale, for Blanche's expression became concerned again and she did not stay long to talk. Catherine gave her a reassuring hug and a smile, but it did not erase the worried look from her sister's face. She patted her hand.

"Blanche, do not worry. I shall be well. It is only my late illness, and the fatigue of my journey."

Her sister looked doubtful. "If you say it is so, I will try to believe it," she replied. "I have heard in stories of women whose faces have all the blood drained from them, but I have never seen such a thing until now when I looked on you." She paused. "If you wish me to stay with you, I will, so that if you become more ill, then I may call for a maid and have our brother call for the doctor."

A doctor. Fear crept into her. No, she could not have a doctor examine her. She had spent a long time away—more than seven months, at least. Of course her brother and sister would be concerned about her health, but her brother had already brought up the subject of marriage, and he would think also of her virtue, as any responsible relative would. She was no longer a virgin, but the blame would probably fall on Jack, not the marquis. Adrian clearly did not know the circumstances of her disappearance; he suspected their father as the cause, and her brother obviously admired de Bauvin. Should a doctor be brought to examine her? It would be natural to request that she be examined for damage to her health, but the doctor would no doubt bring a midwife to determine if any damage had occurred to her maidenhead.

Catherine gazed at the bed in her room, then at Blanche. It would be safe for now, she thought. The marquis was not a guest of the house tonight. She needed to think and rest. She shook her head.

"No, truly, you are very kind and sweet, sister, but I will be well. Indeed, I had excellent care in restoring my health when I was in Paris." It was true; Felice had been an excellent nurse and knew much about herbal tisanes and salves. She doubted any doctor could do better. "If you insist, however, I will call for you if I do feel ill, I promise it."

Blanche nodded reluctantly. "If you wish." She shook her head. "It probably would not make much difference, for I do not think doctors do anything but give potions that do nothing."

Catherine gave her a questioning look, and Blanche's face became full of grief. "They did not help Tante Anna, after all." Catherine looked sharply at her sister. "Tante Anna? What happened to her?"

Blanche raised hopeful eyes to her. "Do you remember her, then? She was very kind to me, and gave me presents. She..." The girl swallowed and shook her head again. "She fell down some stairs and did not...did not...." She pressed her lips together, clearly trying not to weep. "She is in heaven now, I am sure."

Catherine closed her eyes. Her aunt had suffered greatly under the hand of her husband. She was fairly sure it was not an accident. Her uncle and her father were of the same nature, though they were not of the same blood. "I remember," she said. "She was good to us, and I am sorry...." Her voice halted, choked by tears, then she swallowed and patted her sister's hand. "Well, you are right, a doctor will do me no good, and I promise I shall call for you if I need you."

Blanche smiled a watery smile at her. "If you promise, very well." She gave Catherine another hug. "I am very glad you are home. I remember you told me wonderful stories when I was very little." She went to the door and paused, looking back. "Good night, and rest well."

"Good night, Blanche."

Her sister closed the door quietly.

Catherine did not call for a maid to help her undress, but managed, slowly, to do it herself. She was glad her maid had laced her loosely and that the bow on her corset was easily undone. At last, she was free of her clothes and in her shift, and sat on a chair far away from the bed.

She closed her eyes and began to shake. Her hands trembled, and she closed them into fists to control them, but then her whole body shook. A low, keening sounded in the room; she realized suddenly it came from her and that she had crossed her arms and was rocking back and forth as if in deep grief.

Stop. Stop this. Control yourself. She took a deep breath and made herself stand and move to the bed. *It is only a bed, something to sleep on, where you will get your rest.*

But it was not.

It was where she had been forced, more than seven months ago, to lay, her shift pushed to her neck while her body had been violated. It was where she had knifed her attacker and left him for dead. It was where she had first felt the pain in her hands and her back as they bled and bled, and where her blood had joined the blood of her rapist. She remembered it all now, the instant she had touched his hand again this evening.

Her rapist.

The Marquis de Bauvin.

Chapter 10

❧ THE FROSTED BARREN TREES LOOKED like black lace against the cloudy late afternoon sky, but Jack took no note of it. He had ridden for five days as if the Devil were after him, riding until he wore out one horse after another, until one thought blurred into another out of fatigue. But fatigue did nothing to fade the images that repeated in his mind, particularly those of Catherine.

Her welcome at her home showed him, as nothing else did, that he had no place in her life. The de la Fer mansion was the ancient home of a high, noble family. All he had claim to was the title of a landless baronet and a vagrant's life. At dinner, she had worn her noblewoman's rich clothes and had sat in the company of other equally well-dressed nobles, while he must needs wear a borrowed suit and sat at the other, inferior end of the table. Her family welcomed her with open arms. He had no family, and he was certain he'd be as welcome in hers as he'd been at

King Louis's court—which was not at all, since the French king well knew why Jack wanted to see him.

And, more fool he, he had left the Comte de la Fer without collecting his reward for bringing Catherine back.

Idiot, sopping, drooling idiot. He'd had eyes only for Catherine, and had had a devilish time not snatching her away from the side of the Marquis de Bauvin.

He hated the man. His smoothness, his practiced manners, his rich clothes and beringed hands, his title and obvious influence over Catherine's brother. The devil of it was, Jack knew it all came from envy and jealousy, and the only redeeming feature was that his sins arose from loving Catherine.

He had sat there at the dinner table, watching how she had looked, with her white shoulders rising out of her dress like pristine clouds above stormy green seas, her red curls touching her skin like the colors of sunset.

She was beautiful. He had seen how the marquis had looked at her, first in surprise and then with clear interest. All of the man's cool demeanor could not hide his interest from Jack. The marquis wanted Catherine, and if Jack knew anything of the measure of a man, the marquis would get her.

And, damn him, he knew she'd be better off with such a highborn man.

Which was why he left so quickly. He knew the marquis would wed her, and that was that. There was nothing for Jack to do but leave...and collect his money, which he had neglected to do in his haste, damn it. He pounded a fist on his thigh in frustration. The truth was, he could not bear taking any money for Catherine's return. He didn't deserve it;

he hadn't acted with honor toward her, but had used her for his own pleasure and used her skill for money. Hell. Money was a wretched thing. It sucked the honor out of a man and made him a slave to seeming necessity.

It did mean, though, that he had an excuse to return and claim the funds from the Comte de la Fer, however, and to see Catherine again. The thought lightened his mood, but only momentarily. No doubt she'd be wed to the marquis by then.

He tried to turn his mind to other things, but he could only wonder what he'd tell the king when he met him. That he'd failed, that he had not even brought more money than a pittance for King Charles's threadbare and wandering court. As it was, he'd be at least a day late.

The land varied more in character as he neared Lille. Jack had to slow his horse to a walk from time to time so that he could traverse down steep winding paths through woods that led to hidden brook valleys. One of them took all his concentration, and he dismounted, for it was too steep and gravelly. He heard his horse emit a sigh, and he grinned ruefully. He'd ridden the poor animal hard, and it deserved a decrease in its burden, at least for now. Changing horses often was expensive, and he'd best try to spare this one for a while, even though it'd make him even later meeting the king. He let himself feel the irritation that was always under the surface when it came to thinking of the king. Granted, it was his duty to attend His Majesty and do his bidding, but sometimes he wondered if Charles forgot what it was to have human limitations.

There was indeed a brook at the foot of the steep wooded hill, not wide or deep from the looks of it, and there were wide, flat stones across it that looked easily traversable. He looked around instinctively before crossing; he was not in the midst of a war now, but he'd learned often enough not to let himself walk into a vulnerable position before he looked carefully around.

The woods were quiet, with only a slight breeze rustling the few dry leaves in the trees and the bracken along the floor of the forest. He frowned. A little too quiet; the day had darkened, and there should be the calls of birds and movement of animals readying themselves for the evening. He pulled out powder and ball, primed his musket, and carefully moved out into the clearing.

"Stand and deliver!" cried a voice on the other side.

Jack grinned, pointed his musket above the sound of the voice, and fired.

"Damn you, Jack, put that musket down! You almost killed me." A tall, devilish-looking, dark-haired man emerged from the woods on the other side, frowning.

"And you would have deserved it, Nick, for trying a bastard trick like that. Besides, did you think I was stupid? You called out in English, not French."

Nick winced, then grinned. "Very well, it was a stupid trick. I wanted to see if you'd jump out of your shoes." Lord Nicholas Devere was far from stupid, though. Jack had been in more than a few campaigns with him, and a bolder and more dependable comrade-in-arms he didn't know, with the possible exception of Fichet. He had saved Nick's life once or twice—Nick said twice, but Jack could only remember once. Nick, on the other hand, had saved the life of the king from Cromwell's spies more than a few times, and it was for that reason that His Majesty kept him close.

Jack frowned. If Nick was here, it meant that Charles probably was near, as well.

Nick's grin became apologetic and he lowered his voice. "Yes, he's not at Breda—at least, not officially. He became impatient, Jack. He's champing at the bit to get back to England, for we've just caught one of Cromwell's spies, and it looks like we have a supporter at home, for there are more than a few tired of the man and his son. We might also get Louis to favor our cause at last, as well, and the king has news for you to give to His Majesty. So, he thought he might meet you halfway."

Jack groaned, half glad that he need not travel all the way to Breda and half apprehensive. If King Charles was so impatient as to travel to meet him near Lille, he would also be very irritated, and he'd have to bear an interview that would have a strong resemblance to being roasted over hot coals.

His friend patted him on the back consolingly. "Never fear. It'll be short, I'm sure. He'll want you to depart as soon as you can for Versailles, to give Louis the message. The hotel is less than an hour's slow ride away."

Hotel. It might mean he could refresh himself, perhaps even wash away the travel dirt, and change into a fresh suit of clothes. He rubbed his rough chin. "It'll be good to get some decent food and a shave."

Nick shook his head. "Don't depend on it, friend. His Majesty is *very* impatient and wants to strike when the iron is hot."

"Devil take it," Jack said, and sighed.

*   *   *

Nick, luckily, was wrong, and Jack did have a chance to refresh himself and even rest for a few hours. It did not make him feel any better about facing the king, however.

Jack entered what served as an antechamber for the king's apartment in the hotel. He noticed it was more threadbare than the last living space in which Charles had stayed, but saluted and grinned a welcome at Nick, who stood at attention by the door. "Still guarding the gates of hell?" Jack asked.

Nick grinned. "Still. He's in a fair good mood today, though. Truth to tell, I'd give heaven itself to trade places with you, but you and His Majesty would kill each other within hours of you attending him."

"I'm no regicide," Jack said, and grinned. "His Majesty would have my head first."

Nick gave him a look more understanding than Jack liked.

"Aye, and you'd give it to him at his bidding."

"As should all loyal subjects," Jack replied, but even he thought his words were more automatic than felt.

Nick gave him a keen look. "Even kings—especially kings—can ask too much."

For one moment, Jack was inclined to agree. *King and country,* he thought. *Have and hold.* He shrugged. "My family has always been loyal. Who am I to be different?"

"The king rules by divine right, but he's not God, Jack."

Jack laughed. "'S blood, I know that. God never had as many women as His Majesty."

"You're a blasphemous man, and you'll fry in hell some day," Nick said, grinning.

"I depend on you to pull me out, old man," Jack said. "Speaking of frying in hell..." He nodded toward the door. "I suppose he wants to know if King Louis will support him?"

"If by 'support' you mean give him troops and money, yes."

Jack let out a deep breath. "I'll need your frying tongs, Nick."

Nick gave a sympathetic wince before he opened the door. "Good luck, friend," he said under his breath.

The king sat behind his desk, busily sorting through papers. For a long moment, he ignored Jack, even though he obviously must have seen him bowing on one bent knee before him. The floor was hard on his knee; he regretted, irritably, that he had not the foresight to have kneeled on the rug closer to the king.

At last he heard the papers rustle again, and the king's voice: "You may rise, Sir John."

Jack rose and looked up; the king had risen to his feet, as well, which was not a good sign. His Majesty was an exceedingly tall man, taller even than Jack, who towered over most men. The king was usually an informal, cordial sort and would meet others sitting—quite the opposite of King Louis, Jack reflected. But Charles also knew the effect of his height, and used it when he felt it necessary.

Obviously, he felt it necessary now. It also meant the king was displeased, hopefully not about Jack.

"Well?" demanded Charles.

Jack raised his brows in question. "Your Majesty?"

"Louis. Has he given you any word about giving me support?"

"Only that he needs to think on it."

The king made a sound very much like a growl. "'Think on it.' Damme, that's what he always says, no matter what he's asked, whether from peasant, noble, and now obviously king."

"My apologies, Your Majesty." Jack sympathized; waiting on kings was the very devil, and *he* had to wait on two. His thought must have been reflected on his face, for Charles's thick brows drew together in a frown as he gazed at Jack.

But then his Majesty's face cleared and his eyes twinkled as he grinned. "Aye, Jack, I'm getting a bit of my own medicine, I know."

This was what made Jack continue working for the king: the admission to his very flawed nature; his genial informality and charm that overcame his homely, thick features; the acknowledgment that yes, he had put Jack to a difficult task.

And, Jack admitted, the knowledge that he was King Charles's man, and loyal to a fault. His Majesty knew it, and took advantage of it. There was no mistaking that. But Jack was born and bred for his station in life, knew loyalty to the throne in his very bones, and he'd never forsake it, for God only knew he'd forsaken everything else. Catherine's face floated before his mind, but he dismissed it and the despair behind it. She was in the hands of her loving family, and did not need him.

"I need you, Jack."

Jack looked up at the king.

"I can't be in all places at once, and King Louis is one I've…well, tapped the least." A rueful look crossed the king's face and he glanced at Jack. "You know how it is. You've been as homeless as I, and more poor, I know." He smiled slightly. "Still making money from your dueling, Jack?"

"Not at your court, and not if you forbid it elsewhere, Majesty," Jack said promptly.

Charles laughed but shook his head. "Most definitely not at my court, for heaven knows it's caused me more problems than it's solved, but elsewhere . . . well, a man must do what he must do in the service of his king."

Jack relaxed. He knew only fighting since he'd been a boy, exiled along with Charles, and he knew no other way to earn a living than by his sword. He knew that Louis—or rather, the Cardinal Mazarin—had paid a certain sum to Charles for Jack's services in war, but that sum was certainly limited. He had once taken a musket ball intended for "Monsieur" Phillipe, that effete brother of the French king, and for that his value had risen. But he had returned with money, half of which he gave to Charles, and he had to be chary with the rest.

"And that includes making another call upon Louis. And no, you may not go openly. I am still talking with the Spanish, after all." His Majesty's face took on an optimistic look, however, and he smiled widely, eagerly. "But look you, we've caught a Cromwell rat that can talk, and did." He sat again in his chair and waved Jack to another. Jack sighed in relief. He was not going to get the dressing-down he expected.

Charles leaned forward, his dark eyes alight. "My cousin-king still fears his nobles, and rightfully so, though in my opinion he'd best keep them busy on their estates rather than demand they attend him. A man's less likely to knife you in the back if he's a league away, after all."

Jack's attention sharpened, and he raised his brows.

"Aye, you've guessed it," Charles said, correctly interpreting his expression. "It's a devilish plot against the life of the king, a conspiracy between Cromwell and a couple of Louis's nobles."

Jack let out a breath. "Very grave, then, in more ways than one. Did your rat give any names, Your Majesty?"

The king grinned briefly at the pun, then nodded. "Aye, two: the deceased Comte de la Fer and the Marquis de Bauvin."

Fear smothered Jack like a black shroud, and his breath left him. The room spun for a moment around him, and he rose slowly from his chair, grasping the back of it to steady himself.

"Jack?"

He forced his attention back to Charles, who had risen again and looked at him with concern. "I am sorry, Your Majesty, but I must go—*now*."

The king frowned, affronted. "You'll not leave until I *give* you leave, Marstone." He peered at Jack, and his face became concerned. "And I think I'll call a physician, for you look more ghost than man."

Jack pressed the palms of his hands over his eyes, then shook his head. "Your Majesty, I've just come from the home of the Comte de la Fer and seen de Bauvin with him."

Charles's expression sharpened and he leaned forward. "So it's true, then. And?"

"I fear there's not just treason, but sorcery." He explained quickly, almost frantically, of his return of Catherine and his encounters with the demon and the supernatural fog.

It was obvious to him now. He had tried to be

objective, had told himself that Catherine could very well have been the source—an unwitting source—of these occurrences. He had no reason to think otherwise; what he had heard of the supernatural had always seemed random and without reason in its movements. But two things were clear: Catherine had a certain power—he had seen how quickly she had healed from her wounds and how she had more strength than anyone would expect of a woman, much less one who had been so severely injured.

And she had been the focus of supernatural attacks.

He had seen no reason for it, and thus had seen such attacks as random, or perhaps arising from her own powers. But it could not be a coincidence that she had once been the betrothed of the Marquis de Bauvin and that the marquis and her brother were conspiring against Louis. Fichet had said that the de la Fer fortunes had declined, but Jack had dismissed the report when he had seen the rich cutlery and clothes of the family. But if it were indeed so that the de la Fers had little money, and since it was clear that de Bauvin wished to marry into the family, regardless of which de la Fer bride he'd wed, it must also be so that he sought some prize other than the woman herself. If the marquis wished to topple King Louis from his throne, he'd want as much power as he could find.

"Well." King Charles leaned back in his chair, steepling his fingers before him. "I have lost my kingdom, my wealth, and have wandered homeless almost half my life. I have been pulled and hammered between Catholics and Presbyters until my own faith has been sorely tested, and I wondered if God has decided to curse the whole of my life." He let out a long sigh. "I tell you, Jack, I can only think that the fact that you have seen de la Fer and de Bauvin together must be divine Providence itself, and proof that God at last will see me home." He gave an incredulous laugh, as if he was not sure whether to believe his good fortune. "It's all come together. The Parliament's dissatisfaction with Cromwell and his son, General George Monck's support—yes, that's the other thing, can you believe it? And now this, a way to convince Louis to support us, to show that God's on our side, not Cromwell's."

He rose, and Jack rose, as well. The king paced back and forth restlessly, his face growing more animated. "Go immediately to Versailles. Tell Louis it's a matter of import, a threat on his life. He'll see you then, by God!"

Catherine. Her image rose before Jack's mind's eye again. She was with that bastard de Bauvin, and God help him, he could not leave her in that monster's hands. He gazed at King Charles with all the respectful firmness he could muster. "Your Majesty, if it please you...I have to see to Mlle Catherine de la Fer's welfare. She's in danger, and could be a pawn in her brother's and de Bauvin's plans."

Charles cut the air with his hand in an impatient gesture. "You will do as I say and go straight to Versailles. We do not know exactly when de Bauvin and de la Fer will strike." The king frowned. "God's blood, Jack, you took your time traveling to me, so I needs must come to you. You'll not disobey me in this over a mere wench, or I'll have your head and your estates, too." He paused and his gaze softened. "Look you, Jack, we all have made sacrifices, even I."

Jack bowed stiffly. "As you say. But Mlle de la Fer is key—"

"By God, Marstone, you stretch my patience!" roared the king. His hand rested on his sword, as if he was ready to pull it out, and he strode over to Jack and stood but inches from him. He seized the front of Jack's coat and pulled him face-to-face.

It was a war of stares. Jack gazed unblinking, teeth gritted, into his king's eyes, and Charles stared angrily back. Silence reigned for a long moment before the king released him.

"You've been seduced by a possible witch, and you won't see it." The king's eyes bored into his own. "If Louis is killed before he sends me aid, then you'll present your head for the hangman's noose, Marstone."

Jack nodded, relieved. "I'll build the gallows myself, Your Majesty."

Charles looked grim. "I'll hold you to it, I promise you." He presented his hand, and Jack took it and knelt before him. "Now go, or else I'll give in to my impulse to run you through now, for I swear I have never met a more troublesome subject as you, Jack."

Jack grinned. He'd been forgiven, he knew, for the king had stopped calling him Marstone and returned to calling him Jack. Charles grinned back. "Damn your eyes." He waved him away, and Jack moved to the door. "And, Jack—"

Jack turned to gaze questioningly at his king. "Yes, Your Majesty?"

"Godspeed."

Chapter 11

CATHERINE CRIED OUT AND SAT UP IN her bed with a jerk. She breathed in frantic gasps, then forced control over herself, taking in deep slow breaths instead. Her heart still hammered, but as she sat and unclenched her hands, her heart slowed. She swallowed and looked about her. There was no one here. It was a dream. It was as Père Doré had said: the touch of a sorcerer would cure his victim of the spell.

She dreamed every night, dreamed the memories de Bauvin had stripped from her. He surely was the one who had done it; there was no other explanation.

She remembered it all now: how she had dressed herself carefully the day before her wedding to the marquis, for her father had beaten her until she had agreed to wed him, and the welts still burned when she put on her dress. She remembered how her aunt, Tante Anna—the Comtesse de Lisle—had visited her in her room. Her aunt had smiled slightly when she entered, but a shadow of fear crossed her face as she looked at her niece. She looked anxiously about her, then focused her attention on her niece and clasped her hands tightly in her own. Catherine had looked questioningly at her.

"Listen to me, Catherine—" The comtesse's voice hesitated. "You must not marry the Marquis de Bauvin."

Catherine wet her suddenly dry lips. Her aunt's voice was full of fear, and she remembered again the rumors that had floated about her bridegroom. She had met de Bauvin once, but though he was handsome enough, there was coldness underneath his civil veneer, and she could not like him. But her father had beaten her when she refused the marquis's proposal of marriage, and she knew she had no choice. Her father would beat her until she either married de Bauvin or another, perhaps worse man. She had hoped that at least de Bauvin would not beat her. She looked at her aunt, and her heart ached, for she knew her uncle the comte was brutal to her, and beat her gentle Tante Anna when he was drunk. At least she had not heard that de Bauvin was a drunkard.

Catherine squeezed her aunt's hand. "Tante, the marquis is not a drunkard—" She stopped and bit her lip, ashamed she had blurted out what must be an embarrassment and pain to her aunt. She gazed at the older woman's tired face, aged more than her forty years, and noticed a bruise on her cheek, barely hidden by her cap atop her curling hair. Anger flared in Catherine and her hands turned into fists at the thought of her uncle. If she were a man, she would fight him—

But she was not. She opened her hands and laid them neatly one on top of the other on her lap as she had been taught since a child, and was glad they did not tremble with the hatred she felt for her uncle ... and her father, for they were one and the same in nature.

Her aunt looked away for a moment, then met her eyes squarely. "My dear, I would spare you worse than what I suffer daily. De Bauvin is an evil man ..." She swallowed, and looked about her in fear again. "You remember my Jeanette—"

Dread crept into Catherine's stomach. "My father said she had a fever—"

Her aunt shook her head, and when she gazed into Catherine's eyes, her own were full of agony. "No. She disappeared. She was last seen—I saw her— in de Bauvin's company. And then she was gone, no one knew where. But then my husband took me to a dinner at the marquis's house, and I found her necklace and rosary, just outside de Bauvin's study. What else could it be but that he took her away?"

Dread clutched Catherine's heart harder, making it beat painfully. "No, no, surely it cannot be true," she said, her voice lowering to a whisper in spite of herself. "Perhaps she dropped it the last time you visited—"

A knock silenced Catherine's words and both women looked toward at the door. Catherine glanced at her aunt's frightened face. "Be easy, Tante, it is no doubt only my maid—*entré*, Minette!" The door opened, and she heard her aunt sigh with relief when she saw it was indeed the maid who entered.

Minette gave a curtsy. "Has mademoiselle decided on the flowers she will wear?"

Catherine itched with impatience and almost blurted out that she would wear a funeral wreath. She kept her face composed and her hands in her lap instead. "Roses," she replied. "We have many in our gardens, and I believe red will do." Rebellion boiled in her gut, even though she kept herself still. She hoped Minette would get some roses that had long thorns that would scratch the marquis should he come too close to her. The thought made her smile, enough so that she could say pleasantly, "Do leave me to my aunt's attention, Minette, for we have not seen each other this age, and I would have a comfortable talk with her." The maid curtsied and left.

She turned to her aunt. "Come, my dear tante, help me undress and put on my other clothes. It is not proper for me to greet guests in my wedding gown."

She hoped the distraction of the maid would turn their conversation in another direction, but it did not. Her aunt clutched her arm.

"Listen to me, *ma chère*. I know my daughter; she would have given me word had she been able, but all she could do was leave behind her rosary. It was a message from her, for she was a clever girl." She shook her head again. "I am not as clever, alas, but at least I can keep you from him, the evil one." She put her hand in the pocket of her skirt and drew out a bag, pressing it into Catherine's hands. "Take this and leave, my dear niece. And if you cannot, then use what I give you to kill him. And if you cannot do even that, kill yourself, for *le bon Dieu* must forgive you if you refuse to live with *le Diable* himself."

Catherine gazed, confused and horrified at her aunt, for the woman's voice grew more frantic as she spoke, her eyes more wild. Her aunt talked of murder and suicide—surely she could not mean it, surely her husband's treatment of her had made her become mad with fear. Catherine swallowed down her own fear and slowly untied the string that cinched the bag. She went to the bed and emptied it there, then looked at the bag and the contents strewn on the coverlet. Money, enough to travel far from home, and . . . a dagger in its sheath. She picked it up and drew out the knife. It was obviously old, its hilt made of smooth wood, but the blade was polished, as if someone had taken good care of it. She wondered from what armory her aunt had taken it—probably from her uncle the comte's. He had many such daggers, however, amd would probably not miss it. She pulled out a rosary peeking from under a part of the bag, and then picked up a cross on a necklace that lay next to it. The cross was very plain compared to the rosary, of grey metal—iron, she was sure—and adorned only with a small pearl and a tiny ruby.

She had slid the cross into her hand, and a small shock made her start, so quickly gone that she thought she must have imagined it—but no, a small drop of blood formed on the palm of her hand. She had wiped it away with her other hand, then carefully turned over the cross, examining it for sharp edges, but found none. Perhaps she had pricked herself earlier while doing needlework, and had not noticed it until now.

That night she had picked up a book she had left on the bedside table, then curled up on her bed and began to read, smiling a little at the fanciful fairy tale a court lady had penned and published. As she neared the end of the story, her eyes began to droop— she had been through much and was quite tired.

She had not known what awakened her—a noise, a presence. It had been dark, and the flickering candle only enhanced the shadows around her bed. Her hair hung down in her face, and she pushed it away, annoyed—she had forgotten to undress it. It would be tangled in the morning without a proper brushing. But she yawned and shrugged. Her maid was very good with a brush, and the tangles would come out quickly enough. She turned to blow out the candle.

And choked back a scream. The Marquis de Bauvin stood in the shadows there, his arms crossed over his chest, staring thoughtfully at her.

Catherine shoved herself away from him. "Monsieur, you should not be here," she said, making her voice as stern as she could. "I may be your fiancée, but I am not your wife, and I have kept my virtue as my father has assured you, and mean to keep it until the day I wed—which is tomorrow. Please leave." She wondered how he had entered—she always locked the door when she went to bed. Had he bribed one of the servants? Her aunt's words came back to her about her father's financial obligations—or, dear heaven, had he bribed her father? She closed her eyes briefly and swallowed down fear.

The marquis did not move from leaning against the wall, and he seemed only to watch her, his face half in shadow, his expression not easy to discern. There seemed to be a sense of curiosity about him, as if she were an interesting species of insect, and he were studying her.

"Please leave," she repeated, more forcefully this time.

He moved at last, but came closer to her, then seized her wrist before she could move farther away from him. He took her chin in his hand and forced her to look at him. She shuddered. His eyes were flat of expression, empty of emotion, empty perhaps even of a soul. Something flickered at his throat, and she became conscious of his state of undress—he wore only the breeches he had worn earlier, and his fine shirt was open at the collar. The flicker caught her attention again—the candlelight shone on an amulet at his throat. The dark crystal seemed to stir with a sluggish, greedy light, and she was drawn into it, pulled as if by a hundred spidery filaments.

She felt herself move toward him on hands and knees, and fear guttered in her stomach so that she felt she could not breathe. She clenched her teeth and a sharp prickling in her hands began. Her nightgown pulled against her back and pain from the weals forced her to gasp....

She wrenched her eyes away from the amulet and looked at the marquis.

He released her then, his brows raised.

"Interesting," he said at last. "You should not have been able to do that."

Catherine scrambled away from him and swallowed down bile. She had not had any control over her own body; she had crawled toward him as if she had been a dog, she who had taken pride in her self-control. The thought made her want to vomit, and the dread that spread from her heart to her gut made her want to scream.

"Stay away from me. Stay away." Her voice sounded unnaturally loud in her ears, but she could not have shouted, for her throat felt closed with tension.

"Tell me, Catherine," the marquis said in a conversational tone. "Do you have a dagger, a weapon of particular...power? Something that gives you more strength than you normally would have?"

He must be mad. He talked to her as if she had not spoken at all, as if they were in a drawing room conversing upon the weather. How was she to respond? She glanced at the door. If she were quick—

The marquis seized her wrist again and pulled her to him. "No, mademoiselle. Neither one of us will leave this room until I find and take the source of the de la Fer power, whether it is a weapon or... something else."

She would scream. Surely someone would hear her. She drew in a breath, but the marquis clamped his hand over her mouth. "Don't. It is useless to cry out. No one will pay attention. I have made sure of it." He looked down at her, and his expression changed, no longer empty now, as he pulled her even closer against his body.

She bit his hand.

A growl burst from him, and then she could not breathe, for he had pushed her down to the bed, his hand now clamped around her throat. She clawed at him, at his hands, struggling to draw in air, then kicked at him. He moved quickly aside, a practiced move, and Catherine wondered with horror if he had done this before.

"I will release you—slowly. You will tell me what I want to know. If you tell me, I will be generous."

She could feel the blood pulsing in her ears, her senses fading into black, but managed to nod. He released his grip, and she coughed as she gasped for air, but he still kept her immobile with his body on top of hers.

"There is a power in the household of the de la Fers," he said. "I have sensed it, and I desire to have it. I have heard that the blade that pierced the side of Jesus of Nazareth passed through this house, and then nothing was heard of it since. If anywhere, it is here. The power is stronger around you than anyone else here. Therefore you must have it." He looked deep into her eyes and reached between them, pulling out the amulet. "You will tell me where it is."

He was mad. She had no power. Neither did she know of any in her household who did. If she had had any, she would have used it to render her father and her uncle powerless.

The marquis must have caught something of her thoughts in her expression, for he smiled ironically. "What, did you think I desired to marry you because of your looks? You rate yourself too high." His hand gripped her chin, forcing her to look at the amulet again. "You will tell me where the source of power is."

The tendrils of darkness drew her will to the amulet again. She twisted against him to get away, but it did nothing but make his eyes half close and let out a soft breath. "Yes, I will be generous if you tell me." He moved his hips against her. "Be still, and tell me."

She wanted to vomit. "I . . . don't know. I know nothing about power," she said, struggling for control over her fear and her roiling stomach.

"Don't lie. Your will is strong, but it will break in time. I will make sure of it." He pulled up her nightdress and trapped her hands above her head.

"No, no, don't, please, *mon Dieu, Jesu, Marie—!*"

Anger flamed in his eyes at last, and he put his hand over her mouth again. "Don't say those things. Tell me about the power, the blade."

The blade—was it the dagger her aunt had given her? But it was the only thing that would help her escape. She remembered she had put it under her pillow—but he had her hands trapped, she could not get it—

She got one hand loose from his at last, but it

was useless, for he forced her to look at the amulet again, and her muscles went lax.

"Tell me about the blade of power."

"I . . . have . . . no . . . blade of power." The words came through her lips, stiff and sounding so harsh it seemed not her own voice.

The marquis stared at her for a moment, his body stilled and resting against hers. "Then there is no dagger. And yet I still sense the power strongly about you. I sensed it from your cousin, as well."

The amulet's influence faded enough for Catherine to close her eyes briefly in despair. It was true, then. The marquis had indeed taken her cousin Jeanette and perhaps killed her, killed her for some indefinable power neither she knew nor anyone else had told her of.

"You are mad!" she cried, gasping. "I know nothing about this power."

He forced her to look at the amulet again. "Tell me that you have no power, mademoiselle. Tell me, and I will make this pleasurable for you." He moved against her, touching her in her secret places, and her forced gaze into the amulet caught a red spark in its depths that seeped into her loins, enflaming them and making her press herself into him against her will.

"No!" she cried. She felt ill. She opened her mouth to tell him she knew of no power within her, but no words came forth. They were stuck in her throat—out of terror, out of pain, out of despair, she knew not what.

"So I thought. There is power in the de la Fer women, if not in the men, and I will take it now," de Bauvin said, and thrust himself inside her.

Pain. Screams. The prickling in Catherine's

hands became sharp as knives, and she jerked as if she were newly beaten.

She could not see. Darkness enveloped her, though she fought and fought and fought the pain, the darkness, and the terror. The palms of her hands were pierced with agony, dispelling the red darkness, and she opened her eyes and saw her hands become fists, striking the man above her. Pain again as he hit her, and hands fell above her head on the pillow.

There was nothing she could do. Nothing. She was Catherine de la Fer, of an old and noble family, but she could do nothing. The place between her legs burned harshly; even moving a little brought more pain, so she did nothing...but keep herself from weeping. She would not do that. No, she would not give him that satisfaction, at least.

She turned her head and looked away as he worked on her...she felt as if she were not in her body, as if she had somehow floated away. She wished she did not have a body, not this one, not this one so full of pain.

She wished she were dead.

Pain lanced her again, the palms of her hands, her back, and now her womb. She glanced at him and looked away—the marquis's eyes were closed and his face harsh, his amulet...

The amulet had ceased its hold on her. De Bauvin was not looking at her, was not asking about the power or the dagger...

The dagger. Slowly she moved her hand beneath the pillow, remembering her aunt's words to kill herself rather than be the wife of de Bauvin. Her hand felt metal, then the haft of the knife that had fit her hand so well earlier. It fit well now.

The marquis had asked her about her power—she

had it not then, but somehow her hand struck and struck again, hard, she knew not how many times.

He only groaned, stiffening once, then was a dead weight. She struggled under him, pushing him forcefully away, and his head struck hard against the corner of the bed table and then against the floor.

Catherine rose to her knees on the bed, the knife still in her hand. There should be screams and cries now, there should be alarms sounding. But no sound came to her ears except the snapping of the fire in the hearth and her breath coming harsh through her teeth.

There was blood. Blood on her gown, blood on the bed, blood flowing from her hands—had she cut her hands with the knife? She did not know.

All she knew was that she was not Catherine de la Fer any longer. She was not the girl who was about to be married, she was someone else whose body was different, whose soul was not the same as it was.

She looked at the dagger in her hand that did not seem to be her hand; it was a stranger's, for it was covered in blood. The dagger dropped from the hand to the bed—see, it could not be her hand, for it was numb, and she felt nothing.

Nothing but a terrifying ache between her thighs—no, no, she would not think of that. Her back did not pain her, or the palms of her hands, and that was good.

She moved to the edge of the bed and slipped from it to the floor, stumbling on something that lay there. The guttering candlelight flickered over the floor and the body slumped against the bedside table. Blood shimmered in a pool next to it.

Nausea filled her throat and she spewed her supper on the floor.

Jesu, Marie. God help her.

Panic rose. She had to get away. She could not stay here. Her father would beat her if he found out what she had done—

An hysterical laugh cut off her thoughts. Her father's beating would be nothing compared to what she would receive. She had killed the Marquis de Bauvin. The thought pierced her numbness, and flooded her with fear. He was an important man, with connections at the king's court. She was nothing, less than nothing. She would be taken away, imprisoned, executed for murder.

She wanted to die, she deserved to die, but the thought of being imprisoned, of being cut off from the open air, perhaps to be beaten again—

The stench of her vomit came to her, and she realized she was on her hands and knees on the floor, in the same way she had been on the bed when de Bauvin had forced her will to his. She forced herself to her feet, her knees shaking. No. No. She could not let herself be imprisoned in a lightless cell, and she would never be beaten again. She would not let anyone touch her.

She looked about her again. It was dark and quiet. Someone had screamed; it should have roused the servants, but she heard no voices, no running feet. She swallowed nervously—her throat hurt.

She had screamed. She shook her head dully. No, it was someone else, someone who had belonged here. She did not belong here, she was sure.

There was a bowl on the washstand near the fire, and water within. She would wash herself there, and she would leave this place.

She worked steadily, washing and cleaning, and setting the bed as neatly as she could. There was nothing she could do about the man on the floor, or the blood. She would leave it for the servants.

She had to leave. She took the dagger and washed it carefully, then put it in a velvet bag she found on the bedside table. There was something else in the bag—yes, money. A lady had given her money so that she could go away, and the lady had given her something else—ah, the dagger, a rosary, and a cross. She put her hand between her breasts and pulled up the cross in front of her eyes. It lay over a wound in the palm of her hand. She frowned. She must have cut herself somehow...but no matter; the wound faded, and the skin of her hand became smooth.

She tucked the cross between her breasts again.

She knew there were men's clothes in the wardrobe next to the fireplace. Someone...someone named Catherine had put then there at one time when she wanted to practice fighting.

It was fitting that she put these on; she was not as she was before. She tucked the bag and the dagger in one pocket of the coat she put on, put on sturdy shoes, and left the room.

The hallway was quiet; the people who lived in this house must be asleep, she thought. She walked down the stairs and past an open door.

It was an armory. A vague remembrance of some unpleasantness came to her regarding this room, but she pushed it aside. It would be good to have some kind of protection, she thought. She remembered she had learned something about weapons.

The candles were faint in their sconces, but she could make out the various weapons on the wall. Daggers—she had one already, so needed none. But there was a fine rapier she remembered she had used once, and she took it in her hand. It felt comfortable, and strength seemed to flow into her from it. She also took a belt and a scabbard, for she could not let damage occur to such a valuable weapon. She settled the belt around her, slipping the rapier into the scabbard, and as she walked, the scabbard rested in a satisfying way against her hip.

The summer night air was cool but not overly so, and she was thankful for that. She walked to the stables. If she were to leave quickly, she would need to take a horse. She halted at the entrance for a moment, listening for movement, but there was none. She supposed the stable boys were probably sound asleep. She went inside to a stall that contained a familiar horse. It nickered at her, and she stilled, looking about her in case the noise might have wakened anyone. But nothing stirred.

She took the mare and wrestled a saddle on it. When she went astride, a sharp pain formed between her legs, and an echoing fear, but it only made her dig her heels into the horse's sides and ride away as fast as she could from the memory.

Memory...Catherine forced herself to remember everything, even review once again the dream of her rape. De Bauvin had tried to take her power from her, and now he might try to take what power Blanche might have, in the same way. She knew he must be the one who had cursed her so; did not Père Doré say that one way of identifying a sorcerer was if an affliction disappeared upon touching that sorcerer? All her memories had returned when she had at last touched de Bauvin's hand that evening she had returned home.

Catherine pressed trembling hands to her face. *Jesu, Marie,* what was she to do? De Bauvin wished to take some power that she had—he had thought it was in a dagger, but she did not know of any that contained power. But she did know that the supernatural had touched her and that she recovered from her wounds very quickly, more quickly than anyone else, and that she gained strength in only a few weeks once Jack had found her. It spoke of some kind of power within her, or about her, and perhaps that was what the marquis was after.

She did not know much about such power or of sorcery, but there must be some reason de Bauvin wanted to wed Blanche when she, Catherine, had disappeared. It was clear to her in the week since she had returned that the de la Fers' financial affairs were not as stable as the fine clothes and cutlery they owned seemed to imply. Certainly the marquis was far more wealthy than the de la Fers. He could have his pick of brides, as noble as she, and more rich.

Therefore, he wanted something else the de la Fers had, and it must be the power he had spoken of. And if he was willing to wed Blanche, then it meant she, also, had it, as well. She thought of the marquis's character and what she had heard of him from her poor aunt. He was not the sort to simply seek power only to hold it. He was someone who would use it and wield it. She remembered the conversations Jack would have with Fichet about the affairs of countries, and remembered the reason why her own King of France kept his nobles so close at court—so that he could keep his eye on them. She swallowed. Surely the marquis did not think to take the king's power, as had the nobles during the Fronde revolt a decade ago?

Catherine forced herself to think over when she had the first manifestations of supernatural forces. She had never been aware of it growing up, nor as a young woman. It was only after she had been... violated. She closed her eyes and forced her body to relax, and her mind to be objective. It was only after she had been subjected to the marquis's violence that she had found the strength to stab him and shove his body from hers onto the floor.

She swallowed. There had been much blood. Blood on the sheets, on the floor, some of it hers and some of it de Bauvin's. The household must have known of it, for there was not one spot of it on the floor or on the bed when she returned. Someone had ordered it cleaned, but no one had mentioned the incident to her, and except for Blanche, who was at the convent at the time, everyone must have known. Including her brother.

She wondered how her father had died. She remembered now his blustering, his bullying abuse. She was glad her brother was not like that, at least not on the surface. But if her brother had known of her stabbing of de Bauvin, why then did he not tell her he knew, and why did he consent to have the marquis wed Blanche instead?

Either Adrian must know and approve of whatever de Bauvin planned to do with the power that existed in her or Blanche, or he was under de Bauvin's arcane control. Either way, she could not mention anything to him of what she knew. She had to pretend that she still did not remember anything and find out why it was that Adrian had said nothing of the incident, and why de Bauvin still desired to marry into her family.

Catherine looked about her room, then rose from

her bed and went to the window. She could hear a rooster crow in the distance—it must be the morning, though she could see no light on the horizon. Her brother had insisted they would go to Versailles to be presented to the king soon, though he had not stated exactly when.

So far, the marquis had not visited either Blanche or her for any long length of time, for which she was thankful. She wondered what he waited for, if he wanted the power that existed in her and in Blanche. He had not hesitated to try to seize it before when he—

She put away the memory for now. She had gone over it with as much objectivity as possible, and had even controlled her fear. She allowed herself to feel a bit of pride in that—she had vowed she would control her fear, and she had. Felice would be proud of her, she thought.

She wished she were back at the inn, with Felice and Fichet, and . . . and Jack.

She wished he had not gone, but she had as good as pushed him away. She had not wanted him to stay, thinking that she had been the source of the supernatural attacks.

Now she knew she was not. She groaned. It was just as well that Jack had not stayed; he could not love such an idiot as she was. She looked out the window again—useless. He would not come for her, although he might come back for the money her brother had promised him. She had made it clear she wished to stay at her home and that he was to go on . . . and he was at the beck and call of his king, after all. No, he would not return for her, but he might, to claim funds for his king. She could hope for that.

She found herself watching the darkness; she was not sure for what, exactly. Jack, perhaps, though she knew it was foolish. If she were to watch the night, it would be better if she looked for an intruder.

She turned back to her bed and flipped over the pillow. Her dagger was there, and her rapier beneath the bed. She was better prepared now to defend herself than she had been before. She knew how to use both a dagger and a sword.

Her expertise was something she kept hidden from her family, and of course de Bauvin. The less they knew of her training, the better. Her brother had seen her practice, but she made sure she looked clumsy at it, and had been so successful, he had laughed at her. She had grinned, shrugged her shoulders, and asked that he humor her, which he had.

She replaced the pillow and gazed out the window again. She frowned. Something moved out there, shifting back and forth in a pattern she remembered, and dread crept up from her stomach to her throat. She made herself lean forward and peered into the dark.

The hairs on the back of her neck rose, and her hands began to prickle with pain.

It was the demon, she was sure of it. Catherine gritted her teeth against the pain that seeped into her back, and ran to her bed, taking out her sword from under it. If it came to the house...

The pain faded, and she gazed out the window again. The weaving, shifting shape was gone.

She was certain it must have come from de Bauvin. Perhaps he sent the creature to keep guard over her and Blanche, to make sure that they did not leave without him knowing of it. Which could mean, of course, that he did not believe that she had totally lost her memory. She had been very careful, however, to reveal nothing, for both her life and Blanche's depended on it.

Or it could mean that he sent the demon to guard against others.

Jack.

She swallowed. If Jack came back, the demon might attack him. It made sense. If de Bauvin had at all sensed that there was anything between her and Jack, he would wish to prevent it. How was she going to keep the demon from him?

She slowly went to her bed and put the rapier back underneath it. If the demon was set to guard her and Blanche, then it made sense that if they left their home, the demon would be sent after them.

It meant, then, that if Jack decided to return for the money, it would be best if she and her sister were not here. She swallowed. She would have to convince her brother to go to Versailles as soon as possible . . . and watch de Bauvin very carefully. It would mean, of course, that she would have to keep him close by.

She closed her eyes. *Dieu me sauve.* It was difficult enough now to see him, knowing what he was, and knowing that no one would believe her. Even if anyone wished to examine her claims of rape, it was possible she herself would have to undergo torture during investigation to ensure she was not lying. She could bear much, but by the time the investigation was done, de Bauvin would have done his damage.

But she would do it. She would watch de Bauvin, even flirt with him, if need be, to keep him under her eye. If she could find solid evidence of sorcery, she would turn him in and work to free her brother from his influence. And if she did not . . .

She would find some way to kill him before he hurt Blanche.

Chapter 12

ALL JACK WISHED TO DO WAS SLEEP, FOR his body felt wracked with fatigue from traveling so long and so hard on horseback. But Catherine was in danger, and he needed to make sure she was safe.

He cursed himself for denying the possibility. He should have stayed long enough to see that she'd be unharmed. He had seen the wounds on her back when he had found her—he should have considered the possibility that she had acquired them at the hands of her family, or perhaps even de Bauvin.

But he had seen for himself that her brother the comte was of a pleasant disposition, and seen the joyous welcome of her younger sister. He had not liked the Marquis de Bauvin, but he had discounted his dislike and put it down to jealousy, for God knew he felt as jealous as the Devil himself. He'd even left before the dinner party was done, for he could not bear to see the marquis court Catherine again. And by doing so, he'd abandoned her to a traitor and most likely a sorcerer.

He had little doubt of that now. It fit; Mme Felice had said that the demon had attacked her and Catherine as they had left the church after their confession. If it were so that they were in a state of grace, then it made no sense that Catherine would be the source of summoning the demon. Felice had said, after all, that they had done nothing but walk home, and certainly he nor Mme Felice had heard any conjuration from Catherine. Therefore, it had to come from somewhere or someone else.

But he'd been skeptical. He had had little faith in the claims of any religion after seeing how the adherents had caused bloodshed and strife, and caused him and his king to be exiled.

But King Charles's information had brought together all the parts of the puzzle in his mind, and if he could get back to the de la Fer estate, he might be able to take Catherine away and keep the marquis and the comte from overthrowing Louis.

Fear for Catherine almost choked him, but he pushed it away. He had to think clearly, regardless of fatigue, regardless of his fears. There was always the chance that the marquis and the de la Fers had already left for Versailles. He hoped not. But he was not such a fool not to cover the possibilities. Charles had delayed him yet another day after their interview, but it was necessary. After they had spoken, he had to carry a letter in Charles's own hand as well as his seal, to help ensure Louis would believe his news. But Jack made sure to send a letter by fast courier to Paris as soon as he quit Charles's presence, with the hope that Fichet would travel to Versailles and with any luck gain access to King Louis's court. He grimaced. The chances were not great that a common innkeeper would gain King Louis's audience, but Fichet was clever and had a way of circumventing bureaucracy better than most...if Fichet did not determine another course of action was superior. He hoped that his friend would follow orders.

The day was fading, the colors of twilight touched the sky, and he could see ahead of him the way to the de la Fer estate. Just beyond the silhouette of the trees, the mishmash of Gothic and Norman architecture arose, and he prayed that Catherine was still there.

He called to the gatekeeper when he came to the entrance of the estate, and managed not to curse while he waited. The thought of stinting on curses made him smile a little—he was grown cautious of profane language all of a sudden. But he did not want to tempt fate—or the devil—not when proven supernatural doings had been afoot.

The gatekeeper shuffled to the gate at last, holding a lantern aloft, for the sun had fallen beneath the horizon. He squinted up at Jack.

"You are the one who returned Mlle de la Fer."

"Yes, yes," Jack said impatiently. "And I wish to speak with her brother or with her. Let me in."

The gatekeeper did not move. "You cannot, monsieur. They are gone."

"Where?"

"To Versailles."

Jack bit back a groan and managed to tamp down his fear and disappointment. He turned to go, but stopped. "Do you know whether the Marquis de Bauvin has gone with them?"

The gatekeeper shook his head. "I do not know. I had heard the marquis left a day after them—or was it a day earlier?—but it was only thirdhand that I heard it."

"When did the de la Fers go?"

"Two days ago, monsieur."

"And de Bauvin's estate—where is it?"

"It is past Rouen, just south of it."

Jack bit back another curse, wheeled his horse around. He galloped back down the road, then turned toward Paris.

Both fear and hope rode him hard. Two days. He was only two days behind Catherine, and perhaps three behind de Bauvin. He was glad he had changed horses not long ago; he could gallop a while until he came to the next inn that would exchange horses. If he rested four hours at most, he could catch up with them within a day before they reached Versailles.

It was not long before he was past Rouen and on the road on which he and Catherine had experienced the strange mist. It was close to where the gatekeeper had said de Bauvin's estate was.... No coincidence, that, Jack thought. But he'd not be sidetracked; he'd go straight to Versailles, for regardless of whether the marquis had preceded or followed the de la Fer family, he had most certainly, or would, go there.

His horse suddenly shied, and Jack forced his attention back to his surroundings, then cast a glance in front of him.

It was the mist again. Of course. He slowed his horse to a walk. Of course it would be here again, near de Bauvin's estate. But he did not have the supernatural senses that Catherine had, and though he had felt colder than he ever had in a fog, it had not affected him in the way it had affected her, and he doubted it would again.

His horse disagreed, however. The gelding tossed

its head, whinnying plaintively into the mist that had grown denser. Jack kept a firm hand on the reins. He remembered that this portion of the road was straight and that all he and Catherine had done was ride without turning to the right or left until they were through it.

He gritted his teeth. If possible, the opaque formlessness was stronger than it had been before. Still, he would get nowhere if he let it bother him. He urged his horse into a faster walk.

The hairs continued to prickle at the back of his neck, however, and every nerve seemed on end, for the freezing mist curled up his legs and seemed to catch at them, as if they were brambles determined to twine around his ankles and keep him in place. He took in a deep breath and let it out again, then frowned. There was a familiar scent—he did not remember quite where he had smelled it before, but he hoped it would go away soon, for it smelled like a latrine.

His horse screamed and bucked, nearly unseating him, as a dark shape swept in front of them. He gritted his teeth against a curse, and turned it into a prayer instead, but had no time to note if it had any effect, for the monster struck again and his horse fell and became still.

He managed to leap free at the last moment, rolling on the ground and coming up, rapier in hand. His tired muscles protested, but he spun around, trying to see past the mist to the dark shape of the demon. Nothing. God help him. He was as good as blind.

A sound, a whiff of a foul scent—Jack whirled in time to move from a black, outstretched claw. He struck out with his sword, but the claw disappeared into the mist again.

He looked around him at the formlessness—he'd lose his way if he continued to spin and spin again. He looked for his fallen horse, then looked away, swallowing. The poor animal had half its neck torn away... and Jack was sure he'd share the same fate if he wasn't careful and let his weariness overcome him.

He wasn't at that point yet, though. He was in the midst of battle, and he knew he was in the initial energy that always came to him when he first joined a fight, regardless of his condition. It would fade after a while, but at least he'd have a good chance to best this creature for the first half hour or so. He needed only that much time to kill it, and it could be killed—he'd seen Catherine do it, and it gave him hope. He tried not to think that he hadn't been to confession as she had, or that she hadn't fought within a mist.

This mist did give the creature the advantage. He moved closer to the horse's corpse. It had fallen to the side of the road, and its head—what there was left of it—pointed in the direction they had been going. If Jack kept close to the roadside and kept his mind on whatever direction he might turn, he might be able to continue on his way past the mist.

Another dark claw came out of the mist, barely preceded by the stench of the creature. Jack struck out, and a scream came from the demon. He grinned fiercely. That might slow it down.

It did not. The creature came at him again, and again, and Jack barely missed being decapitated twice. He was half thankful for the mist, for it silhouetted the monster's form.

He ducked, and felt a stinking breeze pass over

his head. He struck again, and the creature howled. Faugh! If he did not die from this creature's attack, he'd die of its smell.

He watched carefully as he avoided more of the monster's attacks, and thought he saw a pattern in them. It swiped at him, rather than lunged, in the way a man might use a scimitar or a broad sword. It meant that Jack had at least one advantage—he could cut as well as pierce it with his rapier. Very well!

The monster swiped at him again, and this time Jack did not strike, but moved back—luckily in the Parisian direction, as best as he could tell—letting the sweep of the monster's arm pass over his head.

Now! He lunged.

He could feel the rapier sink into the monster's body, and a foul stink followed it. The creature howled again, and for a moment, triumph made Jack grin—

Only to have his breath squeezed from him in a crushing grip.

He could not breathe. The stench and the grip made him cough, and then pain seized his chest. He gritted his teeth, and found that one of his arms was loose...darkness came over his vision and a freezing chill over his body. No, no, not now. Dear God, Catherine, please not now.

Warmth seemed to seep into him, and he opened his eyes and felt the hard haft of his dagger in his hand. He must somehow have seized it even as he had run the monster through, and he was glad he had trained himself to do so until it was second nature. His rapier had done little good, but at least he could do more damage to the demon before he died.

He managed to move his arm between them, and thrust the dagger in the demon's throat.

A strangled scream ended in a burble of reeking slime, and the monster's hold loosened. Jack gasped in agony as he pushed away from it, and fell on the ground with a clatter of metal.

He shook his head to clear it of pain and chill numbness, then opened his eyes. *Thank God.* He had landed next to his rapier. He seized it and rose quickly to his feet, gritting his teeth against the pain in his ribs, and putting all the strength he had left in the stroke to cut off the demon's head.

He fell again. *Jesus.* This time it was not a curse, but a prayer. Dear God, he hurt. He opened his eyes. A dark, stinking puddle formed not far from him— he remembered this was what had happened when Catherine had killed the demon they'd seen in Paris. It was dead, then. Thank God.

Pain struck when he rolled, trying to get to his feet. Vomit choked him, and he spewed it out, groaning in pain as the heaves hit his ribs. Dear God, he hurt. Dear God.

He forced his eyes open. He was curled up on the side that seemed to hurt less. One of his arms tingled, as if on the edge of freezing and warmth. He touched it—it was wet. He did not remember the monster clawing him. Perhaps it had, or perhaps he had cut himself when he fell.

He could see darkness in front of him when he lifted his head, but when he looked down, his feet were still encased in clinging fingers of grey. He had somehow gone past the edge of the mist. Not enough, though. Not enough. The farther away he was from it, the better.

He managed to push himself to his knees and

fumbled on the ground for his rapier. His hand felt metal—yes, there it was, and his dagger...

Never mind about his dagger; he had his rapier, and he was not about to feel around in demon-slime to fetch it out. He could still smell the stench of it on him, and his stomach heaved against his ribs again, making him groan with pain. He pushed himself up onto his feet, clutching his ribs, and moved away from the mist.

Walk. Walk. He knew he needed to go forward. Forward. Forward, or else he'd fail. Fail Catherine. He couldn't fail her, God help him. He had failed everyone else, but Catherine was his last chance. His last chance.

He was not sure how long he walked. He only knew that he had grown colder until he could not feel his legs, and that he could see dawn just at the edge of the horizon.

He opened his eyes, and found himself on grass. He was on the side of the road, most likely, though he was not sure how he had come there. He could not feel his hands, and was glad he had thought to put his rapier into his scabbard, so that he'd not lose it. It was relatively soft grass, and perhaps he would rest for a minute. Just a minute, and then he would go on—go on to find Catherine.

He thought he heard the sound of horse's hooves, but somehow he could not open his eyes. The sound stopped, close to him. Perhaps Catherine had come to find him. Perhaps they were on the road to their next duel, where they would fight for money.

"Catherine," he whispered. "I am glad you are here."

A sad sigh sounded nearby, but a masculine voice answered. "It is not Mlle de la Fer, M. Sir Jack."

Jack let out a weak laugh. "Damn you, Fichet, you are supposed to be in Versailles."

"It is a good thing I am not," Fichet replied.

Jack tried to rise, but pain struck again, and he groaned. "Dear God," he whispered, and darkness claimed him.

Catherine allowed de Bauvin's hand on hers as he bowed over it, and was glad she had enough control over herself not to reveal how her skin crawled to be this near him. She even smiled pleasantly at him as she ordered refreshments in the parlor of the hotel suite in which she, her brother, and her sister stayed while in Versailles.

She still had her dagger with her, however, hidden in the pocket of her skirts. It made her feel more secure, and more able to bear the marquis's presence. The only thing that kept her from killing him now was the lack of sure signs that de Bauvin intended to use what power he had gained. She needed proof, and witnesses.

She had kept watch on him, just as she was sure he kept watch on her. He stayed at apartments just across from the hotel at which she stayed. She had one advantage, however; she was sure that he did not know she had regained her memory.

He was paying more attention to Blanche, however, and that she could not allow. She had seen Blanche's reaction—half pleased at the attention of such a high noble, and half uncertain and a little fearful. Even if she did not see this uncertainty, that her sister was so young made the alliance disgusting, and that it was to one such as de Bauvin made it abhorrent.

She gazed at de Bauvin, who looked to the door when a footman and maid came in with the refreshments. He was ever watchful, this man. Very little escaped him. She would have to tread carefully to make sure he followed the path she wanted him to follow.

"I am pleased you decided to come to Versailles," she said. She was becoming a good actress—she said it with light pleasantness. "Do you stay long?" She made her voice sound hopeful.

He smiled at her, and she noticed the smile did not reach his eyes. His expression had a measuring quality about it, as if he weighed her worth every time he looked at her.

"Yes," he said. "The king wishes his nobles near him, and I expect he will wish the same for me." He picked up a glass of wine.

"Good. I know that Adrian and Blanche—and I—are glad of your company. We are so much of the country, we are not at all certain how to manage so near court."

"I would think that after your sojourn in Paris, you would know more of how to live in a city." He watched her closely, she noted. She thought carefully before she replied. . . . It was the opening she needed so that she could divert his attention from Blanche to herself.

She made herself frown, then shook her head. "No. Paris is not like Versailles, and I did not attend court or any high function. Indeed . . ." She hesitated, putting on an uncertain expression. "I must say it was more strange than instructive of the ways of the court."

His hand paused in bringing the wineglass to his lips, and he looked over the edge of it before he sipped. "In what way?" His voice was bland, but she was sure his attention was caught.

She gave a hesitant laugh. "You will think me very silly, monsieur, but..." She watched as he leaned forward. Yes, he was all attention, she was sure. "Some very strange things happened to me in Paris."

He smiled, and this time it did reach his eyes, for an avaricious glint appeared there briefly before his expression turned bland again. "You may tell me, mademoiselle. Am I not your brother's friend, after all?"

She bit her lip, lowering her eyes, for she did not want him to see the triumph in them. She sighed, then shook her head again. "When I stayed with Sir John Marstone and with the inn-wife, they said that the wounds I had when they found me healed very fast. A miracle, Mme Fichet had said. She had never seen the like, and she had nursed many." It was an exaggeration, of course, but essentially the truth. "Indeed, even M. Marstone said that I have become stronger than any woman he had known."

She looked up with a guileless expression, and noted that the marquis's body had tensed, and that his hand clutched the wineglass so that his fingertips showed white against the clear surface.

She wrinkled her brow in a frown. "Do you remember if I had any such powers, monsieur? Before I was kidnapped to Paris?"

He gazed at her for a long, assessing moment, then his eyes slid away to gaze at the wine in his glass. "No, I am afraid not," he said. "Our betrothal was shortened by your abduction."

She sighed. "It is a mystery, then." She held out her hands to him. "I even went to a priest while in Paris, for I began bleeding from my hands, though I had not hurt them. Oh, they do not bleed now," she said, when he raised his eyebrows, "but they did."

"To what did the bleeding respond?" The marquis leaned forward, clearly interested, and Catherine forced herself not to pull away.

He was caught now. He did not even try to pretend she was imagining it all. She made herself frown as if in thought. "I...I am not sure. My hands bled when I encountered men attacking a girl in an alley. It happened again when— When I was attacked by a dark monster." She swallowed and closed her eyes; she did not have to falsify her dread at the memory. "You will say that it was my imagination, but I tell you, M. Marstone saw it, as well." She opened her eyes again to see the marquis's gaze upon her, intense with interest.

He leaned back in his chair after a moment, seeming to make himself relax, but he still seemed all attention. "And what happened to this...creature?"

"M. Marstone killed it," she said. "He is a prodigious swordsman." It was a lie, of course. She had killed it, with Jack's help, but she did not want de Bauvin to know it. She smiled, and sighed as if in relief. "I am glad you do not doubt my story. I told Adrian of it, and he brushed it off as a fantasy."

"You told your brother?" There was an odd note in his voice, and she wondered if she should have mentioned it. She had only vaguely mentioned her adventures in Paris to Adrian, nothing as specific as she had just told de Bauvin, for she wanted to protect her brother from feeling more guilt than he already felt. But she wanted to see what effect such

words would have on the marquis. It turned his voice
sharp, as if he had not expected her to tell her
brother.

"Why, yes," she said, putting surprise in her
voice. "He is my brother, and of course would be
curious about what happened to me while I was
away." She shook her head. "But he did not believe
me, and M. Marstone was not there to verify it."

The marquis nodded and seemed to relax. He
shot a glance at her. "I would not put much thought
into it, mademoiselle. You were ill, and your mind
had been affected so that you remembered nothing
of your life. It could well be fantasy. Perhaps we shall
talk of this again."

She frowned again, but only to cover her triumph. He was caught, indeed, and if this did not divert his attention from Blanche, she did not know
what would. "I would be glad to talk of it again," she
said. "The bleeding is a nuisance, and I would like to
be rid of it."

The marquis smiled, and this time it looked gen-
uine. "I will be glad to be of service, mademoiselle,"
he replied.

A clock chimed then, and the marquis rose and
took his leave, for he was meticulous about his outward manners. Catherine smiled fiercely as the door
closed behind him. The marquis had exposed himself and his interest well. He was not aware that she
had regained her memory, so he would be that much
more vulnerable to her. She would be willing to wager that he would visit more often now, and then she
would be able to discern more about his purpose in
coming to Versailles. She was relieved to note that
her brother did not go to de Bauvin's home in the

evenings but a few times, and then it was only for dinner, after which he soon returned.

She frowned. Adrian was looking more tired, more worn these days, though he did not spend his time in dissipation as young men often did at court. Were the matters of their estate worrying him so? It was clear that they expended a great deal of money traveling to Versailles, and though she had tried to conserve as much as she could, being at Louis's court demanded more than she suspected her brother could afford. She had tried to offer her help in managing estate affairs, but Adrian had brushed her off, and a stubborn look had come into his eyes. He clearly felt responsible for running the estate and their financial affairs. And yet he had insisted they come to Versailles, which could not have helped.

De Bauvin must be behind it; Adrian did nothing but sing the man's praises, and any argument Catherine tried to raise was firmly dismissed. She wished she knew how she might pull her brother away from the marquis's influence, but she did not know how. Should she tell Adrian the true reason she ran away from home?

Dear heaven. She did not want to, but if it meant she could release him from the marquis's thrall, then she must. She still needed to find out more about the marquis, and then in a week's time, she would be presented in court, since that also was the time de Bauvin was to attend the king. If he did anything, it would be then. She wanted to expose him as a sorcerer in front of as many influential witnesses as possible, and if the king did nothing, she would kill the marquis herself.

She swallowed down despair, pressing her lips

together in determination instead. She wished Jack were here, but it was a stupid wish. It was necessary she deal with de Bauvin alone. She did not wish for Jack to know what the marquis had done to her; it was a shameful thing, for she had not been able to resist him. It was enough to know that whatever happened to her, her brother and sister would be safe.

Catherine rose and went to her room, and brought out her sword from under her bed. If she dressed in the new military fashion for ladies when she went to court, she could carry the sword, as well, and perhaps tuck it underneath her skirts. It would be awkward, but she could do it. She had tried it, and most of it was well concealed underneath a stiff over-dress, and a long shawl draped over her shoulders would conceal the guard and haft. She preferred her trousers and jacket to a dress, of course, but she had practiced a few times with her dress and she could still fence well if her stays were loose and her bodice not constricting.

It was vengeance, she knew. Vengeance for what the marquis had done to her. But she hoped God would forgive her if it was also to save her family.

Chapter 13

THE MARQUIS DE BAUVIN PUT HIS SCRYing mirror on his dressing table with satisfaction and gazed pensively out his room's window at the hotel across the street. There stayed Catherine de la Fer, her sister Blanche, and their negligible brother Adrian.

They were in his control now that they were well isolated from any true relationship. They went to balls and parties, to be sure, but the associations were manipulative at least and shallow at best, as most noble associations were. And any that threatened to become more, he made sure they would not last.

For example, Sir John Marstone. He was a nuisance, and now the marquis was rid of him. The man was obviously the one who had destroyed the first dark seeker he had sent out in Paris to search for Catherine de la Fer, so he had dispatched this second one. But the combination of the bramble-mist and the seeker had done the trick: Sir John was severely disabled, if not dead. Dead, more likely. He'd seen for himself the fool's lifeless body tossed along the side of the road.

The marquis gazed for a long moment at the hand mirror he had placed on the table, frowning. He would almost have thought that M. Marstone had some power of his own, for a similar obscuring light had been about him as had been about Catherine de la Fer in the hand mirror. But it was of no import now; the man could not interfere with his plans.

Now he would turn to other, more important matters. In a few days, he would be in the presence of King Louis. He had both the de la Fer sisters within his reach; even better, the elder had no memory of her past, and her power had increased to such a point that his sorcery could feed from it without even having to take her. He could use a simulacrum, or summon an incubus, and send it to her room to draw the power through it to him.

He half closed his eyes, remembering the night he had taken Catherine, so as to find the source of and draw off her power. He was not certain which way he would rather do it. There was a certain deliciousness in watching her struggle in fear, but then doing it from afar by incubus would mean he could watch her helplessly unable to resist the power of the demon as it sucked away her power night after night and left her an empty shell.

Or no. There was the younger girl to consider. She had the power, as well. Why not make it last? He would take Catherine himself—he would enjoy that. Meanwhile, he would use the incubus on Blanche, slowly, over the course of a few months. That meddler Cardinal Mazarin would be dead, and he would have control of the king by then, or perhaps even be king himself.

Yes, he would do this. He must be patient, however. The power was best wielded when freshly taken. He'd use an incubus on Blanche for now, and use her power to continue influencing the Comte de la Fer as well as other nobles in Louis's court. The night before the revolt, he would take Catherine's power, and then...

The marquis smiled. And then he would be king.

Sometimes Jack thought he was in heaven, and sometimes he thought he was in hell.

Mostly hell.

Something squeezed his lungs so that he could not breathe from the pressure and the pain, and his skin felt burned and stretched across his bones. He'd hear voices, sometimes Fichet's, sometimes his father's, and sometimes the slippery smooth voice of the Marquis de Bauvin, telling him he was nothing but a failure, a rogue, and a dammed idiot. The hellish thing was that it was true, and no doubt the pain and burning he felt was his punishment.

But then he'd hear Catherine's voice calling to him, telling him to come to her, soon, and the pain would lessen. That was heaven.

He tried to block out the sounds of the others, and reached for Catherine's voice. But soon her voice faded and, oddly, became Fichet's, though they were nothing alike. It disturbed him, and at last he opened his eyes.

It was, unfortunately, Fichet. The innkeeper stood over him with a wet towel, a mug of what looked suspiciously like hot tea, and a frown.

"We had better be in Versailles," Jack said. It came out as a whisper, and he noticed his throat felt sore.

Fichet thrust the mug at him. "Drink, M. Sir Jack."

"*Are* we in Versailles?" Jack asked, not quite putting the mug to his lips.

"Drink first, then I will tell you." Fichet's frown grew deeper.

Jack drank, then almost spit out the tea before he swallowed it down. "It's a damnable draught—what is it, piss?"

Fichet's lips twisted downward even farther than Jack thought possible. "No, monsieur, it is a tisane, from Felice's own recipe. It is for the fever and to knit broken bones, and look you, if I had not given it to you, you would still be very ill. Drink the rest." He eyed Jack grimly. "And be grateful."

Jack drank, tamping down his impatience. "There," he said. "Now. Are we in Versailles?"

Fichet said nothing, pushing Jack back down on the bed, and applying the cold towel to his forehead.

"Well?"

Fichet sighed. "No, we are not. We are in an inn on the road between Rouen and Paris."

A long string of expletives burst out of Jack, and halted only when he remembered he had resolved to try not to curse so much. He threw the cold towel from his forehead and glared at Fichet. "I can understand why *I* am not in Versailles—I have been to the north, at the command of my king. However, I distinctly remember I sent word that *you* were to go to Versailles and *why* you were to go. Or did you not read my letter?"

Fichet's expression was disapproving as he picked

up the towel, pushed Jack down again with insistent force, and placed the towel on his forehead again. He gazed sternly at Jack. "Monsieur, I did indeed read it, and thought it foolishness, and so did my *dulce* Felice."

"Foolishness!"

"Yes, and idiocy, as well."

Anger flared, and Jack pushed himself off the bed, then almost vomited from the vertigo and pain that slapped him down again. He caught Fichet's amused look.

"Very well, you've had your revenge. But at least you owe me an explanation for why you are not watching over Catherine."

Fichet looked haughtily down his nose at him. "Because your message was foolishness. It was obvious to me and my good wife that you were in more need of protection than mademoiselle."

"Oh, really?" Jack snarled. His head pounded, and it did nothing for his temper, but the experience of pain just minutes ago kept him from reaching out to wring the innkeeper's neck.

"It is truth," Fichet replied calmly. "You said that you had seen de Bauvin at dinner while you were at the home of the de la Fers. Since you were very sure in your letter that de Bauvin is a sorcerer—and you are a skeptical man of all things religious and supernatural, M. Sir Jack—then it must be so. Felice and I knew immediately that if indeed de Bauvin was a sorcerer, he would do all he could to keep you from mademoiselle, and thus your life would be in danger."

"And what brought you to that conclusion?" Jack itched to throttle Fichet, but he remembered that patience was a virtue, and besides, he might feel like vomiting again if he rose from the bed.

Fichet sniffed as if offended. "It is clear to anyone who looked at you that you are in love with mademoiselle, and she with you, although she is better at hiding it. Since it is reasonable to assume the study of sorcery needs much perception, it follows that the marquis must be a man of such parts. Therefore"—Fichet smiled triumphantly—"the marquis would see your affection for Mlle de la Fer, and do all to keep you from her. He might not do anything if you left, but he would do all in his power if you returned." The innkeeper looked at him critically, his gaze resting on the bandages wrapped across Jack's chest and more on one arm. "You returned. Therefore, he must eliminate you."

Jack pressed his lips together in frustration. "Very well. But does this not even suggest to you that Catherine would be in even more danger than I?"

"No."

"Enlighten me," Jack said, his voice dripping with sarcasm.

"I have sent Père Doré to Versailles to attend her." Fichet went to the other side of the bed and examined the bandage on Jack's left arm. He nodded approvingly as he pressed on it, and when Jack only winced from a stinging sensation.

"A priest!"

Fichet looked at him gravely. "But of course. If the marquis is a practitioner of the dark arts, then it is reasonable to send a priest to counter the evil with whatever holy rituals he may know. Also, mademoiselle told Père Doré about her condition before you left for Normandy, and the good *curé* decided under the circumstances to see the cardinal about it, regardless. The priest already has entrée to the king's court, and since I have informed him of your message, he also knows of de Bauvin's sorcery; it is therefore much more useful for me to search for you than for me to attempt a very useless entrance into the king's court." He smiled a very self-satisfied smile. "You must admit it was useful."

Jack rolled his eyes. "Very well. It was useful." It did make sense, and he felt more of a failure than before. But he held out his hand in apology, and Fichet grasped it. " 'S truth. I'm grateful, Fichet . . . and if I'd half a brain, I would have thought of it."

The innkeeper raised his brows. "I do not see how. Not even I, Robert Fichet, would have seen it had Felice not told me after you left that mademoiselle had allowed Père Doré to consult with the cardinal about her condition." His gaze was kind and wise. "You cannot know or do everything, M. Sir Jack. Not even I. We can only seize of life what we can and be grateful for the good, *hein*?"

Jack shrugged, a resistant gesture, but Fichet's words gave him a measure of comfort. His life from a youth had been full of regrets that always led to more regrets, and it was a burden he'd worn so long he did not know how to release it. It spurred him to loyalty and to duty, as well . . . and were these not honorable things?

He thought of his loyalty, born, he knew, from the inadvertent but very real betrayal of his family to Cromwell's men. At the very least, he had tried to make up for it . . . somehow.

He pressed his lips together in disgust at himself. Damme, if he'd let himself sink into a melancholy. It was a useless state, and he'd be better off getting out of bed and seeing to that duty he so prized and to Catherine's safety.

He looked at Fichet, who was preparing yet another tisane. "How long have I been abed?"

"Two days." The innkeeper held out the steaming cup. "Drink more, please."

"Two days!" Two days more behind Catherine and the traitor de Bauvin. He thrust aside the bedcovers and carefully pushed himself up from the pillows. His head was less dizzy now and though he looked at the cup Fichet held out to him with distaste, he took it and drank it down. He had to be practical. The drink obviously worked to make him feel better, and he'd need all the resources he could, to travel quickly to Versailles.

"Rest now," Fichet said, and moved to push Jack down again, but Jack quickly moved off the bed to his feet, though the action made him dizzy again.

"Enough, friend."

Fichet moved away, then nodded slowly, though he sighed, for he obviously recognized the intractable tone in Jack's voice.

Jack touched the bandages around his ribs. "Do you have any more? I'll need to be held together as tightly as a virgin's garter and stays, for I'll need to travel as soon as I can stand." He carefully moved away from the bed, taking a few hesitant steps before it was clear the dizziness would not strike again... yet. "Which is now, since I'm clearly standing." He nodded at the innkeeper. "I'll be grateful if you could find me a fast horse, for I'll be off as soon as I can get my clothes on."

"But you are not well!" Fichet protested.

Jack shrugged again. "I know. I'm well enough to stand, so I'll be well enough to ride. You've taken me out of danger, and I'm grateful, Fichet. But neither of us knows how de Bauvin will use Catherine for his purposes, and the sooner we arrive in Versailles, the better it will be." He swallowed. "I hope to God it will be better." He did not want to think what, if anything, de Bauvin might have already done.

Fichet nodded, understanding in his eyes. "I do not think he will do anything yet," he said.

This was possible. "Not until he is closer to King Louis," Jack acknowledged. "It takes time before His Majesty allows anyone close to him, for God knows I've tried for ages with little result." He sighed and began unrolling the bandage around his ribs. "Help me tie these tighter, Fichet, for we have a long ride before us."

The innkeeper looked disapproving, but he brought forth more bandages and then, for good measure, a leather jerkin. Jack managed to put on the garment, but only with Fichet's help—easing his arms through the armholes brought more pain. The innkeeper had to lace it up for him, but he did it well. It kept his torso fairly immobile and, with luck, would keep him from inadvertently injuring himself more.

He'd been beaten up badly; the monster had had a crushing grip, and had sliced his left arm so that he could hardly move it. The wound, and he was sure the foul stench of the creature, had given him a fever, and his arm still pounded with heat and pain. It meant he wouldn't be able to fight two-handed, or at least not well. He flexed his left hand. It was weak, and his arm was not strong enough to give a killing thrust, but at least he could hold a dagger and annoy an opponent with it.

He sighed deeply—or tried to, for a red-hot poker seemed to thrust itself into his side as he took in a breath. The breath turned into a cough, which also caused the poker to poke into him again. He groaned. "Oh, God!"

Fichet gave him a stern look. "I, also, will pray that you do not die on the way to Versailles, M. Sir Jack."

Jack gave him a grim look. "You are enjoying this."

An innocent look spread across the man's face. "I do not enjoy another man's suffering." His expression became severe, however. "But if your suffering causes you to be more sensible later, then I will do my best not to interfere."

"You *are* enjoying it," Jack said, but grinned. "Very well, if I suffer, I suffer. Let us go."

Fichet frowned again, but took up bags that Jack noted were already neatly packed. His grin grew wider. The man knew him well, and knew he'd want to leave as soon as he could stand. He took in another deep breath and pain struck him hard. He forced himself not to gasp.

If he could stand at all, that is. He gritted his teeth and put one foot in front of the other, carefully, and then more firmly as the movement eased some of his muscles' stiffness. He'd stand, sit, ride, whatever it took to get to Versailles, even if it killed him.

Just as long as he was sure Catherine was safe, and that he carried out his duty to his king.

Chapter 14

"CATHERINE…" BLANCHE CURLED A ribbon around the tip of her finger in a dreamy manner. "Catherine, do you think the Viscomte Visser particularly handsome?"

Catherine looked down at her needlework and hid her smile. Her sister was young. Just past her fourteenth birthday a few days ago, and they had two days until they were to be presented at court, but Blanche was already attracting notice. How else could it be? The girl was beautiful and merry, and had also a kind heart. What man could resist?

"Mmmm. The Viscomte Visser. Which one of the hundreds of your admirers is he?"

Blanche blushed lightly and shook her head. "I do not have *hundreds*! If you mean the gentlemen who come to visit, you know they are Adrian's friends, not mine."

"Any of whom may become your suitor." Catherine smoothed her hand over her embroidery. It was a skill she suddenly remembered upon gaining the rest of her memories, and she was glad to put her hand to it again. It kept her occupied, and kept her mind from horrors and nightmares and the future.

"So, tell me of this viscomte," she said. Her sister's chatter amused her, and helped pass the hours until the evening's entertainment. Catherine glanced out of the window at the afternoon sky. No clouds marred the deep blue, and she had noticed a few brief wisps of warmer air from time to time. She was glad. She would like to see spring once again.

If she lived long enough.

She dismissed the thought from her mind and gazed at her sister, giving her an encouraging look.

Blanche smiled dreamily. "I am sure you must have seen him. He has black hair, and blue eyes so dark they look violet. He is tall, and very handsome, and Marie says he is too handsome to have any virtue in him, but I do not think she is right! He has always been polite, and has never been pressing in his attentions." She sighed. "I am sure he only sees me as Adrian's little sister."

"Perhaps," Catherine said, and smiled. "But you have now turned fourteen, and I am sure it will only be a short time before he—or another, better suitor—will notice you even more than you are noticed now." She shuddered as if intimidated. "I do not know what we shall do when we are then mobbed in the streets by all your suitors. We shall have to hire guards, no doubt."

Blanche laughed. "You are silly! That will not happen." Her expression sobered. "We are not well off, after all, and I know by now that one must have a good dowry to attract suitors."

Catherine lowered her eyes. She felt trapped; she knew what she planned to do to the marquis would put her family into jeopardy if she did not execute it well, and even then, families of good repute might not wish to marry into a family that was associated with such trouble. But she did not see any other way out of ridding the world of such an evil as the Marquis de Bauvin.

She felt Blanche's hand on her arm and she looked up, grateful for the look of deep affection on her sister's face.

"Thank you," Blanche said.

Catherine raised her brows. "For what?"

"For consenting to be betrothed to the Marquis de Bauvin again."

Catherine shrugged and made herself smile. "He is handsome, rich, and will help restore our fortunes, I'm sure."

Blanche nodded, but looked at her searchingly. "But you do not love him."

Catherine bent her head to her needlework again. *Dieu me sauve*. No, she hated the man. But at least she would not have to marry him. She forced a smile on her face again. "No, but very few women do fall in love with their fiancés. At least his ... manners are without fault."

Her sister nodded, but her expression was still doubtful.

"Besides," Catherine continued. "You are still young to be married."

"But Adrian did not think so!" Blanche protested.

"You are thinking of your viscomte again, I am sure."

Blanche's blush confirmed Catherine's assertion.

"Well—if he is the one I am thinking of—he is young, also, and he will wait a few years before he thinks to wed anyone. Adrian thought to marry you off to restore our fortunes, because I . . . had been kidnapped. Now that I am here, it is not necessary that you wed so soon." She cast Blanche a laughing look. "Besides, think of how many years you have left to flirt with gentlemen before you must be married. Indeed, I wonder if it is at all good that you are to be presented to court in two days, instead of next year." She gazed at Blanche a little more sharply. The girl seemed not so animated as she had been at home, and perhaps more pale and tired. "I am beginning to think that the parties we have attended are fatiguing you more than you admit."

Blanche shrugged. "It is nothing. I have not been sleeping well and have had . . . disturbing dreams." She looked away, as if embarrassed.

Unease uncurled in Catherine's stomach. "Dreams?" She did not discount anything that might be of supernatural nature. "Unpleasant ones?"

"Oh, no!" Blanche said, then blushed very pink. "That is . . . they are nothing, to be sure, only dreams."

Catherine relaxed. It was clear they were not at all unpleasant dreams. She grinned. "Of the viscomte, I assume?" she teased.

Her sister's blushes spread past her cheeks to her ears, confirming Catherine's suspicions. "Oh, they are only dreams! Although . . ." Blanche's face grew concerned. "Although sometimes I think they must arise from sinful thoughts, and cannot be good."

Catherine winced. She knew exactly what kinds of dreams they were. She herself had them, and they reflected everything she had done with Jack on their travels. But Blanche had just turned fourteen, and only recently had come from a very strict convent. Any carnal dreams she might have could not be much more than fantasies of dancing and kissing.

She remembered the viscomte of whom Blanche spoke; he was a well-spoken and handsome young man of no more than seventeen years, too young, she thought, to set up a nursery, but not too young to attract a girl's fancy. He also had in his favor no association that Catherine had been able to discern to the marquis, but had been introduced by the mother of one of Blanche's convent school friends. Surely there could be no objection there.

She gave her sister a reassuring smile. "Most girls dream of young men. I am sure it is only that. If it concerns you, you may make your confession when we next go to Mass, and then think on purer things."

Blanche looked relieved, and Catherine suppressed a wince at her own hypocrisy. She had certainly not thought of purer things . . . but it was, after all, all that she would have of Jack.

She pushed the thought away, for it depressed her. Better she keep to her plans, which had worked so far. What she had revealed of her powers to the Marquis de Bauvin had definitely intrigued him; that he renewed his suit for her hand proved that he still wished to seize the power he had seen in her when he had—

She would not think of that part of the past. The future of her family was more important, as was any clear proof she could present of his sorcery.

She looked up at her sister to see her yawn and rub her eyes. Catherine shook her head. "I think our frivolities have taken their toll, indeed. Go up to your room and rest, Blanche." She smiled. "I think your suitors will be put off if they see shadows under your eyes. Although, if you are to dream of your viscomte again . . ." she teased.

Blanche shook her head and laughed, then rose, not reluctantly, and left the room.

Catherine watched after her again in concern. Perhaps she was worrying overmuch, and made too much of what she saw, but it seemed Blanche had gone to her room with an eager light in her eyes, and her movements were almost sensual.

The tendril of unease within Catherine unfurled into dread. Her sister was growing up, of course, and was experiencing the first urges of a woman. But the girl had been well protected, unlike herself. She was an innocent, and had not until recently been around many men at all.

Her hand grew still over her needlework, and she stared out the window to the building in which the marquis lodged. She did not know how far de Bauvin's sorcery could reach, or what exactly it could do...except for what she herself had experienced. She looked down at her lap to find she had misstitched a pattern in her work, and she forced herself to undo it and stitch again, for the discipline gave her mind focus.

De Bauvin's sorcery could reach far. After all, he had sent the demon to Paris while he had been at his home near Rouen. She had defeated the creature, but not easily. The marquis was that strong, at the very least.

Therefore, it would be nothing at all for him to affect her family from across the street.

Fear seized her, and she rose hastily, dropping her needlework heedlessly to the floor. Blanche. No. *Mon Dieu*, let her not be cursed, as well.

She ran up the stairs as quickly as her skirts allowed and threw open Blanche's door. The curtains had been drawn against the light, but at least a dim reflection of the light outside should have shone through. There was no light but the weak, fluttering flames in the hearth, which should have let the cold outdoors in, but did not. It was hot and humid, as if all of summer had poured itself into this small room, and a heady, musky scent permeated the very air.

A moan from the bed made Catherine look toward the sound. She shuddered. A mist floated above it, above Blanche, who lay on the bed, her eyes closed, her head moving restlessly on the pillow. The mist moved down, taking the shape of a man, and little strands of grey curled down from it and touched Blanche's lips, breasts, and thighs.

Catherine swallowed down bile and clutched her cross in her hand. She ran to the bed and struck at the mist, but aside from a brief disturbance of the form, her hand passed through it. Her cross... she took her cross in her hand and punched her fist through the mist again.

The mist-man twisted as if in pain, but it was not enough—he clutched at Blanche as if she gave him life. Frantically she searched for Blanche's cross—it was not on her neck! It sat, tossed on the end of its necklace, on the table next to the bed. Catherine seized it and flung it over Blanche's head.

A shriek sounded in the room, and it tore into her heart, for she feared it came from Blanche. But the mist-creature seemed to take a more solid form, looking very much like the Viscomte Visser, and then faded. The room's air became cooler, and the fire in the hearth began to flicker normally on the wood that was piled within. The heavy, seductive scent was gone.

Catherine sat suddenly on the edge of the bed and put her hands over her face. *Mon Dieu.* It was different from what had happened to her, and it was clear that Blanche did not object to it. But the girl thought it was only a dream, and did not know what was happening. If her sister's fatigue and shadowed eyes were signs, it surely meant that once again de Bauvin sought to steal the power he had tried to force from her those many months ago.

She raised her head and let her hands fall to her lap as she turned to gaze at her sister. The girl rested quietly now and breathed more evenly—a natural sleep, she thought. She touched Blanche's cheek gently—it was cold, as if she had been walking in a winter storm.

Catherine's heart beat wildly, and she felt for a pulse—yes, it was there, very slow and faint, but steady. She let out a breath. She did not want to think what would have happened had she not stopped this... this thing. Gently she drew up the bedcovers over the girl, tucking them in firmly around her, then went to the fireplace and put more wood upon the fire. The flames licked at the dry timber, and the light grew brighter in the room.

She went back to Blanche, sitting on the bed again. She had failed to protect her sister, although she supposed that she should be glad Blanche had not been violated as she had been. She let out a shuddering breath, and shuddered again, and then found that her cheeks were wet, and she could not control her weeping.

Pressing her hand to her mouth, she managed to keep down the sounds her sobs tore from her heart, but the tears did not stop. She gazed at Blanche, so still in the bed, and was glad her sister was so deeply asleep. She did not want to have to explain her sorrow, her fears, or why she was here in this room.

She let herself weep a little longer, then dried her

face. Gazing at Blanche, she touched the cross that she had found on the bed table. It was very like hers, plain, with a tiny ruby and small pearl set in it. She turned it over, then set it down on Blanche's chest again. Had her Tante Anna also given one to Blanche? Perhaps. It comforted her a little to think that she and her sister had crosses that were alike.

She would tell Blanche tomorrow that she had bad dreams and that she wanted to share a room until the nightmares disappeared. She did not really need her sister's presence, but she was sure Blanche would need hers. She would also make sure her sister wore her cross at all times.

Catherine rose and went to her room. Soon they would be presented to court, and the marquis would be there, as well. It would be her opportunity to accuse him of sorcery and of being a possible traitor. She had no tangible proof of the latter, but she could send a message to Felice and she at least could be a witness to the sorcery.

She gazed again at Blanche, at how very still and pale she was, and once again felt her pulse. It was there, and steady, but the girl still did not move except to breathe very slightly.

Catherine swallowed. She hoped she had done the right thing and that Blanche would awaken after a few hours. Closing her eyes, she focused her mind, concentrating on any sensation that might indicate evil. The air remained cool and the scents she smelled were only those of woodsmoke and the faint lavender scent that Blanche always wore. No prickling sensation touched her hands, or sharp ache came to her back.

She opened her eyes. For now, all was safe. Blanche would be better for some rest. In another hour she would check on her sister again, and then if she was still not awake, she would have Marie watch over her. Unless Adrian insisted and unless Blanche awoke, she would not attend any balls or parties tonight.

Adrian. Fear hit her sharply again. Her brother, also, had looked tired and worn . . . perhaps it was not only estate affairs that had made him seem so weary. Dear heaven. Did de Bauvin sap Adrian of his life, as well? She thought wildly of taking her brother and sister away quickly, but she knew it would be of no avail; de Bauvin would only follow them. She had to expose his sorcery as soon as possible. But how? How?

She shook her head. For now, she needed to pretend she suspected nothing. Now that it was possible Adrian was also under some kind of spell, he might tell de Bauvin of her suspicions if she revealed them. Despair tugged at her spirits at the thought of one more obstacle, but she suppressed it. She could not give in to hopelessness.

Catherine left the room, going down to the parlor again, for it was possible they might still have visitors. But there were no more, and she was glad to be alone. She was content plying her needle and plotting the downfall of the Marquis de Bauvin.

However, the next morning, Blanche was the same as before. Catherine had thought that perhaps sleep would help her recover, but if so, she was far from recovering. She gazed at her sister resting peacefully. Blanche still had not moved from the tucked-in position that Catherine had set her. Even at her most fatigued, the girl had never slept so long or so still.

"Mademoiselle, she has not moved except to breathe—I would almost think her dead if not for that," Marie said, when Catherine had summoned her.

"Hush! Do not say such things," Catherine said,

for a shiver of dread crawled up her spine at the maid's words.

"I wonder if she is ill, mademoiselle."

"I... I do not know. We must find a physician immediately. Go, call a footman, and send for one." Marie left.

Catherine sat on the edge of the bed and took Blanche's hand in hers. It was lax, but warm. She leaned over and shook the girl's shoulder, then slapped her hand. No response came from her, only the still-steady breathing. Desperation choked Catherine, and she seized both of Blanche's shoulders, shaking her whole upper body. "Please, please, Blanche, wake up. Please!"

The girl responded no more than a rag doll might, her head rolling back, and her arms flopping to each side.

No. No. Catherine clenched her hands into fists. This was her fault. She should have insisted on leaving Blanche behind in Normandy... but if she had, for all she knew, the marquis would have done worse. She did not know what to do. Pressing her hands over her face, she moaned, rocking herself back and forth. She needed to do something, something to revive Blanche.

A knock sounded at the door; it was the doctor, and Adrian followed him, gazing at Blanche with clear worry.

The doctor was a portly and intelligent-looking man, who bowed in a competent manner and looked with concern at her sister sleeping so still in the bed.

Hope rose. Perhaps it was something of natural origin—perhaps it was something easily cured by cupping or bleeding, with some medicine. Quickly, she told him of Blanche's condition the night before, leaving out the supernatural aspects, for she was not certain the man would believe her.

She watched as the doctor bent and listened to the girl's heart, felt her pulse, but after the long, silent examination, he shook his head.

"I can find nothing wrong, Mlle de la Fer, other than her unresponsiveness. She does not even seem to have a fever."

Catherine nodded.

"It could have been a fever the night before." He shook his head again. "I will give you a tisane in case the fever returns, and then I will bleed her only a little, since she is not in a fever now." He looked at her and Adrian kindly. "Do not worry. She should awaken soon, I think. If she still does not, then send for me again and I will see what can be done." He nodded toward Blanche. "If you will help me with the bleeding, I will be most grateful."

Catherine stepped forward and held the bowl, and she closed her eyes briefly and gritted her teeth at the sight of the blood that dripped slowly down her sister's almost snow-white skin. Anger and grief pounded behind her lips, wanting release. But she swallowed it down, waiting for the doctor to be done with the bleeding.

It was, indeed, only a little blood, but it seemed to Catherine to take too long. The doctor seemed satisfied, however, and she helped press a small pad to the wound as he wrapped a bandage around it securely.

He bowed again before he left. "I will admit I have not seen the like," he said, shaking his head. "But she is only a little pale, her breathing is normal, and her temperature is neither too high nor too low. If I did not know any better, I would say she is merely sleeping."

"But she does not waken when I shake her," Catherine said.

"Yes," the doctor replied. "That is the thing. She does not waken." He hesitated. "It would not hurt, I think, to have a priest say prayers over her."

Dread chilled her. "Are you saying she might die?" There, she said it.

He shook his head, smiling kindly. "No, I do not think so. But prayers would not hurt. I have seen many strange things, and even seen such evils as the plague strike some and avoid others who lived in the very same house. For all that we doctors learn what we can of the body, there are things that are also beyond our knowledge." He sighed. "As I say, having a priest pray for her cannot hurt." He bowed once more, then left.

She turned back to the bed and found Adrian sitting there, Blanche's hand in his. The room's drawn curtains cast a shadow on his face, making him seem aged, even skeletal. He *was* thinner than he had been before, Catherine thought, alarmed. He looked up at her, clear grief in his eyes. "Will she be well, do you think, sister?"

He does care for us. The thought brought a certain relief to her, for at least what influence de Bauvin had over her brother had not stripped him of affection. Adrian cared at least for Blanche.

"I wonder if you are feeling well yourself, Adrian. I think I shall ask the doctor to return to attend you," she said.

He waved a dismissive hand. "I am well, only tired. Do not concern yourself with me—I need only rest for a while, *after* I am sure Blanche is well." Stubbornness sounded clearly in his voice, and she remembered he would argue into the night if he felt he was right. She gazed at the shadows beneath his eyes, and grief filled her heart. She could not weary him any more than he already was; he needed whatever strength was left to him.

Perhaps Adrian's care for their family was stronger than his loyalty to de Bauvin. Perhaps he would help her if she revealed to him that the marquis was behind Blanche's illness and that she suspected the man of sorcery.

She went to her brother and laid her hand on his arm. "I think Blanche will recover, but we should also call a priest."

He frowned, clearly perplexed. "Why a priest? If she will recover, then what is the difference whether a priest attends her or not?"

She wet her lips, wondering if she should tell him her suspicions now. "It . . . it could be sorcery."

He stared at her, incredulous. "'Sorcery'? I think not."

She sat next to him and clasped his hand. "Why not? I tell you, I have seen supernatural things while I lived in Paris, and this smells of the most dark enchantment. *En vrai*, we have had sorcery very close to us." As close as across the street, she thought.

He stared at her skeptically. "Catherine, you have been ill, as well, and have lost your memory. I have never seen any such, and to assume that Blanche's illness was caused by some sorcerer is foolishness."

Anger flared, and she released his hand, moving back from him. "Then what do you think it is? She had no illness before this, and in fact is a very healthy girl. It was not until the Marquis de Bauvin came to live in the rooms across from us that she became ill."

Her brother stared at her for a long moment, then shook his head. "You are joking, but this is no laughing matter, sister. Are you saying that the marquis—my friend, and friend to our family, your *betrothed*—is a sorcerer?"

Catherine gazed him firmly. "Yes."

He rose suddenly, anger clear in his face. "You know nothing, Catherine. You know nothing of what happened in the nearly eight months you were gone." He walked to the fireplace, his back to her, staring into the fire with his hands clenched into fists.

"I did not tell you," he continued. "You were ill, and just returned to us." He cast an unreadable glance at her before he returned to gazing at the fire. "You think that kidnappers beat you and took you away."

Catherine sat, frozen. Did he know her story for a lie, then?

"I am sure it's not so for I found no trace of strangers when I questioned our neighbors about your disappearance. Our father—" He said the word as if he spoke a curse. "Our father beat you. He beat you severely, before you disappeared." He waved a dismissive hand. "If you ran away, I do not blame you. I hated him, our father. He was stupid and let our land go to ruin, so that we had nothing but our name to marry off." Adrian's voice was full of loathing, breaking Catherine's heart. "He beat all of us, except for Blanche, and that was only because she was with the convent sisters from the time she was very small. I think the beatings eventually killed our mother and her unborn child."

Catherine felt ill. She had thought Adrian too young to have known about their mother. She thought she had protected both her brother and sister, but it was clear she had not. Perhaps that was why she had acquired her affliction—it was punishment for not caring for her brother and her mother well enough. She gazed at Blanche, so quietly asleep on the bed. Or her sister, for that matter.

"If you knew that our father had beaten me, and that he had agreed to my marriage with the marquis, why did you agree to Blanche's betrothal, and then to mine when I returned?" She turned to look at her brother, and saw that he had moved away from the fire, gazing at her earnestly.

"Because you did not seem averse to him, and because it was to reward him."

Unease seeped into her. "Reward him for what?"

He stepped to her and took her hands, smiling at her. "For ridding us of our father, Catherine, and protecting you."

Faintness made her close her eyes, but she managed to take a step back and pull her hands away from him. "Protecting....Rid us of him...." She swallowed. "What do you mean, Adrian?"

"What do you think?" His voice turned harsh. "Our father is dead. Did you not wonder about it? The marquis found our father beating you severely, and intervened on your behalf. Father attacked de Bauvin for his trouble, and wounded him badly. I saw the bandages on the marquis myself when I returned home, and he explained it all to me."

Catherine felt ill. The marquis had explained everything away—the blood, the attack, her disappearance. He was now a hero to her brother. It was no wonder Adrian would hear no ill of the man.

"I...I did not remember. I thought perhaps Father had died many years ago." It was true, at least at first. But then she had not questioned, for she had been too occupied thinking of the marquis's threat to them.

And thinking of Jack. She wished he were here; she wanted his warmth and generosity and strength as she wanted heaven itself. But she had to fight the marquis without him. It was clear that the marquis would attack or use anyone close to her. Jack, at least, was safe; he would be in Breda with King Charles at this moment. As long as he did not return to her, he would be no threat to the marquis, and would no doubt be left alone. She could not even send for Fichet or Felice—they were her friends, and she had burdened them enough.

She forced herself to take her brother's hand—it was cold, as cold as that of a man who was on the point of death. She looked into his eyes. There was a feverish look in them, and she knew that she could not tell him of what she knew of the marquis, nor of her dread, knowing that what was left of her family was under dire threat. If the marquis was not drawing out the life force from her brother, as well, at least his influence was still very strong. She would not be able to convince her brother of anything, not even that whatever the marquis had done to kill their father, it was still wrong.

"I am sorry," she said. "I did not know."

Adrian's expression softened. "Of course you did not, poor Catherine! I would not be surprised if you lost your memory because of our father's brutal treatment of you. I tell you, I wished to kill him myself when I found what he had done to you. But the marquis told me all would be well, and that he would help ensure our fortunes would rise again." He paused, his expression looking lost and alone. "I tried to kill father myself after our mother died." His face suddenly crumpled in grief. "She looked very much like Blanche, you know. But I was too small, and I was in bed a week from our father's beating."

Tears came to Catherine's eyes, and she took Adrian into her arms, holding him as if he were still a little boy. He was a young man, but younger than she, and had only a month ago reached his nineteenth year. She remembered Adrian being ill in bed, but had been kept away from him because she was told his illness was contagious.

"I am sorry," she said softly. "So sorry. Forget what I have said. It was foolishness."

Adrian parted from her, and he smiled. "It is nothing, sister. You could not help any of it—what could a girl do against one such as our father?"

"I was the oldest—"

He held up his hand. "And I was the heir and now the Comte de la Fer. I am almost as old as you." His expression grew earnest and fierce. "I swear to you, I shall not fail this time. Not this time. Our estate shall grow richer, even if it means I work the fields myself." He smiled, and humor returned to his face. "Although I doubt it will come to that. Our friend de Bauvin will help us, you'll see."

It was clear she could say nothing against the marquis to convince her brother of the man's evil. Even if she were to tell him what the man had done to her, he would say that it was because her mind had been disordered . . . and it was clear her brother was as burdened by her father's legacy as she had been. She gazed at Adrian's determined face, and knew that it would kill him to think that he had failed to protect her from de Bauvin, as he had failed—impossible as it was—to protect their mother. It was not his fault, after all; he had been too young, only a child. She took his too-cold hand and brought it up to her cheek in affection. "I am fortunate, indeed, to have a brother such as you," she said.

His grateful smile was her reward; it warmed her, and she knew that once de Bauvin was exposed, all would be well. She was not at all sure what she planned would succeed. There was a large possibility that she might be killed. But even that would achieve her ends: at least it would show de Bauvin for the sorcerer he was; and if she died in the attempt, it would ensure that the marquis would never bother her family again.

But meanwhile, Adrian needed protection. She thought of the cross she wore, and the one Blanche wore. They were alike, and certainly seemed to banish the spirit from possessing Blanche, in addition to giving her own self a sense of protection and guidance.

She squeezed her brother's hand. "You will think me foolish . . . but do you wear a cross?"

He shrugged. "I did once. But I seemed to have misplaced it."

Putting her hand to her neck, she held her cross tightly, then took off the necklace. She placed it around her brother's neck instead and smiled. "Wear this for me, and keep it with you always. Never take it off." He began to shake his head and opened his mouth to speak, but she put her fingers over his lips. "No, say nothing. I know you think it foolishness. But wear it for me. I have nothing to give to you that is my own except this."

An embarrassed but pleased expression crossed his face, and he took her hand in his. "I thank you, then, and will wear it always, as you say." He grinned. "I will even find a priest to pray over Blanche. As the doctor said, it cannot hurt."

Catherine smiled and squeezed his hand again.

"Thank you." He gave her another hug and turned to the door. She looked after him as he left and let out a long sigh.

She felt too, too vulnerable without her cross. But it was necessary that her brother be protected. She should have noted earlier the changes in him, but she had been too concerned with the imminent threat to Blanche.

However, she had changed, as well. She had grown stronger since Jack had found her in the alley, and more skilled with the sword. She knew she was stronger than most women—Jack had said so himself. Tomorrow she would be presented at King Louis's court, and before she went, she would make sure she went to confession and received absolution for her sins. If she were to fight evil, she would have to be in as pure a state as she could be, especially if she did not have the protection of her cross.

Tomorrow she would fight the Marquis de Bauvin and would need all the aid she could gather. Jack would not be there, and she was glad, for it meant he would be safe. She thought of Adrian and went to Blanche's bedside to hold her hand. With luck, her strength and her faith would be enough to save them all.

Chapter 15

GETTING ON THE HORSE THRUST THE red-hot poker sensation once more into Jack's side, and it did not stop when his horse started moving. In fact, it made everything worse.

He was sure he still had a fever, and was frankly glad of it; it blurred the days of travel into one. The fog of fever dulled his mind so that the fiery pain turned into a numbing ache—dear God, his whole body into a numbing ache—that only flared into intensity when he got up and down from his horse, and when, damn it, Fichet insisted they rest.

Rest. There was no time. *Two days*. Two more days behind than he had been. Impatience coupled with fear and gave birth to speed, or as much as Jack could stand, given his dizziness and pain. He'd not give in to it, though, for he'd been on marches before and as badly injured. He tried to remember that when he almost fell from his horse at one stop.

"Food," Fichet said firmly, and the sternness of

his voice was laced with anxiety. "You must eat, and then rest."

Two days. "I'm two days behind, Robert."

Fichet's frown was clearly anxious now, and Jack vaguely remembered he almost never used the man's first name unless he was *in extremis*.

"You will have however many days *le bon Dieu* desires, and I am sure He desires that you rest and eat."

Jack began to laugh, but the hot poker in his side cut it off. "God told you that, did He?" he managed to say.

"I have the common sense, M. Sir Jack, which is given all men if they so choose to use it," Fichet said severely. "Which you have not." The innkeeper nevertheless held him up gently as he almost fell from his horse, and took him into the farmhouse at which they had stopped.

More of Mme Felice's tisane was forced into him, and he managed to swallow down food, but he remembered very little of anything else. He might have slept; he did find himself jerking awake once more on his horse. He congratulated himself; he had managed to stay on the animal, at least.

Not, however, for long, although the days and nights had run together, and he had stopped counting the passing days or even acknowledged that time had passed. Once more he dozed, and a shout roused him—he was falling.

He could not open his eyes, though he tried. Hands caught him, and he felt himself carried into somewhere warm. He tasted more of Mme Felice's tisane, and did not resist swallowing it. He had learned by now that it gave him some surcease from the constant pain.

He dreamed.

Catherine was in his dreams. She smiled at him, her green eyes alight with love for him, dear God, yes, love. But he could see fear in her eyes, as well. She was in danger, he knew. It was why he traveled to Versailles, to save her. He remembered he was supposed to do something else—tell King Louis of treason. But Louis was horse's dung compared to Catherine, and King Charles, too, by God.

"M. Sir Jack! You may be delirious, but you will not say such things of our king!" It was Fichet's voice.

He opened his eyes. This time he was clearly in a well-to-do inn or hotel, though it was not Fichet's.

Fichet's expression was a mix of indignation and relief. Jack gazed at him, then glanced around the room. "Are we in Versailles yet, and how many days have I been unconscious this time?"

Fichet clutched his hair in clear exasperation. "This is my reward, *par Dieu*! I nurse you, I almost carry you myself on my back from Rouen to Versailles—"

"Oh, we're in Versailles? Excellent." Jack pushed himself gingerly upright, remembering the first time he had done so, and managed to avoid the extreme nausea he had experienced earlier. "And carry me on your back? Unless you took the form of a horse, you exaggerate, my friend."

Fichet gave him a bitter look. "Each time we have come to a lodgings, I have taken you from your horse and then back onto it again. It is *une merveille* I have not broken my back by now."

Jack pushed himself to the edge of his bed, and though he winced at the pain in both his ribs and his head, the wince also held remorse. "Aye, I'm a damnable patient, Fichet, and I'm grateful to you."

The innkeeper sniffed haughtily. "*Pardonnez moi,*

M. Sir Jack, but you are not. Later, perhaps, but you are never grateful when you are ill."

"Very well, I'm an ungrateful wretch," Jack replied impatiently, irritation banishing his remorse. "I'm whatever you wish. Just help me get this jerkin on, will you?" He pushed himself up and almost vomited from the dizziness that struck him. He gritted his teeth and swallowed.

Fichet sighed. "You are still ill. You still have the fever. And yet you will not rest unless you fall from your horse in a faint. Where is the sense of it?" He held out the jerkin and helped to guide Jack's arms through the armholes, then quickly laced it.

Jack took a careful breath—the pain seemed not as bad as it had been, but he noticed it was becoming more difficult to breathe regardless of whether he wore the bandages or the jerkin. He caught Fichet's worried expression, and shook his head at him.

"Just after I find Catherine, Fichet, and deliver King Charles's message to Louis... just after that, and I'll do as you'll say. I promise you." He briefly pressed the palms of his hands to his eyes and then caught sight of himself in the window's reflection. "God's blood, I look like the very Devil, and feel like I've come to hell."

"*C'est bonne chance pour moi!*" Fichet said, his voice dripping with sarcasm. "Instead of being in hell, we are in Versailles, which means I need not carry you upon my back any longer. How stupid of me not to have mentioned how ill you are before!"

Jack groaned. "Enough, Fichet! Just get me on a horse once more and point me to Catherine's lodgings, and I will leave you be."

Fichet gave him another disgruntled look, and let him lean on him out of the room. "If you had not slept for two days, I would not let you leave here."

"Two days! You should have awaken—" He caught Fichet's sharp look, and closed his mouth. No use aggravating the man any more than he had already done, and he knew he'd tried Fichet's patience throughout their journey. He bore Fichet's grumbling, therefore, as he helped him onto a fresh horse, and said nothing when he followed him on another. Besides, he was not sure his friend would show him the way if he protested.

In truth, he was not sure he'd make it to the de la Fers' lodgings, much less to King Louis's court. He held the reins of his horse tightly in one hand, and the other held onto the horse's mane. It gave him some stability; he felt he might fall any moment from dizziness. He was glad, though, to be outside. The silhouette of the king's chateau showed in the distance against the twilight sky, and a cold breeze brushed his fevered skin. It felt good after the inn, which he thought had been too warm.

But the gladness quickly passed. The pain in his ribs had become a fire, and his head pounded. He wished he had taken more of Mme Felice's tisane before he had left, but it was too late now. They'd come to Catherine's lodgings soon, and then perhaps he could rest for a little before he'd go to Louis's court and demand entrance.

He saw with relief that Fichet rode to the middle of a long line of buildings and stopped. But Fichet only dismounted and then stared fixedly at him, not coming any closer.

Jack rolled his eyes in exasperation, then closed them, for the motion made him dizzy. "No, you do not have to help me down this time. I will allow you to knock at the door and see if they will admit us."

Fichet gave a satisfied nod, turned to the hotel door, and entered.

Jack let himself lean forward on his horse, resting his head on the animal's neck. Fatigue washed over him, the world twisted and turned around him, and he struggled for breath.

Dear God, he was ill. He hadn't wanted to show how badly off he was to Fichet, but he suspected the man knew. They'd fought in wars together before, and had tended each other's wounds. He could hold on for a little while, just a little while, and it would all be done. Then he could rest, and perhaps Catherine would see him. He drew in a shallow, unsatisfying breath, and was glad of a sudden cooling breeze that wafted across his face.

He wanted to see Catherine again. The pain in his ribs was nothing to the pain of wanting her and knowing she would most likely marry the marquis . . . or worse. Was there something worse than marrying that traitor, that sorcerer? He did not know. He needed to save her from it, soon, whatever it was.

A faint voice pierced the fog that seemed to cover his senses. "M. Sir Jack!"

He lifted his head, and Fichet's face swam into view. "Just resting a bit," he said. "I'll be well in a moment." He looked about him—yes, they were in Versailles. Catherine. She was supposed to be here, but he did not see her. "Where is she?"

"She is at court—she is to be presented this evening."

"Hell." The air around him seemed to spin in bright swirls. "Hell." He made himself sit upright and took in a deeper, painful breath. "Very well. We'll go. I've got the message from the king to go to the king . . . the other king."

"Give me the paper, M. Sir Jack. I will bring it to the king."

"No." Anger flared, bringing the world into sharp focus. He took in another painful breath and stared at Fichet's grim face. "Has the marquis gone, as well?"

Silence, then: "He has. He is betrothed to her, so must accompany her to court."

Betrothed. The word echoed in his skull, but he shook his head. If she was, it was unwillingly, he'd stake his sorry life on it. He remembered something else...treason. If the marquis was going to use Catherine in some way to strike at the king, this would be the time to do it. He forced himself to sit straighter in his saddle. "I'll take the paper. Then I'll be done. Just a little while longer."

"You might die, M. Sir Jack."

Jack gave a laugh that caused him to gasp with pain. "Then I'll take down the marquis before I do, and we'll dance in hell together." He leaned forward and spurred his horse forward to the darkening silhouette of the palace of Versailles.

He'd get the message to Louis, never fear. But first he'd see Catherine. That would be heaven enough for eternity.

She had worn a similar dress the day before she was to wed the Marquis de Bauvin. It was the same in color—a deep green that did much to enhance her coloring and show off the whiteness of her shoulders. Catherine did not care. It suited her purposes—decorative enough for the king's court, and voluminous enough to hide a dagger.

She had hoped to wear a dress of a more masculine cut, so that she could possibly wear a sword for decorative effect. But she had argued in vain with Adrian, and she thought it best to stop persuading him when she saw a suspicious expression on his face. She was sure that he had not told the marquis of their conversation about sorcery the night before. However, she was not certain he'd not warn de Bauvin of her suspicions if she persisted.

The dagger might be enough. Jack had taught her how to use it, although she had not perfected her aim in throwing it. She could now fight two-handed, however, with a sword in her right hand and a dagger in her left, and could even switch hands. If necessary, she would see if she could seize a sword from a courtier, if the sword was not merely decorative. She hoped it would be enough.

"Magnificent."

She gazed at her brother, who looked enthusiastically out the coach window at the chateau of their king. The setting sun set the stones to fire, and the palace glowed as if it were made of gold. It was appropriate, she thought, for Louis, who had been compared to Apollo, the Greek sun god.

"Yes," she said. "I only wish Blanche could see it." Her sister was still in her deep sleep; another visit from the doctor yielded no results, and prayers from the local priest only made her shift a little and breathe deeper. Her pulse had not slowed, however, though she was still pale. That was something, at least.

She felt Adrian's hand in hers. "I wish she were here to see it, too," he said. "She would have liked it and marveled over everything." He paused. "She will be well soon, I am sure." His voice did not sound hopeful.

Catherine knew better than to try to convince him that Blanche's sleep had its source in sorcery, however. He still would not hear of it, even after the doctor himself declared that he could do nothing.

It would not matter shortly. Soon she would be at Louis's court, and then she would do her best to kill the marquis. She had thought it might be enough to accuse him of sorcery. But Blanche's unnatural sleep needed a cure. She could not have the marquis touch her—the thought made her ill, and who knew what he would do if he had the chance. She could, however, kill him, and that must end the spell.

Catherine had gone to confession, and had dared ask the priest there if he knew anything of sorcery. He knew perhaps a little more than Père Doré, and he was clearly curious why she had asked. But she had slipped out quickly to the sanctuary after being given absolution, and if the priest had come to look for her, there were enough penitents who sat in the pews so that it would be difficult to single her out.

It made her remember Père Doré, however. She wondered if he had received word from the cardinal regarding her stigmata, or if he had even traveled to Versailles to consult with him. She would be glad to see the priest again; she had appreciated his candor and his kindness, and she suspected that it was he who had let bread fall among the pews when she sought a place to sleep away from the alley.

The coach halted with a jerk, pulling her out of her memories. She took in a deep breath. It was time. She smiled nervously at her brother as he handed her down from the coach.

He smiled in return. "I am nervous, as well," he said. "It is not every day one is presented to one's king." He looked to the steps of the palace. "The Marquis de Bauvin will be there; he may already have arrived, in fact." His expression lightened a little. "It's fortunate we have a friend already at court."

Catherine made herself smile and nod, tamping down the despair she felt. "Fortunate, indeed," she said, and walked forward. The dagger in her pocket tapped against her leg; it gave her an odd reassurance.

The doors to the palace opened silently and she would have almost thought they opened without human aid, for the footmen were entirely quiet and their attire seemed as one with the magnificence of the king's home. She glanced at her brother, and amusement at his round-eyed wonder pierced through her despair. "We must not stare so," she said, her voice teasing. "We will seem like country peasants."

"We are as good as country peasants compared to this," Adrian replied, his eyes still round and taking in every detail. "However, I will refrain from pointing."

She managed a chuckle. "Good."

They walked forward, and she gave her brother a nudge when she encountered the haughtily expectant look of yet another magnificently dressed servant who stood at a large, imposing door.

"Adrian, Comte de la Fer, and his sister, Mlle Catherine de la Fer," he stammered. The servant bowed and moved aside.

Light flowed out in beams as the doors opened. Everything glittered with light, and there must have been a million candles, Catherine thought, to have achieved the effect of noon in summer. Her eyes went directly to the focus of the light, and she could not help sinking into the lowest of curtsies in front of the king. She was supposed to, of course. But this was so much the opposite of her time in the dark rankness of the alley in Paris, it seemed all a fantasy, unreal.

She glanced from the corners of her eyes at her

brother; he, too, had sunk onto his knees in a very low and elegant bow, and did not move until a slight gesture of the king's hand bade them rise.

Catherine rose and stole a look at Louis. He seemed very young to be a king—he *was* young, she realized in surprise. He could not be much older than herself. The king had a solemn expression on his face, but it lightened as he looked at her, and then he transferred his gaze to Adrian.

"We welcome you to our court."

"My sister and I are grateful, Your Majesty, to be allowed in your presence," Adrian replied formally, and made obeisance again, according to protocol. "May I present my sister, Catherine de la Fer." She curtsied low once more.

"You have another sister, do you not?"

Another surprise. She had heard the king worked hard to be informed of everything in his kingdom, but she did not think it extended to a very young sister of a provincial comte.

Adrian bowed again, formally and precisely. "I give you my great apologies, Your Majesty. We were commanded into your presence, which we of course could not refuse. But my youngest sister is ill, and we wished nothing but health to attend your court, as is fitting."

There was silence, then the king inclined his head in approval. "Your loyalty and inconvenience to yourself are commended. We are pleased you have attended us, and wish you to enjoy the pleasures here in Versailles." The king inclined his head again; it signaled the end of their audience, and Catherine let out a breath she had not realized she was holding. They had passed the king's scrutiny, it seemed.

It also signaled the end of an opportunity to

inform the king of de Bauvin's sorcery. Frustration made her grit her teeth, but she knew there was nothing to be done; the protocol of court was strict, and if she had spoken out at any time, she and her brother would have been severely reprimanded, and her chance to inform the king of anything would have dropped to nil.

She curtsied low once again and gazed at the courtiers to either side of Louis. There was a cardinal—Cardinal Mazarin, his prime minister, who stood just to the side and a little behind the throne—and a priest stood beside the cardinal. She recognized him—it was Père Doré. The priest gazed at her gravely and gave a slight nod, and her depression lifted a little at the sight of a familiar face. Perhaps Père Doré had come to Versailles to discuss her stigmata with the cardinal, as he had promised, although she had thought he would write to his superior rather than come to court himself. Hope rose. Surely she could speak with him as soon as the ceremonies were over.

But it took a long time for the ceremonies to be over. More than a few nobles and dignitaries were presented and put forth their concerns, all of which were duly written down. Catherine noted with amusement that the king's refrain was mostly "we shall see." No wonder Jack had been so frustrated when dealing with King Louis.

Thinking of Jack depressed her spirits, for she wished he was here. She focused her mind on the ceremonies and those people who were presented to the king.

A prickling of her hands pulled her attention from the proceedings. She looked about her for the source. There. The Marquis de Bauvin entered, elegant in red and gold, and carrying a gold-topped black walking stick. He made a low, precise bow before the king as he was announced. She watched the faces of the king's courtiers as the marquis was presented, but there was no change in their expressions. He was just another noble who had come to attend court.

But the prickling in her hands became an ache, more so when the marquis turned to look at them. She glanced at her brother; Adrian looked eagerly at de Bauvin, as if he had seen a long-lost friend. Then she looked at the marquis, and the ache in her hands turned into pain.

A dark glint showed in the folds and lace of the marquis's cravat, and she looked quickly away toward the king, as if he took all her attention. She kept her eyes on the throne; it was an excuse not to look at de Bauvin and be drawn in to gazing at the amulet he wore. Despair clutched at her; she had hoped that with the return of her memories when she touched de Bauvin, her affliction would disappear. But it seemed the stigmata came back in response to the evil of the marquis's amulet, and had little to do with the spell he had cast on her to lose her memory.

She cast a surreptitious look at her hands. She was glad she had chosen to wear sturdy gloves—they would conceal for a while any blood that might seep from her hands. The weight of her dagger in her pocket comforted her; if he tried to take control of her, she could use it to defend herself.

The threat was wider than merely to herself, however. De Bauvin must be behind Blanche's illness; there could be no other explanation for the misty visitation. De Bauvin sought power. It was reasonable to assume he had used his sorcery to take what he could of it from Blanche.

And now he had the amulet. She recalled that it was after her cousin Jeanette had disappeared that he had used it on her, to subdue her in her bedroom. Now he wore it again. Her reasoning brought her to rising dread. If he wore it now, then it meant he wished to subdue someone, and it was wholly possible it was not some woman in a bed.

Catherine once again examined the king. He seemed distracted, his attention drawn away from the petitioners. From time to time the king would glance at the crowd of people in the audience chamber, frown, then pull his gaze back to the person in front of him. She saw de Bauvin move closer to the petitioners by the king, and Louis's gaze flicked to the marquis. . . .

There was a pause in the proceedings, and she saw Louis give an impatient gesture. "It is enough for now. We will continue on the morrow."

There was a surprised silence from the officials surrounding him, and Cardinal Mazarin looked disapproving. This was not according to the usual process, and King Louis was one who was very conscious of routine and duty. But he was the king, and the courtiers gave way, bowing politely.

She noted that the marquis moved toward His Majesty slowly, speaking with various other guests as he worked his way closer. Catherine glanced at Père Doré again . . . he was not far, and perhaps she could talk to the priest before the marquis got any closer to the king.

She turned to Adrian—he was watching the marquis as if compelled, his eyes looked more tired than ever, and her heart sank. She could only hope that the cross she had given him would protect him somehow. She touched his arm and shook it a little.

"Adrian...if you do not mind, I would like to talk to Père Doré—he is the priest who stands next to Cardinal Mazarin. Père Doré was my confessor while I stayed in Paris." She glanced at the marquis from the corners of her eyes. He was moving closer to the king—no, she would only pretend to see the priest. She would not be fast enough to speak to Père Doré first. She would have to try to get to Louis before the marquis did.

Adrian drew his gaze from the marquis, slowly, as if in a daze. "What?"

"The priest, Père Doré, he was my confessor, and I wish to speak to him," she said, her voice unsteady.

Her brother waved her away as if she were an annoying fly. "Go," he said.

She did not wait any longer, but moved as quickly and as decorously as possible. She was not sure what she would say—accuse the marquis baldly of sorcery? Begin by explaining her presence? Whatever she said would sound insane—her whole existence had been insane from the time she had lost her memory.

No—it had gone mad the moment her father had forced her to betroth the Marquis de Bauvin.

Fierce anger rose at the memory, and she remembered her vow not to be afraid. She would have faith that what she was doing was right, and not foolish, and that all would go well. She put her hand to her throat—no, she had given her cross to Adrian, for protection. She would go on faith alone, then, and the conviction that she would prevent the king from falling under the most vile sorcery.

She stole a look at the marquis—dear heaven, he had already come up to the king. The ministers and courtiers surrounding His Majesty seemed about to protest, but Louis said nothing and merely gazed curiously at the marquis.

De Bauvin bowed low. "Your Majesty—I intrude, I know," he said, his voice low and apologetic. "But please forgive my eagerness in wishing to present you with a token of my deep reverence for Your Majesty, and all the magnificence you have bestowed upon our nation." He put his hand to his cravat, and pulled the amulet from it. "A rare gem, Your Majesty, if you would consent to look at it."

Jesu, Marie. Horror made her freeze. He was making the king look at the amulet, the one that had taken her mind and allowed him to force her to his will. She watched as he lifted the amulet before the king, lifted it high enough so that not only the king looked at it, but the courtiers around him, as well.

Despair and anger sped Catherine's feet until she was running, pushing past the ladies and nobles surrounding the king, heedless of decorum or the rules that ran the court. The thought that the power of the amulet would move the king, no older than herself, of an age almost with her own younger brother, to do de Bauvin's will, made her stomach turn.

The ache in her hands pulsed, and she gasped as a sharp pain seemed to slice her back. *Mon Dieu, I do not know the purpose I bear these things, and I care not, but help me save the king,* she prayed.

"Stop the marquis!" she cried out. "He does sorcery through the gem he gives to the king!" No one moved. She looked about her; all eyes were on the amulet. A glance to her side caught the glint of a courtier's sword hung from a highly embroidered baldric, and she seized the haft and pulled it away from him, ignoring the man's protest. She pushed aside a lady who cried out and tottered on her high heels, and she slipped past a gentleman who tried to seize her.

Please let me come between the king and the marquis before it is too late. She lifted her head—she had leaned forward in her rush—and the sword in her hand rose to slap the amulet from the marquis's hand.

The crowd around Louis gasped as the dark jewel flew into the air—all eyes seemed to be fixed on it, on the seething red center of it, and Catherine felt the pull, as well. She closed her eyes and forced her attention away. She would not be sucked into its influence or under the power of the Marquis de Bauvin. She heard the sound of it falling to the floor—a sharp rocky sound, not a shattering as she had hoped. She opened her eyes to see that the marquis had stooped to pick it up and held it in his hand.

"She is mad."

She was standing, facing him, the sword outstretched, her back half to the king. Fear struggled to seize her—she could be executed for this disruption, for putting her back to the king. She met the marquis's eyes—cold, empty but for a chill light that promised death.

"No I am not." Her voice came out a whisper, and she cleared her throat, forcing herself to speak loudly. "I am not mad. I seek to defend our good king from sorcery."

No one spoke into the chill silence except for a few gasps from the court guests on the fringes of the group around them. She turned slightly to plead with the king, and her heart sank. He looked confused, lost, and she feared that he had already been caught by the power of the amulet. She looked about her—the other courtiers also looked dazed and confused, and some alarmed, but she could not tell if they had also been caught by the sorcery or if they did not know how to react.

The king seemed to struggle, shaking his head slightly. "What?"

"It is nothing," de Bauvin said, his voice soothing. "Mademoiselle is disobedient to the wishes of her brother the comte. She is betrothed to me, but I must say I am having second thoughts." The marquis moved back a little and her hands burned with pain, and her back once again stung. She forced the sensations to the back of her mind and raised her sword.

"If you try to hurt King Louis, I will kill you," she said.

"See, she is indeed mad," de Bauvin said, raising his voice. "I only offered a gift, and she threatens me."

"It is a sorcerous thing," she said loudly, and her voice echoed in the room. "You have used it on me to strip me of my will, and it is only by the grace of God that I escaped it." She knew her voice had an edge of desperation in it—had all the courtiers here been ensorcelled? It seemed none of them moved or even said anything in protest. She measured the distance between herself and the marquis. He was a sword's length away, but the king was near, and her brother had come up closer, next to de Bauvin. Adrian's face was pale, his eyes just as dazed. A young woman stepped closer and put her body against the marquis's. Catherine felt ill; the lady could not be more than sixteen, but she had placed herself over the man's heart, and so protected him from a killing thrust. He would use anyone to get what he wanted, Catherine thought.

"I would suggest she be arrested," de Bauvin said softly, and a pulse of darkness seemed to seep from his words.

Another wave of pain seized her, but strength

also came, and she somehow shook off the hands that grabbed her.

"No," she said, and anger was a fire in her heart. "No. You coward, you fiend. You use young girls to fuel your sorcerous power and to protect yourself from an honest fight. You cannot even face a woman who dares stand against you." She sneered at him. "Coward. A snake that crawls on his belly, pretending to offer gifts, but bites like a viper. A slime-filled, offal-filled sack of a man; no, not even a man, but a sniveling eunuch who cannot even get a woman in his bed unless he uses sorcery."

Sudden fire dispelled the empty coldness in the marquis's eyes, and he thrust the girl from him. Something bright flashed, and Catherine jerked aside as cold air brushed her neck. A cry beside her made her glance down—an elderly man had taken the marquis's dagger in his throat.

The girl who had stood at de Bauvin's side cried out. "Grandpère!" She rushed to the man's side, shaking her head, screaming in short pants.

Fury seized Catherine, and she leaped forward, willing the sword to pierce the marquis to the heart, even as pain sliced her hands and her back at the sight of the fallen man and his granddaughter. But another flash came up and parried her thrust. The marquis had his sword out at last.

A fierce satisfaction surged through her. This she understood and was trained for. Jack had taught her this, it was his gift to her, and she loved him for it, this gift of survival.

She moved, carefully, so that she stood between the marquis and Louis. She could not risk that he would try to kill His Majesty. The marquis had planned his attack well; the king's brother Phillipe was away, and if he could control the king or even kill him, he could seize power and perhaps raise enough of a force to eliminate the king's brother.

The marquis feinted to the left, but she refused to be drawn by it. He clearly wanted her to turn away so that the Louis would be exposed. She attacked instead, and de Bauvin barely managed to parry it, and it forced him back, away from His Majesty. She smiled grimly. She was glad she had concealed her expertise. It would give her an advantage, at least for a while.

Still too close to the king. She wanted to save her strength, for the darkness that oozed from the marquis sapped her of it, and each time she felt the darkness, she also felt pain in her hands and on her back. That she wore skirts did her no good, but at least she had made sure that her stays had been loosely tied.

She gritted her teeth against the pain, focusing on the movement of her body, on the minute shifts of balance that would propel her and her sword forward or to the side. The pain receded, and strength grew, and she let out a little laugh of relief.

The marquis gave her a sharp look, and then it became calculating. "Mlle de la Fer, give it up. You know I will win."

She parried a thrust that would have pierced her throat if she had not been watching for it. "I know of no such thing," she said. She was glad to see that she breathed heavily but easily. Her pain was almost gone now, though she was beginning to tire. The sword she wielded did not fit her hand as the one she was used to. She thought of the dagger she had in her pocket—it was in her right pocket, not her left, for she had thought she'd only have her dagger rather than a sword. Useless, for she dare not feel for it in the pocket of her skirts while she was fighting.

King Louis's court had formed a wide circle around them, and she was glad they were well away from the king. It was one less thing to fear. The marquis lowered his voice, nevertheless. "I will win, mademoiselle. You see how they are in my control. You think you disengaged my influence from your sister? You are a fool if you think it." His voice grew mocking. "I am taking her—and your brother's—power even as we fight."

Fear struck her again, almost choking her, and she faltered as she glanced at her brother who had fallen to his knees, and then to the floor. The marquis lunged, but she parried—barely—and stepped back, breathing harshly.

"Do you seriously think I cannot take your power even now? I still have the amulet. You *will* look at it, whether you like it or not." He held up the stone in his left hand, even as a ripping sound and a sharp pain lanced her left shoulder.

She had deflected the thrust in time, but her eyes were still drawn to the dark amulet. The red spark in the midst of the darkness crawled within like a living thing.

No. No. She forced her eyes away from it and deflected yet another thrust. Her hands hurt now and felt moist, and her back pained her. She had almost let the amulet's evil into her mind.

She cast a quick look about her before she parried another thrust—she was being forced back to the edge of the circle. The marquis may have the court in his thrall, but she doubted he could do anything but keep them from moving. Surely if he could animate them to harm her, he would have by now.

She gritted her teeth and looked for a weakness, any opening in the marquis's defense. She tried not to look at the amulet, but it was difficult. If she were to fight de Bauvin, it meant that she had to look at him. He knew what he was doing when he waved the amulet before him as he fought; he smiled coldly, confident that her gaze would be caught by it. Every time her eyes were drawn to it, the pain in her hands and on her back increased. The sounds of the girl sobbing over her grandfather added to it; the girl's grief poured into Catherine's heart and she felt like weeping.

She heard a low chant, and a relief from the pains came to her; it was Latin, a prayer, and it sounded like Père Doré's voice. He must have been able to avert his eyes from the amulet.

Another lunge from the marquis, and this she also deflected. She whirled around, hoping the edge of her sword would catch him, but it swished by harmlessly.

Time passed; she did not know how long. The courtiers, the king, her brother, still seemed frozen, unmoving. The spell of the amulet was strong, but the sound of prayers stayed in her ears and sustained her, though she could feel her muscles aching with effort and fatigue.

She gazed at the marquis—he did not seem to be tiring at all. *Blanche.* Dear heaven, did he speak the truth when he said he was drawing power from her still? Fear seeped into her at the thought, and the marquis's amulet caught her gaze.

The red depths seemed to strike at her, strengthening the fear pouring into her heart. She saw another flash of steel before her and deflected it, then deflected another, but it was all that she could do, for her hands became slick with blood and hurt, hurt with a fiery agony. She managed to move her gaze from the amulet and stared at the marquis instead, but it did no good; the same sickly red light was in his dark eyes, and forced all the fear she had ever experienced, had ever felt for her brother and her sister, for the girl in the alley, for the girl and her grandfather here in the court, deep into her bones.

She trembled, and the amulet loomed large in her sight. It pulled her into the depths of it, until a fog entered her mind. She could still hear the sounds of steel against steel—she must still be fighting, her body reacting to whatever sense she must have left.

But a sharp shock shot up her arm, and her knees hit hard on the floor. She shook her head, blinked, and tried to focus on what was before her. The sounds of prayer continued, but she could hear uncertainty in the priest's voice even as he prayed.

The Marquis de Bauvin seemed unaffected by the prayers, and hope began to seep from her. He smiled coldly at her, his sword still in his hand. He kicked another sword—she foggily remembered she had used it—to the side, beyond her reach.

"Stupid, stupid Catherine. You should have yielded to me, but you did not. It is a pity." His smile grew wider, and he lifted his sword. "For you see, you have been too much of a nuisance and so must die."

The world whirled around Jack's head, but he bit the side of his cheek—the street steadied and he could focus on it again. He was on another horse, and the presence of the red-hot poker in his side was permanent now. He was, frankly, glad that Fichet was with him as they hurried their horses down the avenue to the chateau of Versailles.

Fichet said nothing, merely glancing at him from time to time. Jack was grateful for his silence. It was trouble enough to ride, much less speak.

He hoped Catherine was not in danger, but he feared she was. He had tried to reason it out, had tried to convince himself that even if she was in danger, it was not immediate, that he would bring King Charles's missive to Louis in time to prevent any harm. He did not know whether it was his fever or his gut feeling that countered his reasoning, but either way, he feared he might be too late.

He almost rode his horse up the steps of the palace before a shout roused him. He opened his eyes, and blearily noticed that a footman stood, looking agitatedly up at him.

"What are you staring at, you idiot? Help me down."

"We cannot have—this is not according to protocol—"

"Silence, you fool!" Fichet came up to Jack's horse and held up a hand to help him down. "This is Sir John Marstone, a courier from His Majesty, King Charles of England."

"How do I know—"

"He has a paper, which you will see as soon as he dismounts." Fichet managed to keep steady as Jack almost fell upon him as he came down from the horse. "He is ill, attacked by a foul traitor to our king. We must see His Majesty immediately."

"But this man is dirty, and is not properly dressed—"

The footman fell as Jack's fist connected with his chin. "Dribbling idiot," he gasped, trying to force down the pain in his ribs. "Let's go, Fichet." He fished out King Charles's letter and waved it at another cowering footman. One of the king's uniformed guards came forward, sword out. Fichet's sword came out, as well.

"M. Guard, I pray you let us through. This man has an urgent letter from His Majesty, King Charles of England, telling of treason against our good king. If you do not let us pass, we fear our most noble king will die, and you surely will be blamed."

The guard looked indecisive, and impatience and anger seized Jack harder than the pain in his side. "Damn you man, let us through!" He thrust the paper in front of the man's face. "It's King Charles's seal and his written hand, as well. As God is my witness, I'm telling the truth. If you must, follow us to see that we do not lie."

The guard still looked indecisive, but nodded and opened the door to the palace. He followed behind, but Jack ignored him. He had to get to Catherine, to see if she was safe.

The hall down where the footman led them was long, too long. Though he managed to stand upright and walk, he was glad again of Fichet's arm supporting him, for he hurt by God, more than he ever thought possible, and his lungs burned when he breathed. A familiar sound echoed as they neared the end of the hall—the clash of steel—fighting. Dear God, fighting. The footsteps of the guard quickened, and he shouted down the hall for other guards.

The doors opened at last, and Jack was glad of his height, for he could see over the heads of the crowd. They seemed frozen, unmoving, all attention to the center, where stood King Louis to one side, the Marquis de Bauvin, and—God, oh, God.

Catherine.

He watched as her sword flew from her hand, as she sank to her knees in a daze. The marquis said something—he did not know what, and did not care, for all his attention was on her. De Bauvin lifted his sword.

No. No.

A desperate burst of energy flowed through him, and he surged forward, pushing past one courtier after another. His sword was in his hand, and he pulled out his dagger. He managed to reach the edge of the crowd. Catherine looked dazed, drained, pale. The marquis's sword lifted higher, then dropped.

"Catherine!" Jack shouted, and threw his dagger at the marquis.

It missed de Bauvin's throat, the blade sinking into his sword arm instead. It was enough; with one last burst of strength, he tossed his sword to Catherine.

She blinked and turned at the sound of her name, and managed to catch Jack's sword. The dazed look disappeared, and she seized the sword more firmly and swung it with all her might.

It sank into the marquis's side and he fell.

A low groan arose from the crowd around them, and then cries of surprise and horror, as some rushed to the king's side and some with their swords out to de Bauvin. Jack's sword fell from Catherine's hand and clattered on the floor as she fell, barely supporting herself on her arms. Her gloves were soaked with blood, and she knew it was her own. She pressed her hands together—it would not stop. Her back prickled with pain and dripped with moisture, though whether it was sweat or blood she did not know, nor did she care. At least the pain was gone.

Jack. She had heard Jack's voice, and she had held his sword. Fatigue almost made her faint, but she gritted her teeth and forced it away. He must be here, of course. She pushed herself upright, looking in the direction in which she had heard his voice.

Fichet stood there, then he bent over a motionless form, his face full of grief. She recognized the clothes—she had seen them on Jack a few times, though now they looked travel-stained and dirty. She crawled to him...she felt she could not stand, and was grateful to see the crowd of people who had been around her move away.

"Jack," she said. "Jack."

She came to him at last; he lay on his side, and she pushed him over.

Fear struck her again. *"Jesu, Marie,"* she whispered. He was pale, and his lips almost blue, as if he had no blood in him. She touched his face—she could not feel it, of course, for she had on gloves. Frantically, she stripped them off, ignoring the blood that seeped from her hands and the gasps from those who stood around her. She touched Jack's face. "You must waken, *mon cher.* Please."

He did not respond. She took his hand—it was too cool. His chest rose and fell fitfully, but there was a coarse, rattling sound. She waited for another breath. *Breathe, breathe,* she prayed.

She felt a touch on her shoulder. "Mademoiselle, he is very ill, and I fear he will not last long." It was Fichet. His face was creased in grief. "He is a stubborn man, and would not stop until he had done his duty."

Fichet's words passed around her like a niggling breeze, almost incomprehensible, for all her attention was on Jack, willing him to breathe. She put her hands on his chest—it barely rose and fell; every breath seemed a struggle. No, no, he must not be so ill, he must not die. "Please, Jack, be well, be well." She could feel tears flow down her cheeks, and her hands wept blood, as well, dripping on his chest. She could hear prayers again—Père Doré's voice as well as Cardinal Mazarin's behind her. "Hear me, Jack, you will be well. You cannot have come back to me only to die. You will be *well*." She lay her head on his shoulder, weeping. "You will be well, or I pray God I shall die with you." Her hands began to sting again, but they did not hurt as they had when she had fought the marquis. It was as if an astringent balm had been put upon them, and her whole hand tingled and became hot to the tips of her fingers. A hand pulled at her shoulder. "Mademoiselle, he is very ill, you must get up—"

"No!" she cried, wildly, angrily, grief pulsing through her like a hot knife. "No, I will not leave him." She put her hand on Jack's face—it was cold, too cold, but her hands were warm, even hot. The blood from her hands stained his face, but though the bloodstains faded after a moment, she thought only that he was too cold. Surely she could warm him, as he had warmed her when he had taken her out of the alley, had fed and clothed her. "Jack, listen to me, I will make you warm." She put her arms around him. "You are too cold, too cold, and it is not right, no, for you gave me so much, so much." Tears flowed from her unheeded; it was only important that Jack be warm again, that he speak to her.

His chest lifted again, then heaved, a low, rumbling cough burst from him, and a moan of pain. "I hate coughing," she heard him whisper. "It hurts like the very devil." He opened his eyes. "And how you expect me to feel warmer when you pour tears over me, I don't know."

She gave a half-sobbing chuckle. "They are very warm tears, Jack."

He lifted a hand and touched her face, and she almost felt her heart stop, for there was a heat in his eyes that looked very much like love. "They *are* warm. I don't remember anyone ever weeping over me, sweet one, and I wish you would not, for I don't deserve it." He frowned then and rose on one elbow, looking about him at the courtiers who gasped when he rose. "Where the devil am I?" He peered at Fichet, who stood above him, his expression half joyful, half full of awe. "Fichet...dash it all, are we at King Louis's court? Where's King Charles's letter?"

"It is here, M. Sir Jack." Fichet's voice faltered as he bent to pick up King Charles's letter, which had fallen to the floor next to Jack.

Jack tried to rise, but groaned and lay down again. "Fichet, I'm hurt, and as God is my witness, I don't know if my legs can hold me up. Give it to him—His Majesty."

Fichet stood, his self-assurance fled as he nervously held out a paper to King Louis, who stood staring at them, pale and with mixed horror and relief in his eyes. Fichet kneeled low in front of him. "Your Great Majesty, forgive us this intrusion." He gestured at Jack and Catherine, and at the fallen marquis. "There has been a plot against your life, as you can see. His Majesty, King Charles of England himself, has sent his own man to you to warn you of it, and sent those loyal to you to protect you."

Louis came forward stiffly, and then with a quicker step, and took the sealed letter. The young king gazed at the seal on it, then broke it and opened it, reading quickly. He grew paler, then he frowned and his face grew red with anger. He turned to the cardinal and thrust the letter at him, and while Mazarin read it, turned to the guards that stood stiffly at attention. He pointed at the marquis's body.

"Take...that thing out of my sight. Burn it." He turned to Fichet, and his face softened, though it was still grim. "You have our gratitude, Monsieur— What is your name?"

Fichet bowed low. "Robert Fichet, Your Majesty."

"Fichet. You will be well rewarded." The king made a gesture and servants suddenly appeared at his side. "Take the King of England's courier and Mlle de la Fer to rooms near mine. I wish them well taken care of, and if any desire of theirs is not fulfilled, you shall know my displeasure."

Hands came together to lift Jack from the floor, and Catherine could not help giving a watery chuckle when he muttered what must have been English curses under his breath. It was not good of him, but it was much better than his struggling breath, his deathly pallor. He seemed to breathe easier now, and for that she was thankful.

She looked for her brother—a groan made her turn her head. Adrian lay on the floor nearby, and he slowly rose to his feet, looking dazed. He was breathing, alive, *Dieu merci*, and his cheeks gained a pink that had been absent before. It gave her hope that Blanche would arise out of bed soon.

She pushed herself up from the floor, but she almost fell again, for fatigue hit her hard and her sight darkened in a near faint. Hands gripped her arms on either side.

"Breathe, mademoiselle," came Fichet's voice.

She opened her eyes. Père Doré supported one arm, and Fichet the other. She took in a deep breath, and the room lightened. "I am very tired," she said. She shook her head. The words did not describe the depth of fatigue she felt, but it was all she could say for herself. She summoned up as much strength as she could, for though it was clear her brother would recover, she was not sure about Blanche. She looked at Fichet and then at the priest. "My sister—Blanche—Fichet, you must see to her, make sure she is well, for the marquis ensorcelled her."

Père Doré patted her hand. "To be sure, we will, and I will do an exorcism if it is necessary."

She nodded, and weariness finally consumed her. She moved as if in a dream, supported by Père Doré and Fichet until she came to a room, and then two ladies who were clearly well born and a few maids took her within. She let them move her about like a doll and clean her wounds and change her from her court clothes into a warm shift and robe. Only two things occupied her mind: the need to rest, and Jack.

"Jack." She looked at one lady, one of the noble-women, who smiled at her kindly. "I must see M. Marstone, the man who gave me his sword, King Charles's courier."

"Rest first, mademoiselle," said the lady, but Catherine shook her head.

"I must see that he is well. He saved my life, and I did not thank him."

The ladies looked at each other, then nodded. "He is in the room next to yours." They guided her to a connecting door and accompanied her as she walked slowly to the bed in which he had been lain.

"Jack," she said softly. "Are you well?"

He turned slightly, and she could see dark shadows under his eyes, his unshaven face looking dirty and mussed. He smiled, however. "Eh, you're here. I thought it was a dream."

She went to him and clasped his hand. "I am here; I will always be here, just as long as you want me."

He gave a chuckle, then groaned. "Don't make me laugh, sweet Cat, it hurts. Not as bad as it did, but it still hurts." He shifted until he seemed to find a more comfortable spot on the bed, then sighed. "Want you? What, are you mad? Why do you think I rode all this way from Lille and chased you halfway across France?"

She chuckled. "You are very duty-bound, my love. I thought it was to deliver your king's message to mine."

"Kings are the very devil," he said, ignoring the ladies' outraged gasps. "They are nothing compared to seeing you safe."

The ladies sighed sentimentally at this clear sign of devotion, then cried out in indignation when he said, "And if you'll rid me of your devilish female Greek chorus, I'll be grateful."

Catherine bit her lip to suppress her laugh, then gave the ladies an apologetic look. "He is feverish, and does not understand what he is saying," she said. Jack opened his mouth, and she put her hand over it as she continued, "I shall be in my room shortly." The ladies gave her dubious looks before moving to the other room.

"You are ungrateful!" she said. "His Majesty has been very gracious in setting us near his own rooms and lending us his courtiers to help us."

"Aye, and he should," Jack said, but his voice was

weary. "I stand by what I said: kings are the very devil. Both Louis and Charles owe me—owe *us* a great deal, and I shall make sure to wring it out of them." He patted her hand absently, yawning, and his eyes drooping. "Make a list of your wishes, my sweet Cat, for I shall see that between the two of them, they grant every one."

She chuckled in relief now—this was the Jack she knew, and she was sure he was better, else he would not have spoken so. "I shall, *mon cher* Jack. Rest now. If you need anything, only call for me."

He said nothing, but she saw that he slept and his breathing was slow and deep. Relief made her sigh deeply, and she turned to the door that connected to her room.

She did not protest when the ladies bustled about her and urged her to bed, for she was tired to death, and wished only to sleep now that she knew Jack was safe. She let them pull the covers over her and tuck her in as if she were a child, and let herself sink into the soft bed. Her body ached as she relaxed, but she welcomed it, for the sensation was no more than what anyone might feel after much strenuous work.

She smelled the scent of candle smoke as the ladies and the maid snuffed the candles and drew the curtains around her bed. Her stomach rumbled from hunger, but she ignored it, for sleep called, and she wanted it more than anything right now. Tomorrow she would eat and be filled, and . . .

She let out a last, sleepy chuckle. And she would be sure to make that list of wishes for Jack.

Epilogue

July 1660

SHE BASKED IN THE SUMMER SUN, FEEL-ing the warmth soak into her clothing and into her skin. Catherine closed her eyes and breathed in the warm air scented with the flowers from the abbey's garden. It was quiet but for the sounds of a bird chirping in its nest in one of the trees nearby.

The silence was restful, and she valued it. It seemed the only place she gained any peace away from King Louis's court and the only place where she would be left alone.

A rustling sound made her open her eyes, and she was prepared to be irritated, but it was only Père Doré. He smiled at her, and she rose, curtsying before she extended her hand to him. He took it and nodded over it.

"I am glad to see you well, *mon Père,*" she said.

"And I am glad to see you are much less ha-rassed," he replied, his smile amused.

She grimaced. "Does it show? I have tried to be patient, but the Jesuits have asked me over and over

again the same questions, and I can only give them
the same answers as I have given them before." She
held out her hands. "It does not help that they do
not bleed any more, though I am thankful they do
not."

"It helps that the king is fully convinced of the
divine nature of your condition and of your appearance in his court, however," the priest replied, and he
chuckled.

"To be sure," she said, and sighed. It was indeed
useful, for though her brother was implicated in the
accusation of treason, her intervention and Louis's
own experience of de Bauvin's sorcery absolved
Adrian of all blame. "I can scarce leave this place any
more but that I am pursued by those who think I
have some kind of divine gift."

Père Doré looked at her gravely. "Do you think
you do?"

She gazed back at him, and her lips pressed together in impatience. "I do not know, and if I do, I
wish to be rid of it as much as I wished to be rid of
the stigmata. Who am I, after all, to have such a gift?
I have not sought any kind of special treatment from
God, only to be left alone." She looked away, gazing
at the roses that bloomed in the sun.

Or to be with Jack, she thought. If she had any
wish at all, it was to see him again. He had left Versailles as soon as he was able, for his king had called
for his services again; fueled with funds once more,
King Charles had left Breda and joined General
Monck to take the throne of England again. Jack had
laughed when she had given him her list of wishes,
for it was long and some of them impossible, she
thought. He had tucked it in a pocket of his coat and
promised he would give it to King Charles himself,

and then he had kissed her long and hard before he left once again. But he had said nothing of the relationship between them, and there had been no offer of marriage.

"Miracles happen for a reason," the priest said.

She turned to him and shook her head, remembering the year that had passed, so full of pain and despair, with only a few barely grasped instances of joy. "It is certainly not because I am better than anyone else, so tell me another reason," she said.

Père Doré smiled mischievously. "God may work through anyone, saintly or . . . not," he replied. "Perhaps He wished to turn the hands of kings to better things than with what they are normally occupied."

She could not help feeling a little chagrined, for there was a little part of her that had thought perhaps all the things that had manifested had been because of some virtue in her. But she grinned at the priest; it did not matter to her, for she had enough of supernatural things for a long, long time.

She thought of King Louis's many mistresses and how the nobles aped him in his manners. That had not really stopped, but the court had become more subdued and thoughtful for a while, and she had heard rumors that King Louis had secretly sent funds to King Charles after wavering for so long. No doubt this was why it all happened, to persuade her king to support the King of England in regaining his throne.

Only one thing disturbed her, however. For all that she, Fichet, and Père Doré searched for it, they could not find the marquis's amulet. It seemed to have disappeared the moment he died. She was not surprised; the jewel seemed made of the darkness of his soul, and the red light within it was the violence he inflicted on others. It was just as well. The world was better off without such a vile thing.

A sound at the other end of the garden took her attention and she looked up. One of the Benedictine sisters waved at her. "Mademoiselle, you have a visitor," she called.

"I hope it is not another Jesuit, or someone wanting a blessing," Catherine muttered, but she grinned when she saw Père Doré bite his lip to suppress a laugh. She gave a last curtsy to the priest, then smiled at the nun as she followed her to the abbey's parlor; the sisters had been kind to her, and there was something comforting and normal in their daily rituals and work. It gave her a certain peace.

But she had felt restless lately; she wished to be doing...something. She had thought of returning to her home in Normandy, but there would be little there to greet her but unhappy memories. Her sister was well again, but had returned to the convent school she had left when Catherine had returned home. Her brother was still in Versailles, doing his best to be agreeable to the king and to dedicate himself to whatever task Louis set him. Though Adrian had been cleared of the charge of treason, the king still wanted to keep his eye on him, and Adrian was eager to clear his name of the stain that had been put upon him.

She could, of course, stay with him at the king's palace. He called it a mere hunting lodge, but it was so large that she could think of it only as a palace, and she had heard that Louis liked it so much he was wont to stay there rather than in Paris.

The door to the parlor opened, and at first she thought the dark clothes she saw were that of a priest's frock. But the cloth had much embroidery on it, and as she entered the room, the tall figure turned.

She stopped, her heart beating wildly. "Jack," she whispered.

He hesitated, looking at her uncertainly, as if he did not know whether to move toward her or step back.

"I am glad you have... are visiting," Catherine said, feeling awkward. It was not what she wanted to say, but all that she could let out, for the words jumbled themselves behind her lips.

"I brought the list of wishes," he blurted, and frustration crossed his face. "Damme, but that's a stupid thing to say."

She laughed and ran to him, reaching for his hands. "Yes, but it is no more stupid than what I said."

He took her hands in his and brought her fingers to his lips. "I've missed you, Cat," he said, and she looked at him, her heart full. "There were a thousand times I wished I were here instead of in England."

"But duty called you," she said.

He groaned. "Damme duty," he said, and pulled her into his arms. "Dear heaven, I love you."

His lips were hard on hers and his arms nearly crushed her, but she did not mind. "You'll marry me, won't you?"

She parted from him a little, and smiled through her tears. "Did I not put it on the list?" she said.

He laughed. "A hundred times, I think. I believe King Charles gave me one task after another to torture me, for I did show him the list as I promised you I would."

"Did he agree to any of the wishes?"

Jack grinned. "Not to the one about bringing

down the moon, but he did agree to most of the others." He paused for a long time, and she fidgeted, wondering which ones his king had agreed to. "The marriage one, of course." He grinned.

"And—?"

"Greedy." He kissed her again. "I've got my estates again, and a reward from both kings." She did not ask how much—she did not care, but she knew that the return of his family's home meant a great deal to him. "It's enough to support a large family," he said. "If you'll agree to marry me."

She let out an impatient breath. "Agree? Now I wonder if I should, for it seems writing it on your list one hundred times has not made any impression on you." She hesitated. "Is it that you do not really wish to marry me?"

"It's just that it's cold in England, and you like to be warm," he said, and grinned. "Of course I wish to marry you." He sobered, and sighed. "I've not lead a good life, Cat, and I've failed those who trusted me."

"Where you are, that will be warm enough," she said. "And you have never failed me. You gave me warmth and food and love from the day you found me, and now you have given me all except the moon." She kissed him. "I cannot wish for more."

A sound just outside the door made them part, and Catherine remembered that there was, no doubt, a nun waiting outside for propriety.

"When can you leave?" Jack said, not letting her move from his arms.

"Soon," she said.

"Good. Fichet is waiting outside, and there is plenty of room in the coach he procured for your baggage. Oh, and did you know they are going to have a child? Mme Felice is sure that it's because you've said a blessing over her."

Catherine groaned. "No. I have discussed it with Père Doré, and we agreed that I have no such powers."

He gazed at her, a twinkle in his eyes. "Are you sure? I thought I saw a glow about you, and by heaven, I thought an angel entered the room when you did."

She put her hand over his mouth. "Shh! It is nonsense. It is no such thing. I am very ordinary, and wish nothing more but to marry, have children, and fight you with swords."

He laughed, and kissed her once again. "Very well, you shall have your wish." He opened the door and pushed her toward it. "Get your belongings. I'll be waiting for you."

She gave him one last smile and shut the door behind her.

Jack gazed at the door for a moment, then sat down on a chair near the fire. He thought about the woman he was to marry and shook his head. He'd grant her every wish her heart desired and keep mum about whatever she wanted, but she vastly underrated herself.

He put his hand to his left cheek and let his tongue wander to the tooth that had pained him for the whole of the trip from Le Havre to Paris. It had stopped hurting as soon as she had kissed him.

He grinned. She thought him a prize for attempting to get everything on her list of wishes, but he knew she was worth more than anything a king— or two—could grant him, gift or no gift, affliction or not, for better or for worse. He thought he heard her hastening footsteps past the door—he'd better go after her or else he'd miss her in her haste.

Jack paused as he passed the sanctuary of the abbey, and he eyed the font of holy water at the entrance. He fished around into his pocket and brought out a dark crystal, as black as night, but there was no longer a red fire in its depths. It had resisted smashing, burning, everything he could think to do to destroy it, so he had buried it near Fichet's inn. Misfortune took the inn as soon as he had left it there, and so he dug it up again.

He slipped it into the font of holy water and watched as the water boiled about the amulet. The boiling subsided, and the water became clear. Jack nodded. He thought that might do it. He'd have to tell Père Doré they'd need fresh holy water in that font.

Whistling, he walked out of the abbey into the noonday sun, and into Catherine's arms.

About the Author

KAREN HARBAUGH lives in the Pacific Northwest with a wonderful husband and an alarmingly intelligent son. She has found that being a romance writer, wife, and mother is a lot more challenging than being a freelance technical writer or a Quality Assurance Analyst for a major HMO. On the other hand, she does enjoy challenges, and spinning tales for profit allows her to wear multicolored socks and Birkenstocks while she works, which is a definite plus.